Stryke
Book 4, New Vampire Disorder

Marie Johnston

Cover by P and Graphics
Developmental Editing by Tera Cuskaden
Copy Editing by Razor Sharp Editing
Proofing by HME Editing
Book Layout © 2017 BookDesignTemplates.com

Stryke/Marie Johnston. -- 1st ed.

To my editors who help me clean this mess up. And to my unofficial proofers, those friends I can message and say, "Oh crap, I have this book that's releasing, like, really soon. Can you…" and they always do, and they always turn it around in less than a week.

Chapter One

S tryke stared at the roof of the cave he was being tortured in and almost laughed. *Why yes, it was possible to get fucked to death.*

He puffed out a breath and suppressed the following groan. He hadn't been tortured like this in… Well, in the underworld, it was like picking which day he polished his horns. Last Thursday? Friday? At least as a second-tier demon, he could control something like horn maintenance.

The demon bitch Hypna rolled off him onto the gritty floor of her cavern. "You don't disappoint, do you," she purred in a garbled voice that was as unsexy as she was. Although by underworld standards, she was an eight.

And yes, he disappointed himself all the time, but no need to dredge up regrets. His personal mission—the female vampire he suffered for—always came first.

Hypna stood and stretched. He couldn't do the same. Blood ran in rivulets down his arms and torso where her claws had gouged him. Sex with Hypna wasn't an erotic experience, it was a special form of hell in the underworld. It'd take a while for his poisoned penis to dwindle. Stryke didn't orgasm, a rare ability that would get him killed if Hypna discovered his treachery. But he could fake it, make all the grunts and faces, even go so far as calling her name. He should win one of those human acting awards. Sex with Hypna was like pretending to be ecstatic about having his skin flayed off in one-inch strips.

He'd had to fuck demons before, even purebloods like Hypna, sometimes willingly, sometimes not. But she was the first to have an actual reason beyond inherent evilness. A reason that he would do everything in his power to circumvent.

Hypna's horns wrapped themselves around her head and smoothed down her back. One of the fantasies that kept him going was cutting off her horns and shanking her with them. Their turgid, purple hue reminded him of a flaccid cock, the way his would be if she hadn't stabbed him with those damn things and infused a libidinous chemical into his bloodstream.

Fuck, he hated her. He hated all the purebloods. And most second-tiers. Some might assume he'd have an affinity for the weaker demons like himself, those who could claim humans or vampires or the odd shifter in their family tree. They'd be wrong. At least he wasn't chattel for the rulers of his kind to do with as they willed. With his powers, he was often fought over, the prized servant of the thirteen members of the Circle.

He shifted his glare from Hypna's skanky features to the cave walls. Who would've thought he'd miss his former boss, Rancor? The male had been as cruel as they came, but the glee he'd taken in violence had often distracted him, allowing Stryke much more time to himself.

His fellow second-tier demon and sort-of friend Fyra totally owed him. If he hadn't helped her and her vampire behemoth kill their boss, Rancor, Stryke wouldn't be in this situation. Rancor had loved lording Stryke over Hypna. But Rancor was dead, so control of Stryke had been transferred to another one of the thirteen who ruled the underworld—and she'd been waiting for him with claws extended.

Stryke clasped one hand over an oozing wound in his flank and willed himself to heal. At times like these, he couldn't allow himself to remember why he stayed. If any of the demons roaming the underworld caught wind of the reason, his vampire would have a gigantic target painted on her. As if she didn't already have one because of who she was, but this would be worse. This would include inducing the maximum amount of pain in order to torment Stryke.

Hypna spun around and gazed down at him broken on the cavern floor. This had been his nightly routine for the last month since Rancor had been killed: getting mutilated by Hypna as she fucked him in hopes of begetting his child.

Over his dead body. And even then, she wasn't getting his seed, thanks to the bond he harbored for another—the vampire who remained oblivious to it. If he hadn't had that bond, he'd have killed himself or died trying to kill Hypna by now. No one was bringing his child into the world to be used for personal gain. History didn't need to repeat itself.

She pushed her black hair out of her face, her lips curled in a sneer. "I bet your dad was a better fuck."

He almost laughed, but he wasn't stupid. His healing had barely begun and a pissed-off Hypna was much more brutal than a turned-on Hypna.

"His claws were bigger than mine," Stryke rasped. Enduring Hypna's attentions in stoic silence wasn't possible, so his voice needed as much healing as his body.

"More than his claws," she scoffed and planted her hands on her bare hips. Her claws fanned out at her waist.

Yeah, she was right, but his father had been of purer demon blood. And he'd had the size and ferocity that went with it. Stryke's diluted blood made him second-tier—powerful enough to be useful to the Circle of Thirteen. He was an energy demon, and a powerful one at that.

It was the only good thing his father's deception had done for Stryke. The Circle coveted his power, yet they underestimated him since his sire had been outed as just another second-tier. Apparently, the diluted blood went further back than his sire had let on.

Hypna cocked her head while staring at Stryke with ultimate superiority. "I can believe you came from him, though."

The sugary sweetness in her voice stalled his healing efforts. Why was she taunting him with his sire? He stared at Hypna, waiting to see where she was going with her comment while he used the extra moments to heal. The bleeding had slowed to a trickle and the pain was beginning to ebb.

She squatted, giving Stryke a view he'd endured too many times. "He thought he was so—damn—powerful."

Because he had been. Stryke swallowed before he provoked her into her own demonstration of power.

"Until we *gutted* him." Her black eyes twinkled as she straightened. "He also thought he was clever. Does that sound familiar, Stryke?"

Cold washed through him. His aches and pains dulled, but a well of blood gushed out of his wounds as his heart hammered.

Shit.

Rage sparked in her gaze. "I've been fucking you for a month. My fertile season is almost over, yet I have no child in my belly. Why is that?"

Stryke forced his breathing to remain even. If she knew of his deception, there was no reason to bluster.

She eyed his mangled privates. "You've been holding out on me, and I have to ask myself why. No—how. *How* could a second-tier," she spat the word, "not spill his seed when he's been injected with my venom, hmm? How, Stryke? Do you know what answer I came up with?"

By now he was well enough to struggle into a sitting position, but he stayed frozen in place. She might suspect how, but she couldn't really *know*.

"An energy demon who can't climax. Who could Stryke be holding out for? Who could he have bonded to?" Hypna circled around him until she blocked the only exit to the hole-in-the-wall cave. "What females has Stryke been around? Fyra's taken, but I never saw you lusting after her like Rancor did."

Stryke's heart pounded. Hypna was a dead demon walking if she determined the female Stryke had bonded himself to. His mind ran through plans. He could shoot a hand out and send a charge through Hypna's body that would incapacitate her. "Incapacitate to decapitate" had been his sire's motto. It had just become Stryke's.

But she stayed out of reach. She feared his powers enough to be wary of them, to covet them, and the baby was the key.

He could transport himself to the human realm. It'd confirm for Hypna that he was bonded to someone in the earthly realm, but he could find his female and protect her.

"Ah, ah, ah." Hypna extended a hand toward him, fingers spread.

Roots sprouted from the floor and dug into his skin. He roared in pain as a hundred needle-like protrusions pierced him and burrowed into his muscles. The agony alone almost made him flee, but he had to know if Hypna was bluffing.

A cloudy, purple horn flexed over her head and angled toward him.

His eyes widened and he envisioned the house owned by the human who had agreed to host Stryke whenever necessary.

Nothing happened. Dammit, he was too weak yet to transport.

As soon as Hypna speared him with a horn, he'd zap her and wrestle against his restraints.

"What's wrong, Stryke? Afraid I'll find out about your bond to another and kill her?" She gave him a throaty laugh and knelt toward him.

He wriggled his wrist, stretching to reach her toe, but the roots held him in place. His energy had no effect on the roots. They were inert, life-less, only controlled by Hypna's power.

"Do you know what happened the last time I was in the human realm? My prime vampire host was killed right before I could terminate the vampire bitch I was fighting. My host was staked from behind and I was sent back to the under-world, but do you know what I remember?"

Stryke's breath came out in pants. Searing pain racked his body, but it paled in comparison with the terror racing through him. She knew. Fucking Hypna knew who he was protecting.

"I remember," her horn inched closer, "the smell of brimstone and it made me ask, what fool demon would save a vampire wench?" A cruel smile stretched her lips. "What? No denial?"

The sharp tip of her horn stabbed through the skin of his chest. Stryke sent all his remaining en-ergy into her horn. Hypna went rigid before releasing a startled shriek and flying back from the force of his shock.

He renewed his struggles, but the edges of his vision had gone blurry. He was undoing all the healing progress his body had made.

"Nice try, second-tier," she snarled. She stormed back and towered over him. "You wait here while I go release you from her bond. Don't worry, I'll make sure I send her your regards when I cut off her head."

Stryke fought unconsciousness, and a last surge of energy spread through him. The bindings weakened and he let out a bellow.

Hypna punted him in the skull, and blackness claimed him.

***

The night was young. The sun had just set and Freemont's nightlife was out roaring their engines. That's probably about as far as they'd get with the temps dipping into the twenties. Zoey wandered along the sidewalk that had been cleared of snow, having parked a couple of blocks from the convenience store.

She sipped on a red Gatorade as she walked. The night was still young and it was her first drink. In her backpack, she had two more, orange and electric blue.

Her team always teased her for her habit, and she just grinned right back. It was in everyone's best interests to let them think guzzling electrolyte juice was a quirk and not her life's necessity.

A vampire with a blood disorder. If they discovered her secret, her position on the TriSpecies

Synod would be threatened. She couldn't lose her spot. Not that she'd wanted to be a part of her people's government at first, but once her bony ass had been plopped onto the board of vampires, shifters, and a fellow hybrid, well, it'd given her broken heart a reason to live.

Her phone vibrated and she glanced at the screen. Her mouth quirked at the oddly formal message.

The Synod requests Zohana Chevalier's presence.

The Synod would have to wait. Zoey texted a reply that she was in the middle of a task and she'd be there in an hour.

Her partner, Demetrius, would cover for her, like she'd done for him countless times. It wasn't like her errand was top secret. She was low on Gatorade and chips: electrolytes and straight-up sodium with a side of fat. Back when she was younger, her blood disorder had been a challenge to handle and she'd eaten more ham than inhumanly possible. A few stolen salt blocks from some offended cows had gotten her through the worst of it because a girl could only drink so much pickle juice. Then modern times had brought processed food packed with sodium. When Gatorade had been developed, she'd died and gone to heaven. The drink made it so much easier to keep her health issue a secret from those closest to her.

Ironically, living was so much less difficult now, but her reason for living had been stolen.

Mitchell's laughing, brown eyes flashed through her mind.

Tears pricked the back of her eyes. She blinked them back. It'd be a useless loss of salt from her body. Her true mate was gone, and every day the crippling pain was a tiny bit less. She no longer broke down into soul-shattering sobs when she remembered him. It had only taken five years to get to this point.

She readjusted her backpack and tossed her empty container into the recycling bin, then entered the convenience store.

"Hey, Zoey," the teenaged cashier greeted. "Exciting night?"

Zoey smiled. "Always."

The young girl thought Zoey was some biker chick because she dressed all in black and leather pants but never questioned where Zoey parked her bike. If the girl ever did, Zoey would have to lie—she didn't own one. Zoey's severe bun and long hair wouldn't play nice with a bike helmet. Not that she needed one, but humans questioned someone who could walk away after getting their head smeared across pavement.

Zoey selected her items and brought them to the counter.

The cashier clucked as she rang them up. "I wish I could eat like this and have your body."

Zoey would kill not to be dependent on anything more than blood, but she smiled and said her standard, "It's not all for me."

Even she saw the "bullshit" in the girl's eyes.

Zoey packed her items away in her pack and strode out of the store. She was a block away from where she'd inconspicuously parked her black SUV when prickles danced along her nape. She didn't slow, but she reassessed where she'd stashed her weapons. Two sidearms in a holster under her leather jacket. One tucked into her waistband at the small of her back. No knives. She'd waited to run her errand before strapping those on. Humans lost their shit when they saw someone walking around armed with guns and knives and the occasional wooden stake.

She tossed her bag into the SUV and discreetly finished arming herself before shutting the door again and wandering into the alley she'd parked next to. Her parking spot had been chosen because one, she'd never parked here before. Any kind of a routine would leave her vulnerable to vampires with grudges against their government, shifters who still hated vampires no matter how integrated they'd become, or demons hiding in human hosts. And two, this spot had several escape routes—including a handy dark alley for fighting without drawing attention.

The deeper into the alley she went, the less the light of the street lamps penetrated. Faint footsteps crunched on gravel.

Zoey spun with a knife in her left hand and a gun in her right.

A tall form marched in her direction, a female vampire from the smell of her. The scent of a pure, strong bloodline flooded Zoey. Ah, a prime vampire. Then a trace of brimstone curled around Zoey.

Oh…shit. She was alone, facing a possessed prime vampire.

"So, you're the one he wants." The vampire's voice resonated with the timbre of a powerful demon.

Zoey recognized the vampire. They'd grown up not far from each other, though Zoey hadn't dealt much with her. Doriana had been a mousy, quiet thing. Why would she turn her body over to a demon to possess? And which demon?

Zoey ran through the list of thirteen. She'd learned their names from Fyra, but they had yet to learn who'd taken Rancor's spot. The thirteen always hid inside a host, would never demean themselves by bonding to a vampire so they could walk freely in this realm. Besides, what got killed in this realm stayed in this realm, a possibility they'd never risk. Cowards.

Still, they needed the host's permission, or coercion, to enter, and Doriana had given it up. But to which demon?

Zoey filtered a deep breath through her senses. She knew this demon. She'd been the one inhabiting Morgana when that rabid bitch had almost bested Zoey in a bathroom.

"We meet again," Zoey said. And who was the demon talking about? Who wanted Zoey?

The vampire stopped and her black eyes swept Zoey's body in disdain. "That's what gets him off, huh?"

Zoey shook her head. Had the demon lost her damn mind? "Who the hell are you talking about?"

"As if you don't know. As if a romance between a vampire and a demon would escape our notice."

Demons were evil and crazy, but could they be genuinely nuts? Zoey needed to at least find out what demon she was dealing with and report back to her team. "I don't know who you're talking about."

"Look at these." The vampire palmed her breasts and looked down with a frown. "My real breasts are much larger, but even this female's bust is a handful more than yours."

Zoey bristled at the insult. "There's nothing wrong with an athletic build. And since you possessed Morgana the last time we met, you heard her taunts about my mate being dead."

She was about to say, *There's no male after me*, but the words died unspoken. The sense of anticipation she'd been stricken with for weeks couldn't have anything to do with what the insane demon was talking about. Maybe she'd just been widowed so long, she was in a lonely, perpetual state of wishful thinking.

Zoey turned her attention back to information gathering. Fyra had named the Circle demon who'd possessed Morgana during their encounter. Hypna.

Surprise brightened Doriana's demon-black eyes. The vampire was present in body only; Hypna had full control. "You don't know?"

Sour dread laced through Zoey. That question coming from a demon wasn't the start to a good day. More footsteps resonated in the night and the smell of brimstone grew thicker. Were the demon's second-tier servants coming after Zoey? They had to be in hosts, too.

"You don't know." Hypna threw her head back and laughed. Her laughter died and she met Zoey's gaze with a Cheshire-cat smile. "This will be fun."

No, it won't. Zoey raised her gun and shot Hypna between the eyes. The vampire's eyes lost focus and she dropped backward to the ground. Zoey cursed herself for not packing a stake to dust the vampire with, but she jumped on the fallen vampire and started sawing at her neck with the knife.

The footsteps grew faster as Hypna's minions rushed to her aid.

Damn vertebrae. Decapitating a vampire would be so much easier if they didn't have spines. Zoey sucked in a breath to smell her attackers. Human sweat and sulfur. No other vampires. Zoey made a mental note to inform her team that another broker had set up in the area to lure humans into being hosts for second-tier demons.

As they approached, three of them lumbering down the alley to block her in, she was grateful second-tiers weren't strong enough to inhabit vampires, much less the more powerful and wealthy primes. She could deal with them in multiples.

"Don't worry, vampire. We're not going to kill you," one male said.

"Just play with you for a while."

Their mistake. Cops would be showing up soon, thanks to the sound of the first gunshot, so Zoey made her next shots count.

Bam, bam, bam. Three head shots followed by clouds of copper-tinged air. There. No more demons to trouble her.

She holstered her gun so she could use both hands to saw the prime female's neck off. She couldn't be allowed to heal and keep hosting one of the thirteen.

The groan of a portal to the underworld echoed off the brick buildings around her. The demons were getting sucked back home now that their hosts were dead. She hacked harder, the vampire much harder to kill. Stealing Hypna's host was worth flirting with the sucking chasm that was opening under the bodies of the three humans, but if Zoey didn't move fast, she'd be taken down, too. She was far enough away from the second-tier's portals but right on top of Hypna's.

Almost. Done.

With a holler, she chopped through the bone and shoved herself backward as far as she could.

The vacuum of the portal tugged on her clothing. Zoey gritted her teeth and tensed all her muscles to resist the force. Her body slid an inch toward the ink-black opening.

She was out of the way of the humans' already closing portals, but the vibrations of the portal sucking Hypna back into the underworld had Zoey scrambling until she hit a wall. The force of the portal kicked up debris and trash, and the creak of the Dumpster next to her was deafening. Her only instinct was to get as far away as fast as possible.

Until she bumped into another Dumpster. The pull on her feet dragged her toward the portal.

Her stomach twisted in growing terror mixed with determination. She clawed against the ground, but her fingernails did little to gain traction.

She kicked, but it only propelled her toward the portal.

She only needed to last a few more seconds and the chasm would close, but as she scraped across the pavement, every second felt like a minute.

Frantically, she wrestled a knife free and slammed it into the pavement. The scrape of metal across cement curdled her eardrums.

Nothing was working.

The lumbering screech of a Dumpster made her look up. It was rolling right for her as it got sucked into the underworld.

Her last thought before she face-planted with the giant trash receptacle was, *He's here*.

Chapter Two

Stryke zapped the last vestiges of roots and concentrated on his no-longer-secret bond to his vampire. He appeared at Zoey's location, in his own form thanks to their link, and reacted without thinking.

A Dumpster had plowed into Zoey and was pushing her into a portal. He lunged and tackled her, wrapping his arms around anything he could get ahold of. The Dumpster flew into the portal as he and Zoey rolled clear.

With a snap, the opening shut. Silence descended.

Zoey hung limp in his arms. He glanced around. Four blood spots on the concrete. He sniffed. One prime female, three human males, all demon-possessed.

He glanced at Zoey. She'd killed four hosts and sent four demons back to their realm, but she'd gotten taken out by a Dumpster.

A smile twitched his lips. Just her luck.

Sweet brimstone, he'd missed her. Looked like they were actually going to officially meet. And she was going to hate him for linking himself to her.

Barely healed himself, he managed to stand while cradling her to his chest. Sirens blared in the distance. With one hand, he searched for her keys and found them in her jacket pocket.

He staggered out of the alley. All the businesses were closed this time of night, but people were home in the apartments above the offices. Humans peered out of upper-level windows. Stryke knew what they'd see: a tall, naked man, covered in blood, carrying an unconscious woman. At least his horns were covered by his hair, so he had that going for him.

He opened the SUV and gently laid Zoey inside. He crawled over her and into the driver's seat instead of going around the outside. She got a face full of his junk, but she was passed out and couldn't hold it against him. When she came to, she'd have issues with much more than getting squished against his bare body.

He stomped on the gas and sped off, heading for his human host's house. Lee wasn't expecting him, but it wouldn't matter. The kid was at a weak point in his life, which had made him easy to possess in the first place. When Stryke had had to step out of Lee's body one too many times and the young man had seen him in his true form, Stryke had used the opportunity to order the stunned man to take care of himself. As a result, Lee welcomed Stryke's interference in his sad, lonely life.

Lee was just one of the many mistakes Stryke had made in his long life. The human was growing too attached, but Stryke just kept dispensing advice. He'd have to sever ties with the human and move onto a host who was less…needy. Despite the bond to Zoey that allowed him to roam this realm in his own form, he'd been using hosts. His real form was too distinct to blend among humans and other demons would know instantly he was bonded to someone in the realm. But Stryke hadn't considered Lee growing dependent on him. His error.

The unconscious female slumped in the passenger seat was another miscalculation.

She was supposed to have been a pawn. Stryke's mission was to use her and her mate to gather information. But Stryke hadn't taken into account how much her mate had loved her, unconditionally.

Stryke had grudgingly compared it to his own dedication to his ill-begotten sire. After the way Stryke had grown up, the big, burly male who'd thrown Stryke a few morsels to keep from starving had commanded Stryke's utter devotion.

But Stryke's diluted blood hadn't sat well with the other twelve when they'd learned Burhn was his sire. Because how could Stryke be a lowly second-tier demon if both parents were pure? Two pure-bloods didn't make a half-breed.

The rest of the Circle had made his sire pay dearly for the embarrassment before they'd killed him—while Stryke could do nothing but watch.

A stately house approached. Lee's parents were wealthy and always out of the country, and they left the care of the three-story monstrosity to their boy, who they always left behind. Stryke might order the kid to paint the place. Canary yellow might've been in style thirty years ago, but it was atrocious by today's standards. Stryke's eyes, used to the dark and dank underworld, throbbed whenever he looked at it. White paint on the trim had long ago peeled away, reflecting the way Lee's parents had treated their son.

Snow crunched under the car's tires but wasn't deep enough to hinder the SUV. Stryke swerved to miss an ornate birdbath and parked behind the shed alongside the trees that surrounded the house.

Stryke jumped out and ran around to gather Zoey into his arms. Cold nipped at his feet. His natural store of energy shrank deep into his body, making the bite on his skin much more acute.

Zoey groaned and Stryke picked up the pace. Jogging to the house, he ran through his plan. Hypna might think she could find Stryke easily enough, but he could wield his energy like no other, including concealing it. But it wasn't foolproof. She was one of the thirteen and not to be underestimated. While her other second-tier minions would struggle to locate him, she might track him herself.

After she found another prime to host her. Stryke smiled grimly to himself. Hypna was probably throwing the world's biggest tantrum in the underworld at being bested by Zoey. Had the demoness discovered he'd escaped his bonds yet? The roots hadn't been easy to wrestle out of, but focusing his energy like a laser searing through his skin, he'd burned through them. How'd the Circle think his dad had gotten his name?

A light on the back porch flicked on and Lee peeked out the window, his avid gaze more appropriate for a five-year-old than for a twenty-one-year-old. When Lee's gaze landed on Stryke and his female load, he whipped the door open.

Excitement and curiosity flooded Lee's expression. "What can I do?"

Stryke's corrupted heart sank. The kid liked to be useful, needed. Human hosts didn't have the best survival rate and Stryke's guilt ratcheted a little higher every time he used the boy. Even with his bond outed by Hypna, a ready host would be handy, but the more he used Lee, the harder it was to think of Lee getting hurt. He'd have to cut the kid loose.

"Get my bag." Stryke stepped in with Zoey and beelined straight to a main-level guest room.

The room, like the house, was stuck in the past. Faded, floral curtains hung limply from a rod, and the matching bedspread wasn't in any better shape. The carpet wasn't shag, but pink wasn't a good color no matter the decade in Stryke's opinion.

He laid Zoey on the bed. The lump on her head was already going down and she'd wake soon.

Lee dashed into the room and threw the black bag at Stryke. Stryke appreciated the hustle and it was probably the most activity Lee had gotten all day.

No, that was no longer correct. Lee's ashen skin had taken on a healthier glow. It wasn't yet robust human flesh, but it looked like he actually got off the couch once in a while. Life filled the boy's eyes like Stryke hadn't seen unless he was possessing him and looking in a mirror.

Humans didn't often surprise him, but this one had. When Stryke had first sensed Lee's weak will, his only thought had been "Bingo!" A rich human whose family didn't give a shit about him, who didn't hold down a job, but who had a house and vehicle for him to use? Hell, yes.

But once he'd manipulated Lee's energy so he could gain access without the boy's acquiescence, he'd been staggered by the boy's inner pain. Lee was lumpy and frumpy and he hated himself more than even demons hated...everything.

The first time Stryke had to step out of him and use his own form to help Fyra, Lee hadn't been horrified. Confused, awed, but not scared. Every time he'd used Lee as a host after that, the human had oozed feelings of usefulness and willingness.

Between possessions, Stryke had maybe thrown out a few suggestions for the guy. Move more. Eat less. Wash your clothes.

Lee had taken to the advice as quickly as his metabolism had burned through his first bag of baby carrots.

Guilt about Lee's safety welled and Stryke stuffed it down. He'd throw his best friend into the fire if it served his needs. And he had, in a way. If he went as far as calling Fyra a friend, then she was his best friend—his only friend. They'd both been Rancor's servants, but her moxie had endeared her to Stryke long before she'd straight-up betrayed Rancor, then killed him. To be fair, he'd also thrown Fyra a lifeline after he'd turned her over to a furious Rancor. And she hadn't died, had she? Her big, blond vampire had rushed in to save her and Rancor had never guessed that Stryke was a traitor.

Stryke yanked out his warded cuffs and bound Zoey's wrists. The cuffs would hold against her superior vampire strength and prevent her from flashing away. Then he stripped her of all her weapons lest they get used against him or Lee. On one of Stryke's last visits, he'd warded Lee's house against vampires flashing in and out and against as much demon interaction as possible. But the Circle never shared all of their secrets, so he wasn't filled with confidence. Demons were like lawyers—masters of loopholes.

Zoey squirmed and moaned.

"Leave us," Stryke ordered and Lee scurried out, closing the door behind him.

He straightened over Zoey and waited. Her lovely brown eyes blinked open. They were glassier than he'd expected and the fatigue radiating off her concerned him. She'd gone head-to-head with a giant metal bin, but she was a prime female, the strongest of their kind. Although in the last few decades, Stryke had started equating prime with rich. Primes were predominantly old vampire families who lorded their power and money over the rest of their kind.

So why the long recovery?

Her gaze landed on him and swept over his body. Her eyes briefly widened and dammit, he hadn't had time to dress. Then she narrowed her eyes on his face and inhaled.

"Demon." Her voice was hard, but it sent shivers up and down his spine.

"Zohana." He used her full name. Mitchell always had, but to Stryke, Zoey fit her so much better.

Her jaw clenched, and she tried sitting up but collapsed back. A string of curses left her when she spied the cuffs on her wrists. "You bastard."

Stryke sat on the bed next to her and palpated up and down her torso. "Why are you not healed?"

His hands were on her. The bond within him sighed at her proximity. What'd she feel?

She gasped and tried to wriggle free. Her pupils dilated briefly, but her anger won over. "Don't touch me."

Ah, she wasn't unaffected either. He couldn't help his chuckle.

She went still. "You're crazy."

She tried to hide her panting, but her lips parted. Why was she breathing hard?

His worry climbed another notch. It wasn't a reaction to him, but because of her health. "Why are you so drawn?"

Her mouth snapped shut and her nostrils flared. She kicked at him, but he easily batted her leg away. It landed with a thump.

He gripped her chin in his hand. "Why? Tell me."

***

Zoey trembled. How humiliating, to be weak and fragile in front of a virile, devastating… demon.

Demons should *not* look this good. Or smell this divine. Was he covered in his own blood? Shouldn't that be a turnoff? And how had she gotten here?

Where was here? She gave up exerting the effort to control her shivers. The seizures would start soon and she'd be completely at his mercy.

But she already had been and she was out of the alley and tucked away in a… Gawd, this place was unreal. It actually looked like Betty's room in the compound. Demetrius's aged assistant had scattered obsessions from various centuries, but the last one enamored her the most.

Zoey struggled to keep her eyes open. Always so tired when she let it go this far.

If the demon had something nefarious in store—and duh, demon—then she wasn't any worse off making her request.

"Gatorade," she mumbled. "My backpack." Her eyelids weighed heavy. His ruggedly handsome face scrunched in confusion at her request.

"What's with you and the Gatorade?" He pushed off the bed and strode to the door.

And she *did not* fight to keep her eyes open to watch his firm buttocks clench with each step.

He jerked open the door. "Lee. Get the backpack out of the SUV."

She didn't hear a reply but sensed movement outside of the room.

Her stomach roiled. She hated wasting energy on nausea, afraid she'd urp her brilliantly colored drink all over. The rest of the world dimmed around her. She closed her eyes only to flutter them again as she was jostled against a warm, hard body.

Instead of struggling, she curled into him shamelessly. It was like he had a well of energy that was inviting her to tap into it.

If she did, would it be as invigorating as a month ago? Another time she'd been unconscious and an anonymous rescuer had given her his blood. Blood so powerful, so full of...everything, Zoey hadn't needed an electrolyte drink for days.

From her team's report, Zoey had determined who'd saved her then.

This couldn't be...

A bottle was shoved to her mouth and cool, berry-flavored liquid spilled over her tongue. She swallowed and sucked down more, repeating the process until the demon tipped it to give her every last drop.

Energy slowly flooded back into her system, and she shifted until she could shove herself away from him.

Hellfire, those eyes of his were exotic, intoxicating. Violet with flecks of black, they tracked her movements. She tried flashing away and no big surprise, she couldn't.

"Who are you?" Strength had returned to her voice, but sheer will kept it from wobbling.

It was like every cell in her body wanted at him, to plaster herself full-length against his bare skin after she shredded every last thread of her clothing.

"Stryke."

Oh. That was easy. She'd expected games, riddles, nonanswers. But he'd admitted exactly who she thought he was.

"Stryke," she repeated and regretted it. Heat flared in his eyes and his gaze grew impossibly more intense. She glanced around, again absorbing her environment. "Why?"

She couldn't be more specific. So many questions and he'd only answer if he wanted to.

"To save you," his full lips quirked, "but you'd taken care of the situation for the most part."

She'd been getting sucked into the underworld. Yet she was still in her realm. And he was nude. Think beyond her hormones! Nude... He'd come straight from the underworld. He didn't need a host to stay in this realm. Someone anchored him here. Who?

Perhaps if she discovered why she'd been jumped tonight, she'd have her answers.

"Why did they attack me?"

"Because you and I are connected."

She sputtered a laugh and beckoned for her backpack. Her brows lifted as he snagged another bottle and handed it to her, like he knew exactly what she needed and wanted to help. She cradled her juice between both hands like a child, since she couldn't separate them.

A glint of humor mixed with confusion in his eyes. "How about we exchange information. You tell me why the juice, and I'll tell you why Hypna wants you dead."

Zoey had been correct. It was Hypna targeting her specifically.

How badly did Zoey need to know why? She hadn't told anyone about her condition, not even Mitchell. Not that he would have thought any less of her, but she hadn't wanted to *feel* like less in his eyes. She'd already chosen a path that had pitted her against most other prime families, and Mitchell had followed her—and died for it. Since she'd been a girl, the way primes did things had bothered her. Once she'd befriended Demetrius and learned of the atrocities their government had been committing against humans and shifters, even vampires, she'd joined his game of infiltration and deception and had gone undercover to stop the enslavement of and experimentation on shifters.

When she'd met her true mate, she hadn't been able to back out and pretend blissful mated ignorance. She wouldn't have made it two months since Mitchell had run in the very crowds she'd worked on undermining. When she'd told Mitchell what upset her about their people and those who ruled them, he'd been concerned, too. As a true mate should. Slowly, she'd revealed more and more until he'd become as deeply undercover as she was with the organization their government had sanctioned to do their dirty work.

And now he was gone. All because of his unwavering devotion to her.

A calloused finger traced the side of her face and she jerked back, spilling blue liquid over her lap.

Stryke dropped his hand. "I feel your sadness."

"Yeah, I feel your…" Damn, she didn't have a comeback. *Keep your eyes off his privates!*

"You can feel anything of mine you'd like."

She bared her fangs at him and rolled her eyes away. She hadn't done that since she was a teenager.

He chuckled. "The juice?"

"I'm thirsty."

"You were close to comatose. I thought your drink was just a habit, but I can see now that you need it. Why?"

"You knew I drank Gatorade?" Her fear spiraled higher, mostly because she forced it to. The thought of him watching her, studying her, made her heart flutter, and not because she was low on sodium.

"I know many things about you, Zoey, and I'd like to share how, but you first."

She studied him. His wood-fire scent scrambled her brains, but she detected a thread of dishonesty. "You lie."

He inclined his head. "I did not say you'd like what I had to say. That's my only hesitation with telling you."

"Did you…" How was she going to ask? *Did you save my ass a month ago? Was that your powerful blood that healed me?* Because she'd crawl over glowing-hot coals to get one more drop.

He lifted a dark brow. "Did I what?"

"Were you at the Godet mansion several weeks ago?"

"You'll have to be more specific. Was I at the Godet mansion when I handed Fyra to Rancor and texted you to tell that big lug to get his ass over and save her? Or was I at the Godet mansion when Hypna was sucking the life out of you in a shattered shower?"

"I was taking care of it," Zoey grumbled, totally lying and he probably knew it. Morgana had pinned her, and Hypna had gone along for the ride, much to Zoey's mortification. Morgana had caught her off guard in the bathroom—damn Gatorade ran right through her—and the prime had cornered Zoey, then used Mitchell's memory to torment her.

"I'm sure you would've," he leaned forward with a wicked smile, "totally died. You're welcome."

Zoey scowled at him. Stryke had a playful side that she wanted to explore, not get the hell away from.

Duty. That was a good excuse, though him being a demon was more than enough. Her team had encountered Stryke on their last few missions. And he'd been helpful only enough to fulfill his own needs.

Her phone started vibrating. She awkwardly reached for it in her back pocket, but her hands were bound. Stryke snaked an arm around her and withdrew it.

His smoky scent crowded her, and the wall of his bare skin sucked the breath out of her lungs.

"You so need to get dressed," she hissed.

Another low chuckle rumbled through his chest. He was sitting so close the vibrations danced through her. He checked her screen. "You're late for a meeting. The Synod?"

It wasn't a secret that she sat on the board that ruled her kind, as well as shifters and hybrids. But Stryke seemed to know about all aspects of her life. It should set off alarm bells, make her cringe with dread, not fill her with a warm glow that'd been missing since Mitchell had perished.

"I imagine Demetrius will come looking for you, since he's your boss and likely sitting in on the same meeting." Stryke frowned and stared at her phone. "I suppose I must tell you how we're connected or he'll keep trying to interfere with your safety."

"I'm better off with my team than in an eighties-reject room with you."

Stryke glanced around the room. "Ah, that's the decade this place is stuck in."

She recalled he'd ordered someone to get her pack. "Who else is here?"

"His name is Lee and he's human. And I'd be very upset if you held his ability to host me against him. He didn't have a choice."

"They always have a choice."

A knowing gleam brightened his unique eyes. "No, not always. Haven't you wondered how I can be in your realm in my own form? Hasn't Fyra explained how it works? I assumed you'd know, since she was able to go on the run in this realm after she bonded to Bishop."

Zoey kept her expression impassive instead of chagrined. The question had briefly crossed her mind. She'd been too busy trying to determine how she'd ended up in a badly outdated home. And ogling his true form.

"Now, about Demetrius," he continued. "I want to talk to him with you, and I'll tell him the same thing I'm going to tell you." He took a deep breath. "You and I are bonded."

Chapter Three

S tryke let his words sink in. Zoey's com-
plexion had been returning to normal
until his announcement. Now, she paled and her
mouth dropped.

"You lie."

"Do I?"

She'd have a better sense than he would.
Vampires could sense emotions better than selfish demons could, though Stryke could sense
more from her because of their bond.

A flush spread up her neck. "No. Impossible.
I agreed to nothing."

He sighed. "You did, but you didn't understand at the time what you were agreeing to."
This…this was the part he dreaded. "Because I
was in Mitchell."

Zoey exploded off the bed, her half-empty
juice bottle spilling blue liquid over the pink carpet. "You *lie*." She prowled around the bed, eyes
intense with rage, her fangs bared. "How dare
you drag him into this mess. How dare you insin-
uate he'd host a demon."

"I said they don't always have a choice."

She stopped in front of him. "You aren't strong enough to possess a prime. Fyra said she can't. How can you?"

He remained sitting. Zoey wasn't clawing his eyes out and he didn't want her any more on the defensive than she already was.

"I'm older," he explained, "and the energy aspect of my abilities is stronger than hers."

Zoey's gaze darted away, then back. Her brow furrowed and she looked away again. He didn't need vampire senses to know she was thinking what he said made too much sense.

She licked her lips. "Mitchell would've known, and he wouldn't have tolerated it."

"He didn't detect me." Almost had, but Stryke had withdrawn enough to remain under the radar. "The undercover assignment you two were on distracted him enough to allow me to hitch a ride."

Color leeched from her face again. She was likely ruminating over whether or not he knew all the details of their ill-fated mission.

"Yes, I was there." Stryke rested his hands on his lap and spoke calmly. "You two were tasked with getting inside Sigma, reporting to Demetrius what was going on, and implicating the Vampire Council in their wrongdoing. Well done, by the way. Your team dismantled a government that ruled for centuries."

Zoey shook her head, her eyes glistened. "No, impossible. Mitchell was too strong to be possessed."

Stryke's lips flattened. Perhaps at one time, but not when Stryke had seized his opportunity. Unlike other demons who needed brokers to prep a host, Stryke used his abilities to sense openings, and he could exit the underworld right into a new host. Zoey's opinion of her mate was the best one possible and for good reason. Her mate had kept his inner turmoil from her, and it'd eaten at him until it had left an opening for Stryke.

"You are correct, he was strong." Zoey recoiled at his easy acceptance. "But I am not one of the Circle, who needs a prime vampire to hand themselves over. I can sense energy, how it moves, the path it takes. I sensed an opening and crossed the realm into your mate."

Zoey twitched like she wanted to cross her arms, but she was still bound. She dropped her hands in front of her. "What kind of opening?"

No, Stryke wouldn't tell her that. He'd actually agreed with Mitchell's decision to keep his inner turmoil from her; by then, Stryke had grown overly fond of her himself. "It's not always identifiable, but you two were carrying out a pretty covert operation. Perhaps it was the stress of betraying his family."

Partial truth. Very close to the truth, actually. Zoey wouldn't detect his lie, and neither would she determine the real meaning behind Stryke's words.

She mulled over his statement. "And one time when you were in Mitchell, we supposedly bonded."

"All it takes is a bite, Zoey. It's all about blood." His words were guttural. She and her mate had copulated many, many times, every chance they had gotten. And he'd been there, too.

A blush stained her cheeks. Yeah, she'd figured that out. Over and over, they'd sworn their loyalty to each other, Mitchell more to justify what he'd been planning. All it took was once for Stryke to insert himself into the equation and bond to her. He didn't regret it; his unrepentant demon genes wouldn't allow it.

"You're like a supernatural voyeur." She swallowed hard. "Did you kill Mitchell?"

Stryke's chest squeezed as he remembered the lick of the flames claiming Mitchell's body. Zoey's frantic pounding on the other side of the door. The stench of flesh burning as Mitchell succumbed. The male had blamed himself for getting murdered and had mourned what it would do to her. Stryke had stayed until the last minute when the portal opened and sucked him back home, the inferno covering his tracks.

"Losing a host does not benefit me." Truth. Not complete, but enough for an answer.

She took a step back, then another. "I'm bonded to a demon." Her wide gaze landed on him, filling with fury. "You *asshole*. I lost Mitchell and now you threaten my job, my profession, my life?"

"What are you—" Oh, her position on the Synod. No, he couldn't imagine they'd take news of Zoey's demon mate lightly. And Hypna had tried to kill her.

She stormed toward him, her face a mask of rage.

She moved so fast, he couldn't dodge her swing. Balling her hands together, she smacked him over the head. Stryke flew sideways and rolled off the bed with a *thunk*. By the time he righted himself, she had located the keys and unlocked herself. Damn her speed.

Fear propelled him into motion. He lunged toward her with a roar. She couldn't get away.

Zoey charged out the door and Stryke skidded into the hallway behind her. Lee rushed to the hallway after hearing the commotion and the stupid kid stepped in her way.

Damn that boy. "Lee, move!"

Lee froze once confronted with a conscious Zoey.

Zoey slammed past Lee, flattening him against the wall without hurting him.

What a female.

Instead of slowing to look for an exit, she kicked up her speed and raced for a window.

Panic flared in Stryke. If she passed the house's wards, she'd flash away.

He stretched out his arm, almost snagged her coat, but she charged through the glass. The shatter interrupted the silent night and he jumped through the opening after her.

She disappeared as soon as she was clear. He attuned himself to their bond. Please work. He righted himself with a grim smile; he could follow her anywhere.

***

Zoey reappeared outside of the compound. Its stark concrete exterior was the best thing she'd seen in ages. Cold air washed over her, cooling the overheated effects of that demon.

Bonded. She huffed. As if. She started for the exterior door.

The air sizzled behind her and because of that damn bond, she knew Stryke had tracked her.

She spun and snapped a fist out.

He ducked back and caught her hand in his.

"By all that's evil, I'd forgotten how fast you are."

She wanted to preen at the pride in his voice. Instead she plowed her knee toward his impressive genitals, but he blocked her. Ripping her hand free of his grip, she dipped and spun to dig an elbow into his abdomen. She couldn't make a connection. He wrapped her in a bear hug, his arms pinning hers to her sides.

The door crashed open and half of her team poured out with guns raised.

Demetrius, Bishop, and Rourke spread out to form a perimeter. Stryke edged backward with Zoey but kept her cradled in front of him. Even flaccid, his impressive genitals prodded her backside.

Zoey stilled, not knowing why. Her crew was here to help, she could fight and kick, and they'd take head shots at Stryke. But she didn't want it to come to that.

"It's a fucking demon," Rourke said.

"Not just any demon," Bishop said, lowering his pistol, "that's Stryke, in the flesh—and a lot of it."

"We've met, then." Demetrius kept his gun trained on Stryke.

Yes, they had crossed paths with him, but Stryke had always been in a host.

Creed stalked out of the compound, his face a mask of rage. Her stomach plummeted, both at his reaction and hers. Because her first thought was that she'd regret ever having slept with Creed if he hurt Stryke. How shameful was that? Creed was a good male, a worthy one, unlike the demon holding her hostage.

But she couldn't deny the draw she felt to the big male behind her.

Stryke's muscles were like granite at her back until he abruptly released her. She stumbled a few steps forward in surprise but angled herself so she could keep an eye on him and her team.

"I didn't come here to hurt anyone." His voice still sent delicious shivers up and down her spine. She had to get over the feeling and fast.

"He says we're bonded," she announced.

"What?" Creed's steady aim remained right between Stryke's eyes. It wouldn't kill him, but it would slow him down enough so the guys could capture him—or worse.

Stryke nodded. "It's true."

Demetrius made a disgusted noise. "We seem to have a rash of unwanted bonds."

Stryke showed a hint of a smile, no doubt knowing her friends' history. Demetrius's mate had been bonded as a child and D had saved her from her fate. Bishop had been bonded months ago but hadn't wanted to be saved from it. And his mate, Fyra, was becoming one of Zoey's best friends.

"He says he possessed Mitchell."

Silence. The four vampires stared at her in shock. They'd known Mitchell. He'd been a part of their team because of her. Like her, her friends hadn't suspected anything.

"How could you do that without us knowing?" Demetrius spoke what the rest were thinking, what Zoey had been wondering since Stryke had spilled his guts. "I thought second-tiers weren't strong enough to possess vampires, and Mitchell was a prime."

Stryke shrugged. "Most of us aren't strong enough. Sometimes, it just takes knowing the limits of our strength."

"That's a shitty answer," Rourke said.

Stryke's gaze slid to Rourke, his expression a mask of calm. Everything about him read like he was taking a Sunday stroll, no stress, unhurried, no big that he was nude. "I'm an energy demon and I'm not young. I've had more than enough time to learn my strength and," he glanced at Zoey, "read other's weaknesses."

Had she been Mitchell's weakness? A lump formed in her throat. He wouldn't have been undercover with her at Sigma if she hadn't been so damn dedicated to her mission, to overthrowing the Vampire Council.

"What do you think, Zoey?" Demetrius asked.

She met Stryke's violet gaze. The black flecks within seemed to move, sometimes slow and mesmerizing, sometimes fast and frantic, like now. He was worried about what she'd say.

She wished she could lie, but it'd do them no good. "I think it's plausible."

"He helped Fyra, after he turned her into Rancor," Bishop growled.

The text. Zoey had puzzled over why *she'd* been notified that Fyra was in danger from one of the Circle. And there was no denying the feeling of being...pursued wasn't the right word. Anticipation? Like someone was coming for her, monitoring her activities. Now that Stryke was here, she no longer had the sensation.

Demetrius holstered his firearm, but his movements were far from relaxed. "He's been feeding us breadcrumbs, but it's been for his own purposes."

"My only focus has been Zoey's safety. Has been since I met her."

Her brows rose, along with her teams'. Stryke had just admitted she was all he cared about. Hell of a thing.

A tap on the other side of the door interrupted them.

"He-ey," Fyra called from the other side. "Is this a bad time?"

Without waiting for an answer, she strolled out with an armload of black clothing, her flame-red hair stark against the lack of color.

"I know how weird you all are about nudity in this realm, so I brought my dear, dear *fiend* some sweats." Fyra smiled at her play on words. "You boys seem to have these in surplus around here." She handed her stash to Zoey to give to Stryke.

Humor played over Stryke's lips, but the look in his eyes was serious. He tossed the sweatshirt back to Fyra and stepped into the pants.

Zoey sucked in a breath. Through his thick, wavy, deep-brown hair, she hadn't noticed his horns. Tucked into his hair, they sprouted just behind his hairline and curved around his head. Did they straighten? Could he fight with them? What did they feel like?

Hellfire, they should *disgust* her. They did the very opposite.

Stryke's hot gaze met hers, as if he knew what she was thinking, or feeling at the very least.

She needed a drink—a shot of schnapps in her Gatorade.

Stryke straightened and crossed his arms, waiting.

Zoey looked to Demetrius. While they both sat on the TriSpecies Synod to rule their people, she deferred to him when it came to their team. He'd led from the beginning, and even after the Synod had requested—demanded—he take an advisory role, he was still their leader. Technically, she, too, had only an advisory role, but she couldn't advise if she didn't participate in the mission. At least that was the excuse she often used.

It was the most she'd toed any line. Her place as D's second and her seat on the Synod had saved her from a slow death of depression and loneliness. She wouldn't risk her place for anything, even a handsome demon and his supposed bond.

There were only two ways out of a bond. One was to bond to someone else, but her true mate had already come along and perished. The other was to kill Stryke.

Chapter Four

Stryke waited. Zoey wasn't jumping to his defense, no surprise, but her rigid body language said she was uncomfortable about something. The others were too honorable to kill him but were torn because it was the easy answer.

"Is it true, Fyra?" Bishop's deep voice broke the silence. "Could this male have possessed Zoey's mate, a prime vampire, and bonded to her without her knowing?"

"It's *Zoey*? I knew it. I knew you had good taste, Stryke. Umm…" she pursed her lips, "possessing a prime is a helluva thing. I mean, I couldn't do it, but maybe in like a hundred years I could, when I'm more powerful. Only thanks to Stryke, because he pointed out I had energy demon in my heritage and it was making my fire wacky."

"I didn't control her mate," Stryke interjected. He could've, but they were right. Mitchell had been a prime and his strong bloodlines could've overpowered Stryke or at the very least notified him something was wrong, at which point he'd have given Stryke the boot.

If the male hadn't been so conflicted about Zoey and her mission, Stryke wouldn't have had a shot.

"As for Zoey not knowing," Fyra continued, "easy-peasy. A little nip, a murmur of dedication." Her face screwed up. "Didn't you notice the sulfur taint to the blood?"

Zoey's jaw ground down. Stryke could imagine how the extremely private female hated talking about her most intimate moments in front of all her friends.

"No, I didn't," she said, like she'd disappointed herself.

Stryke stepped in with a little Possession 101. "Most demons barge into a host, try to take over. There's varying levels. I can be subtle; many others can't."

A cloud of hatred bloomed off the vampire with the dirty-blond hair and surfer-boy clothing.

Creed.

Stryke's lips curled in a snarl that he quickly covered. Zoey might've fucked him, but the male would have a fight on his hands if he thought that gave him any claim to her heart.

Stryke's frustration crested and he pushed forward. "Look, Zoey's in danger. Hypna knows about the bond and is after her."

Fyra growled. "That heinous hag is not going to touch my friend. I will fry Hypna's contemptuous ass. I don't know how yet, but I'll rain napalm down on her head."

Zoey stepped forward and addressed Demetrius. "I was attacked tonight. Three second-tiers and Hypna in a prime's body. I killed all the hosts and almost got sucked into hell, but…" She jerked her head toward Stryke.

"She got knocked out in the tussle." Stryke cocked a brow toward Zoey, whose cheeks pinked with embarrassment at how she'd blacked out. "I saved her."

"That's why I missed the Synod meeting, because he," she slanted a glare at him, "captured me."

Demetrius stabbed a hand through his hair. "We're not going to get ahead of the Circle if we're taking them on one by one with our own personal drama."

Stryke happened to agree. Destroy one demon and so many more were waiting to take its place. The thirteen ruling demons on the Circle were no different. "Hypna's targeted me for breeding."

Fyra gasped. "Bollocks! And when you couldn't impregnate her, she totally outed you."

He nodded grimly and didn't miss Zoey's sharp look. A flare of jealously? Territoriality? Stryke would revel in it if being with Hypna hadn't been such torture.

A female's voice drifted over the intercom. "Bonds keep demons abstinent?"

"That's my mate asking," Demetrius clarified. "She's our expert on demon lore and if you don't talk, we won't be afraid to fire at will. Prove you're not here only for yourself."

Stryke snorted. He never did anything for himself. He had always been farmed out for his abilities, and he'd drifted through life with his give-a-shit meter on zero. Until Zoey. Since then, everything had been for her, for getting back to her without his underworld baggage following him.

He rolled a shoulder. "Not all bonds can prevent sexual culmination. As long as energy is involved, I can manipulate many things. When an energy demon bonds, the connection strictly controls our ability to reproduce. Otherwise, we'd be pimped out left and right for our coveted powers. However, we can still…especially with Hypna's venom."

Fyra nodded. "She's a walking roofie."

Zoey's eyes narrowed and murderous intent rolled off her. Was it directed at him or Hypna? He never felt hope, but Zoey's reaction made him come close.

Demetrius flicked his gaze at the rest of his team and they lowered their weapons. "Who took Rancor's spot?"

Stryke had no issues sharing information. All of it would serve to protect Zoey. "Quution. He barely ascended. As an energy demon, his powers are as coveted as they are feared. But a few zaps, and he was the last demon standing. Then he targeted Hypna."

Fyra sucked in a breath, and Stryke inclined his head. "Indeed, it was an uneasy day in the underworld when he ascended." As if Hypna hadn't been after him before, she'd redoubled her efforts. Because high on power, Quution had more sinister plans for her. He wanted her for himself, and nothing scared Hypna more than being under another demon's control and enduring what she doled out to others.

Fyra filled in the details for the others. "If she could birth Stryke's young, she could sacrifice the child and absorb its powers. Fight Quution with her own energy. What. A. Bitch. Child sacrifices aren't even allowed in the underworld. Otherwise, all demons would breed constantly and fight over the young."

Stryke agreed. More fury wafted off Zoey. A good sign.

"You can see the incredible danger Zoey's in," he said to Demetrius. "A child that's half energy and half Hypna's atrocious nature would be a windfall of power. And"—he addressed Zoey regretfully—"you're in the way."

Creed spoke for the first time. "We'd solve so many problems if we killed you."

"And yet it still wouldn't make Zoey fall for you," Stryke shot back.

A shocked gasp rippled through the group.

Zoey pinched the bridge of her nose. "Well, that's awkward. As much fun as I'm having running through the details of the hit out on me, here's what my plans are: continue doing my damn job protecting the supernatural creatures of this realm. D, you and I need to talk about what we're going to tell the Synod. Otherwise, I'm going inside." She took a step toward the building.

"Come with us." Demetrius motioned to Stryke.

"I don't think so." Stryke flashed back to Lee's place with a smirk. Because he had Zoey's pack and she wasn't going to let her Gatorade go. Sure, she could get more, but she'd come after him. All he had to do was wait.

***

Zoey swore with the rest of her team when Stryke vanished. She almost stormed inside, but then she remembered—her motherfucking backpack. She didn't dare stockpile her juice or she'd have to explain that it might be more than a habit. If her teammates discovered she had special needs, they'd bench her. Her prime blood was powerful, and she'd even fed them her vein before but only when she could replenish her salts. What if they didn't keep her out of the field but then refused to take her sustenance when they really needed it?

No. Nope. She'd come this far hiding her deficiency.

"I'll be right back," she told Demetrius and flashed back to the house.

"No—" The rest of D's words were cut off.

She'd have to face Stryke alone; her money was in that damn pack. And he'd stashed her SUV somewhere. Stryke was an unexpected mess, but she'd clean up what she could.

She appeared outside of the window she'd fled through. She stomped through the snow to the back door, where she spotted their tracks from earlier. Smaller ones from the human, and larger, heavier ones from Stryke, who'd also been carrying her at the time.

A draft wafted over her and she spun.

Rourke stood with an unreadable expression. "What are you doing?"

Not all vampires could follow on the coat-tails of a flash, but Rourke could and had.

"Getting my shit from Stryke. I'll drive the SUV back." She gestured to where the tracks ran behind a shed. "I don't think Stryke will try to detain me if he wants us to think he's really after my best interests."

Why'd that set a pleasing simmer in her insides? She hadn't been looked after since Mitchell.

"I'll wait. It seems that when you all get bonded to a demon, rational thought becomes overrated." His tone was flat, but a muscle pulsed in his jaw.

As if Rourke had been *rational* when his female, Grace, had been possessed. Actually, he had. Angry and betrayed, but he hadn't turned on the team. Bishop had ditched them all to pursue Fyra, intent on "taking care of it" himself.

"Good idea." And it was. Rourke had her back, like he should. Because she should've planned out her backpack retrieval with her team. "I'll be right out."

She turned to face the door and her eyes narrowed. Stryke leaned against the doorjamb, arms crossed over his well-defined chest, his washboard abs peeking out from underneath. His biceps bulged, and since she sensed no tension from him, he wasn't even trying to look bulked up. His gaze tracked her and he didn't move when she approached. He glanced at Rourke and back at her.

"Need your pack?" There was that lace of humor again, but there was no trace of it on his face.

"You knew I'd be back for it, and the vehicle."

"Which one are you really after?"

"All of it," she said tersely.

He chuckled and turned to walk toward the room she'd been in. He'd given her his back. She worried her lower lip with a fang. Was she that transparent, or was he that confident he could thwart an attack from her?

She sensed the human in the house, but Stryke must've hidden him.

Interesting. He seemed almost protective of his host. She ripped her gaze off Stryke's broad shoulders and studied the place. Ornate, but outdated. Floral patterns reigned supreme in the furniture and decor. The smell was almost stale but like it'd been freshened recently. Fresh paint tickled her nose, and as they passed an empty room, she peeked in. Wallpaper hung from spots where it hadn't been fully removed. The house was being updated.

They approached the room her stuff was in.

"You wait out here," she said.

A low rumble resonated from him. Was he laughing at her again?

"Why, Zohana? Worried I'll accost you, or that you'll accost me?"

She glared at him but didn't reply. Then she patted her bun like it was a talisman for strength. And it was, in a way. Just like her black tactical clothing and weapons reminded her she had a job to do.

He entered the room and stepped to the side. She marched in, slung her bag over her back, and tried to leave.

He stood in the doorway.

"Move," she said between clenched teeth.

"What are you going to do about Hypna? She'll be back."

"We'll take care of her like we did Malachim. Like we did Bita. Like we did Rancor."

"May I remind you that only one of those is actually dead? And a more conniving demon took Rancor's place. Malachim will be back. Bita will be back. They'll finish sulking and seek a new host." He crossed his arms again, and like before, it drew her gaze to his chest. "Too many primes are bitter about the way your new government is stripping them of money and power. They can't corrupt the Synod like they could the Vampire Council. It's getting easier and easier for one of the Circle to possess a prime. Pretty soon, they'll line up to compete for one of the thirteen to cross into them."

Zoey's mood soured the more he spoke. It was easier to think about taking on one Circle member at a time, and since demons were so selfish and disorganized, the group didn't pose a huge threat themselves. But the magnificent bastard was right. They'd be back and her team was ill prepared to take on more than one at a time.

"Noted." She attempted to elbow him aside.

He used her proximity to his advantage and encircled her with his arms.

She was about to demand an explanation, but the words froze because in order to speak to him, she had to tilt her head back. She was a tall female, almost six feet in her boots, but he was several inches taller, even barefoot.

He dipped his head down. Her eyes flared, then drifted shut when his warm lips touched hers.

A growl resonated deep in his chest, vibrating into hers. She didn't mean to increase the pressure of the kiss, but his smoky-campfire scent assaulted her and the sensual sizzle when their skin touched was addicting. Her tongue swept out, and deep down she knew his salty skin would sate her craving.

Oh, his taste. With her need for extra salt, she'd always loved cured meat, and he was like a smorgasbord of the stuff. A huge slab for her to feast on. She could lick every inch of him.

His arms tightened around her and his shaft prodded her belly.

Oh, the size of him. Big all over.

He swept his tongue out to meet hers. Her hands, which she'd kept tucked to her sides to prevent herself from doing something stupid—like touching him with bare skin—splayed over his shoulders.

He was so warm under her hands, his skin much softer than she'd expected from his swarthy good looks.

Who was whimpering? Hellfire, was that her? Yes, because she wanted more, harder, deeper.

Their tongues tangled and the bastard scraped her fangs with his tongue. A dab of rich blood landed on her tongue. Her body soaked it up, greedy for more. She fed from others as little as possible. Feeding was what had brought her and Creed together, and it'd been so nice to just share something with someone again that she'd started sleeping with him. But it'd left her unfulfilled. Not like this kiss.

If Stryke kissed like this, what would sex with him be like?

She wanted to know. She *had* to know. How fast could she get her clothes off?

"Stryke, what did you need me to— Whoa, sorry."

Zoey yanked herself back with a gasp. Reality slammed back, along with logical thinking.

She'd been making out with a demon! Her occupation was at risk with his chatter about the stupid bond, but she'd been diving down to his tonsils.

She staggered back a few steps as Stryke glared over his shoulder, another deep rumble in his chest. His upper lip was curled into a sneer that bared a fang.

And it was so fucking hot.

Her gaze dipped down and heat bloomed between her legs. The tip of his erection poked past his low-hanging waistband. More than the broad tip was visible and she could barely tear her attention away.

Flustered, pissed at herself, and angry with him for interfering in her life, she shoved past him.

The young man at the end of the hallway walked backward until he hit the wall. This must be Lee.

"S-sorry to, uh, interrupt…" His light skin turned gray and her heightened senses picked up on his fear. And it wasn't of her, as if he knew of her and that she wouldn't kill him. Yet it wasn't terror of Stryke, but more like a fear of disappointment.

It caught her off guard. She'd expected the human to have a simpering will, his only goal to please Stryke to stay alive. But his smell, his darting looks full of apprehension between her and the demon—Lee was more of a lost man who'd found a mentor and didn't want to be abandoned again.

"You didn't interrupt a thing." She wished she could say something to calm him. Was he even old enough to drink? Why'd she feel protective of the human when he was willingly helping Stryke?

"Leave us, Lee." Stryke must've recovered and was coming after her.

She picked up her pace and wove through the house toward the door, but if Stryke tried trapping her against his hard body again, she'd somersault out the damn window again.

"Zoey—"

"Nothing to say, demon." The door was in sight and she refused to look back. Those violet eyes might make her slow enough that he'd catch her.

She charged out the door. Rourke was reclining against the shed, looking relaxed when he was anything but. Her friend's stare focused on the demon behind her.

"You know what you can have your human do?" she called over her shoulder. "Have him buy you some clothes."

Stryke's only reply was, "We're not done, you and I." He'd spoken softly. She doubted Rourke had even heard him.

She ignored him and trekked across the lawn. Time to go home, without her demon.

Chapter Five

"I-I'm so sorry." Lee's hands shook as he
pulled at his hair and paced the hallway.

Stryke's anger ebbed. "If it wasn't you, it
would've been the vampire."

The one known as Rourke. If Stryke had
kept Zoey any longer, her friend would've come
knocking, without the courtesy of actually knocking.

Zoey had wanted him. Her lust lingered on
his tongue.

Stryke smiled to himself as he entered the
room they'd been in. "I'm going to get some
sleep. Tomorrow, we do as the lady requested
and get me some clothes. Get some sleep, Lee."

Lee's blond head bobbed and he ambled off.

Stryke watched him go. The boy had come a
long way since Stryke had first possessed him.
The human had been lethargic and lacked ambition, left only with a sense of isolation. It'd
driven Stryke crazy, but the kid had possessed
money and assets at Stryke's disposal. So he'd
started guiding Lee toward a healthier lifestyle. If

Lee couldn't be useful to himself, he would be of
no use to Stryke.

"Stryke!" Lee rushed back into view, waving
his phone. "I just got this message." Lee read
from the screen. "B used to visit me in his sleep.
Just sayin', wink, wink. F."

Stryke chuckled and dismissed a perplexed
Lee.

Fyra, that crafty bitch.

Yes, Stryke would catch a few *z*'s. He
stretched out on the bed that still smelled sweet
like his female. Shutting his eyes, he tried to
steady his breathing.

How did this work? He went to sleep thinking about her and woke up next to her? Fyra had
said Bishop had done it. Had she tried? Maybe it
was a vampire thing and not a bonded thing.

He blew out a frustrated breath. Just fucking
sleep. The effort of healing from Hypna's torture
was catching up with him, and he glanced at himself. He hadn't showered.

Running through the shower, he scrubbed
himself off, then threw the dirty sweats back on.
If his plan worked, she'd be more receptive if his
dick wasn't waving in her face.

He settled into bed and steeped himself in
Zoey's fruit-juice scent.

Why the juice?

He drifted off with that thought and didn't
know how long went by before he opened his
eyes in a different dark room.

He was lying on his back, staring at the ceiling, like he had been when he'd fallen asleep.

Zoey's sweet scent surrounded him. Her walls were bare, unlike when she'd been living with her mate. She liked vibrant colors and had always bought fun decorations.

He frowned as he scanned the room. Everything was plain, unadorned, and boring as fuck.

How many years had she been living in this place? The compound itself was fairly new, but he almost expected packing boxes stacked against the wall. There weren't any, but he bet if he searched her room, her drab, dark clothing would be neatly folded in the drawers. Her hair ties and toiletry items would be tidy and organized. He'd find nothing of her real character at all.

As if she'd let that part of her die with her mate.

How many years had it been and she was still that dedicated to Mitchell?

But she'd still fucked Creed. Stryke suppressed a snarl. It had just been physical release. She was lonely. And if she cut off this much of her personality until she was a living shell…no wonder she'd needed comfort.

He heard a contented sigh and a foot prodded his calf.

Turning onto his side, his mouth quirked.

Typical Zoey. He had maybe a foot of the king-size bed while she slept spread out like a starfish.

Ah, sweet brimstone. Her hair was down. Glorious, silky locks framed her face and spread out on the pillow. When her bun was in place, she was all hard-edged warrior. When her hair was down, she was his ultimate temptation.

The first time he'd taken over Mitchell, the male had been almost ready to drift off when Stryke had floated to the front of his consciousness. The male had succumbed to sleep while Stryke had gotten full use of his body without being detected.

He'd done the same thing he was doing now. He'd watched a sleeping Zoey, marveling over how such a fierce female softened behind closed doors.

Stryke frowned at her choice of pajamas. Solid maroon pajama pants and a white tank top. Where were her adorable prints, the ones only Mitchell—and Stryke—had known about?

Much like her living quarters, she'd made herself blah, plain, when she was anything but.

He let out a sigh. The second time he'd managed to overtake Mitchell while sleeping was when he'd bonded to Zoey. He couldn't seem to help himself. An aimless life and suddenly she'd been his beacon.

He'd stroked her like so…Stryke feathered his fingers along her face, but without touching her. Showing up in her bed in the middle of the night, even if he was just an incorporeal dream, wouldn't go over well with her.

She might attack and draw her team in. Or she might not but still tell them about his visit. She was all about duty.

No, for now, he was content to look at her comforting beauty.

A sigh escaped her and she turned her face into his almost touch.

How badly he wanted to wake her. How long had he dreamed of this? Satisfaction like this was forbidden for one of his kind. After Mitchell had died and Stryke had been sent back to the underworld, he'd thrown himself into doing what he could to limit the Circle's effects on Zoey and her team. Then Demetrius had found his true mate, who had been steeped in underworld trouble, and Stryke had worked double-time, all while concealing his duplicity. When Fyra and Bishop had gotten their happily-ever-after, it had led Stryke here. He wasn't sure he was upset. Relieved? Sort of. He wanted Zoey, didn't care about anyone or anything as long as he was with her.

Zoey adjusted her position, curling onto her side, facing him. His chest swelled. She was seeking him out, even in her sleep.

"Mitchell," she mumbled.

Stryke's hopes crashed. For the eight millionth time, he cursed her true mate.

The dream state released him and he woke up in his own bed. He glared at the ceiling for another hour, his mind working over his dilemma. He couldn't go back to the underworld. He was just breeding stock down there, and not just for Hypna, though she was his primary threat. If it wasn't her, someone else would want Stryke's energy abilities. Would Quution hunt him because he didn't want energetic competition? Stryke had to consider him, too, a potential threat to Zoey.

With a gusty sigh, he came to the conclusion that nothing had changed. His only goals were to keep Zoey safe and make her fall in love with him.

**

Zoey downed her Gatorade. Her craving for a certain demon's blood was ridiculous and the juice was almost ineffective. Probably because she didn't feel like she needed as much after just one freaking drop of Stryke's blood.

She wove through the halls of the compound. Creed would be in his electronics lair.

Creed was their electronics expert. Stryke was an energy demon.

Did she have a thing for energy?

Mitchell had had nothing to do with either. But he was gone and she had a long life left to figure out her male troubles.

Before Mitchell, she hadn't been a big dater, hadn't had any long-term relationships. Primes were too superficial, and Zoey hadn't trusted any to get close. Then after she'd teamed up with Demetrius and they'd set about dismantling the way vampires lived in the world, she couldn't trust anyone but her team. So she'd fed and got it on when the urge arose, though it hadn't very often.

Now she was in a freaking love triangle. But Creed wasn't really into her. He was as lonely as she was and it's not like they could run around and make love connections while they worked. Not when their work pitted them against so many of their own kind. Like most in law enforcement, they didn't spend their time with the reputable members of the population.

She sensed Creed in his office and knocked.

"Come."

Her mouth quirked. He played up the casual vibe, but his formal prime upbringing often revealed itself.

She stepped in and he glanced up from the row of screens spread across his desk.

"Oh, hey." He cleared his throat and swiveled around on the exercise-ball chair he used. His voice dropped a few octaves. "Can I help you with something?"

Her smile probably looked as regretful as it felt. She'd cut things off with him over a month ago, and while his suggestive comments were always playful, she knew he'd strip if she said the word.

"I was checking to see if there's anything stirring out there yet."

Creed stared at her for a moment, like he was searching for a deeper reason for her to be standing in his office.

Maybe there was. Maybe she needed a friend. Maybe she was messed up inside after waking up from an erotic dream that had starred her and Mitchell. A memory, actually, one of their many lovemaking sessions. They'd whispered so many sweet nothings to each other, and they'd taken each other's blood, like they had many times.

Could that have been when Stryke bonded to her? No, she'd have known, right? Regardless, her emotions had been a jumbled mess since waking.

"Do you think he's telling the truth?" she blurted.

She snarled with disgust at herself and plopped onto one of the counters that lined his office and held several monitors.

Creed folded his hands in his lap. For once, he was dressed for the field, in black tactical clothing and heavy boots. It was a good look for him, more natural than Hawaiian shirts and board shorts.

"I think there's something between you two, yes."

Her brows shot up at his frank reply.

"Since Stryke has been in the picture *that we've known of*," Creed gave her a pointed look, like it was her fault the demon was tricky, "you've been acting differently. Distant, uninterested—not that you were really that interested in the first place." He muttered the last part under his breath. "And of course I can't forget you shouting 'he's coming' during climax."

A flush crept up her face. Yeah, that was why she'd ended it between them. Those words had been weird and disconcerting for them both. Yelling another male's name might've been more hurtful, but less confusing. But Creed had known where he stood in the love department. She'd never led him on. He'd been a friend with benefits.

Creed scrubbed his face and held her gaze. "I knew I couldn't compete with Mitchell, and this isn't about us anymore. It's about you and that bastard demon. If you're connected to him, we need to sever it. Because we all believe him that you're a target. And if you're a target— Here, look."

He swiveled around to the monitors.

Zoey cocked her head at one screen. The grainy black and white picture showed a brick-and-mortar manor, a common style with prime families. A woman with platinum, insanely curly hair chased two young vampire males around on the lawn. "Is that Melody?"

"Yes." Creed's tone was neutral, bordering on frustrated, like when he had to deal with the human woman.

Melody lived with Rourke's mate's parents as a nanny to Grace's brother and the boy her parents had adopted.

Zoey's gaze drifted over to the next monitor. No one was outside of the elaborate mansion, but from Bishop's reports when he'd been combing prime residences to find Fyra, Zoey knew this was where Ophelia had been staying with her on-again, off-again boyfriend.

"That's Nadair Moiré's place. Have you no-tified Ophelia about the trouble brewing?"

"I left a cryptic message, but you know how hard it is to get ahold of her," he said.

"What about the Blanchettes? Is Grace's family in trouble?"

Melody, her blond curls bouncing, was hopping and jumping around the boys as they frolicked. Happy, normal children. It was after dark, but Melody had adopted a vampire lifestyle to nanny the boys. Grace's parents watched from the front stoop, their smiles wide.

Zoey shoved away the wistful feeling that threatened to plague her.

She nudged Creed. "I'm gonna tell Melody you spy on her."

Creed shuddered and shook his head. "I will hunt you down and decapitate you before the words leave your mouth. That girl doesn't need any more fodder to crush on me." He pointed to a greeting card thrown on top of a stack of papers. "She even sent me a thank-you card for rescuing her when we saved Grace from Rourke's brother. It had little hearts on it."

Yet, Creed had held onto it. Zoey nearly chuckled until she remembered Melody was human and it'd only mean heartbreak for the girl and Creed.

Although being an immortal didn't promise a long and happy life. Sometimes it meant a long life to live with regrets.

"I'm showing you this because I *see* nothing." Creed switched back to the original topic. "But if you're being targeted to get close to Stryke, those close to you may be targeted to get to you."

Zoey's phone buzzed with a message from Demetrius. **Ready?**

The reason for the rest of her tangled nerves. They had decided to go to the Synod about what was going on with Stryke. Her guts roiled. She couldn't lose this position, she couldn't. Her fellow leaders would have to understand. She tried to feel hatred for Stryke, but it just stirred up memories of losing Mitchell. Only desperation pinged around her insides.

Chapter Six

Stryke reclined against the tree trunk that'd been his post for more hours than he could count. It was his second day on watch. Cold winter air didn't bother him and he wore nothing but black jeans and a long-sleeved black shirt. A black baseball hat concealed his horns and the ensemble gave him a little thug appeal but he could still walk around without attracting too much attention.

He wore no guns or knives, unlike the vampires. His claws, fangs, and energy were his weapons.

He sensed Zoey in the compound, but she was probably asleep. After his dream visit, he'd hunkered down in the trees and guarded her all day and through the night—after he and Lee had gone on a shopping spree. In the middle of the night, she and Demetrius had stepped outside, she'd glanced into the trees in his direction, and they'd flashed somewhere. Stryke had been tempted to follow, but she hadn't been roaming the realm alone.

When the vampires had returned, Zoey had stormed into the compound without a backward glance. Demetrius had stared at the gray concrete walls with his hands on his hips for a minute before following her inside.

Stryke could guess they'd had a Synod meeting and it hadn't gone well. Because of him?

He'd dozed, resting against the tree, for the rest of the night, but he couldn't escape the feeling of foreboding. Hypna wouldn't sit on her rage forever.

Daytime would be the most critical for Zoey. The vampires could defend the compound, but except for Bishop with his demon blood, the rest of them would fry in daylight. So Stryke waited.

His senses tingled at a higher level than normal. There were always demons of various levels roaming Freemont, but a group was getting closer to the compound.

Stryke pushed off the tree and glided through the woods. Any others wouldn't be able to sense him that easily, and he wore dark clothing that'd blend in with the shadows cast from the sun. Not much snow had made it through the trees to the forest floor so he didn't worry about leaving prints.

He scanned the woods. Something had arrived. Birds had gone quiet. He withdrew the phone he borrowed from Lee and sent Zoey a text.

Look alive. They're here for you.

He stuffed the phone back in his pocket and removed his hat to free his horns.

Crashes from deep in the trees echoed. Stryke shook his head. Idiots.

He wiggled his fingers and energy danced between the tips. He narrowed his gaze and spotted dark forms darting left and right with a trajectory toward the compound.

Stryke quit moving. He'd nail them one at a time as they left the tree line to attack the building. Then he'd circle the perimeter and destroy the rest.

He focused his senses. The air vibrated with demonic energy and Stryke sorted out the waves. Six second-tiers, all in human hosts.

Wait. He inhaled and tilted his head as if listening to the wind.

Evil approached. Larger and stronger than the six he detected.

Hypna.

He cut off a growl. The demon bitch thought she could get to him through Zoey. Even if he hadn't bound himself to the vampire, he wouldn't allow his seed to be used for Hypna's gain. He wouldn't bring young into the world to suffer. Not much lit a fire under his ass, but suffering under his mother, then his father, had made him homicidal when it came to those who hurt children.

A shot rang through the trees and fire lanced his shoulder.

What the hell? He touched a hand to the area where agony bloomed. Brimstone clouded the air and he looked at his hand. Stained with red.

Fury built. He'd stalled too long and allowed himself to be shot.

Baring his fangs, he charged the attacker, sensing him a hundred yards away. Stryke dodged left and right. Let the fuckers try to hit a moving target. Bullets whizzed past him. There was a second shooter standing feet away from the first, and Stryke would take care of him after he ripped the head off the first guy.

The host's eyes went wide with fright and he spun to run. Stryke jumped him, and they both tumbled to the ground. The human was more agile than Stryke had anticipated and rolled to his back. Drawing his knees to his chest, the host kicked out. Stryke batted his legs away, but the human flipped to his side and lashed out with another kick. His foot caught Stryke's chest and Stryke collapsed backward, trying to catch his breath. His shoulder screamed in agony at the contact.

With a snarl of rage, Stryke lunged and tackled the human. His torso was peppered with fists and elbows, but Stryke gritted his teeth against the pain. He managed to get both hands on him and send a surge of energy into the man's body to stop his heart.

"Take that, Hirsh," he snarled at the second-tier and jogged away to let the underworld reclaim his coworker.

An itch between his shoulder blades was his only warning. Stryke dove to the ground as another bullet whizzed overhead.

He glanced up toward the stark, gray building. Three humans were crouched at its base, searching for a way to infiltrate the vampires' den.

Stryke stayed low and inched to his left, circling around to attack the second shooter. Meanwhile, the sense that Hypna was getting closer and closer sent a wave of panic through him. An answering wave of energy followed his emotions.

Wasting no more time, Stryke drew his arm back like he was pitching in a human game of baseball and flung an energy ball in the general direction of the second shooter. An answering yell of pain put a grim smile on his face.

The ground shook with the second underworld portal opening, but Stryke ignored it and took off to deal with those who had made it to the building.

More gunshots, larger caliber than the gun used to injure Stryke from the sounds of it. Human yells, laced with the deeper voices of the second-tiers who possessed them, filled the air.

Stryke grinned again when he realized those shots weren't coming from the hosts. Of course the vampires wouldn't leave themselves totally defenseless in the daylight.

A charcoal sedan sped down the road and skidded to a stop in front of the compound, almost ramming the Double-D's Consulting sign. More possessed humans spilled out, but Stryke didn't sense Hypna. She was close, though.

A giant fireball exploded from the compound's first-story window. It hit the car, sending it several yards backward. It landed on its wheels but took out two hosts. A massive boom had Stryke covering his ears as the car, toasted by another blast of Fyra's unnatural fire, flew through the air. More gunshots and snow and dirt flew up where the bullets hit at the feet of the humans running for cover.

Stryke threw energy balls in their general direction but stayed close to the trees for cover. He didn't need any vampire—like Creed—deciding it'd be beneficial if Stryke were hit in the crossfire.

Blood seeped from his wound, which was already closing. Lee would have to sear several steaks to aid in his recovery. Maybe add a few burgers.

Unless Zoey offered a vein. Stryke's lust spiked, anticipating the act of taking her vein. The real him, drinking from her.

It'd been erotic as hell as a passenger in Mitchell's body, what would it be like—

"Why the lustful thoughts, Stryke?" a female's voice purred.

He whirled around to face a vampire, covered head to toe in black, gauzy fabric. His nostrils flared. Hypna!

He reached for her. One touch to electrocute the vampire.

With that damn vampire speed, she clapped a bracelet around his wrist.

Bile rose in his throat. He knew exactly what it was, had done the same thing to Fyra. He'd gotten a band on her that had been constructed and warded by the Circle to dampen her powers and force her to obey its wielder. But Hypna, the demented demoness, was clever enough not to use a material that could conduct electricity.

But plastic? He hooked a finger from his other hand under it.

"No breaking it," she said quickly. Then ticked each command off with a finger. "No using your energy. No trying to kill me. No trying to get the bracelet off." She laughed, an evil villain cackle. He was damned with a simple command. A band he could snap with his little finger, but under her compulsion, he couldn't touch it. "I knew you'd hide in these trees. The prime I chose is strong, and on a cloudy day in the shade of trees, well," a casual shrug, "you make some things easy even if you aren't. All creatures in love are predictable enough," she sneered.

Anger at himself throbbed through his body. How could he have not considered...any of it? The Circle limited themselves by possessing hosts and not walking the realm in their real forms, yet they found ways to cause more than enough trouble. He'd seriously underestimated her cunning.

The fight that had raged behind them at the building grew quiet.

The vampire's blood-red mouth, visible under the sheer fabric, spread in a malicious smile. "Now, do be a good little servant and go ask to get let in. Oh, and kill Zohana Chevalier and keep the plan a secret."

Stryke lurched forward, his body helpless to her commands. He fueled all of his energy into overriding the command, but the power infused into the delicate piece of plastic was too much for him. His energy circled like a caged tiger.

"And pretend you don't know a thing about the bracelet," Hypna called in a honeyed voice.

***

In Creed's office, Zoey held her radio in one hand and fisted the other in the lightweight fabric of her pajama pants. The only thing she'd taken time to do was twist her hair into a bun as she'd run to find out what was going on. She'd skidded into Creed's office and watched the monitor of the camera mounted above the main door. Stryke approached with halting steps. Something was wrong. She couldn't claim to know him, but he'd carried himself with confidence during their time together. Had he been injured? He wore all black, and while Creed had excellent equipment, she couldn't see much detail.

He knocked. "May I be allowed inside?" His voice was tight, his mouth in a grimace. Twisting, he scanned around him, his stony glare clinging to one area of the woods.

"Subtle, dude," Creed muttered and aimed another camera in that direction.

She and Creed leaned close to the screen, squinting, as if it would help them see through the branches.

A tall figure stood mostly in concealment, flowing black garments hanging off a wide-brimmed hat, but Zoey imagined the figure's gaze riveted on Stryke.

"Evil lady didn't realize black is shit camouflage." Creed punched some buttons that calibrated the guns they had hidden in panels outside the building. "Tell Fyra to keep her ass inside."

Zoey relayed the request into her radio.

"Got it," Bishop replied.

Creed pushed the intercom button to talk to Stryke. "Why do you want in? Are you cold?"

Stryke's face contorted. "I'm…injured."

Her hand went to her throat. She dropped it to her side. She was *not* worried about him.

"Then heal," Creed replied in the intercom.

Stryke took a step back, then stepped forward again. He clenched his fists and pulled his lips back in a snarl.

Odd. It was almost like he was fighting himself.

Stryke shook himself and craned his neck left and right. His mouth opened. Shut. Opened. Shut.

Yep. Definitely at war with himself. Or being controlled.

Zoey sucked in a breath. "Is he wearing jewelry?"

Creed glanced at her with an arched brow, then understanding dawned. "You think they're using a control device like they tried with Fyra? Are you sure that's not just wishful?" At her hard stare, Creed tapped the intercom button. "Hey, lover boy, hold up your hands."

Stryke stilled and raised his gaze to the camera. He raised his hands.

"Nothing." Creed tapped the camera to zoom in. "Wait. Is that a clear band?"

"It is!" Rancid anxiety washed through Zoey. Stryke was being compelled. To do what?

Nothing good for her or her team.

Creed relayed the information to Demetrius, who was hovering inside in the main door in case he would need to go out and fight.

"Shoot at the vampire in the woods," Demetrius said.

Fyra cut in over the radio. "I'll throw a fireball her way."

"No," Demetrius said quickly. "We can't risk a fire in the trees, especially not during the day when we're helpless to fight it."

Creed's fingers flew over the keyboards. Muffled gunfire could be heard but only because of her sensitive hearing. Zoey watched with morbid fascination as the clothed figure jerked and flinched.

A faint shout floated through the camera's microphone. A female. "Stryke, save me."

Stryke bared his fangs again, his muscles rigid. From resisting?

"Now!"

With a grunt, he pivoted and stormed toward the vampire. Did the mystery vampire host Hypna?

She grasped Creed's hand that was controlling the gunfire. The guns stopped. "We need to find out who that prime is."

Creed eyed her white-knuckled grip, then her. She snatched her hand back.

Demetrius broke into the tense silence. "Why'd you stop firing?"

Creed looked to her to answer.

"I made Creed stop," Zoey admitted. She had no good answer otherwise. She was almost positive that Stryke hadn't been tricking them. Almost.

Worrying a fang with her tongue, she nicked herself and winced. *Way to be hard core.* Stryke made it to the downed vampire and tossed the bundle unceremoniously over his shoulder. He stalked in the direction of the road. They were getting away and Zoey and her team couldn't pursue.

They watched as Stryke reappeared at the edge of the woods by the entry road and a second SUV sped toward them.

Creed zoomed in and scribbled down the plate number. "Now to hack the database and get us an address."

"Send me all the details." She breezed out of his office and back to her room.

Changing into her work clothes, she mentally inventoried what she'd need. An open juice sat on her dresser and she took a long swig.

A thirty-two-ounce bottle, and it was barely as effective as one drop of Stryke's blood. Why was demon blood so good for her condition?

Would Fyra's do the same? Zoey couldn't take the chance. No one knew about her electrolyte deficiency and as much as she adored the fire demon, Fyra spilled secrets almost as often as she left singe marks on the walls.

Zoey trusted her team, but information like that had a way of spreading. It'd start with safer assignments, then a friendly gesture, like a shipment of Gatorade as a gift. Questions would get asked, and with her position on the Synod already in jeopardy because of Stryke, she couldn't risk it. She and Demetrius were on the Synod because the strength of the families they came from had gotten them voted "most likely not to be ignored" by other vampires.

"Zoey, open up," Demetrius called as he knocked.

She zipped out to the door, opened it, and went right back to loading her weapons and arranging them on her body.

His face was drawn, his pale-green eyes tired. "What do you think you're doing?"

She sensed his concern. He wasn't physically fatigued, but his concern over her weighed on him and it was no surprise. He took on all their problems as his own.

"I'm going after him."

Demetrius crossed his arms. He was dressed like her, minus all the weapons. It was daytime so they weren't going anywhere. "To do what?"

She slammed down a knife she'd been about to strap on her hip. "I can't solve any of this without him. And..." Hellfire, should she even say the rest? "I can't let him be used by the Circle. Hypna's making him do...stuff."

That demon bitch touching Stryke made her fangs throb with the urge to rip Hypna's limbs off. Witnessing him run into gunfire to rescue her, even under compulsion, wasn't Zoey's fondest memory. She hadn't experienced jealously like that since...ever.

Demetrius gave her a look that said, *And that bothers you?* "She may not touch him. If they're still in this realm, she can't access her venom. If they go back to the underworld, then she might leave him be, sexually at least, since he can't finish. Torture's still on the table, I'm sure."

"How do you think she'll torture him?" Zoey shook her head. "Does it matter? He's going to get hurt because of me."

"He's going to get hurt because he's a demon."

"Would you say the same thing about Fyra? She likes him, that has to mean something."

Demetrius rubbed his eyes. "Look, Fyra's standards are different, we all know that. And Stryke hasn't proven himself like she has."

"Fuck, Demetrius. It's like you with Mitchell all over again." Zoey gasped at her outburst and put her hand over her mouth.

"I had nothing against Mitchell." Demetrius paused. "But like I said then, he was dedicated to you, not to the mission. I couldn't know that as soon as you were threatened he'd throw the rest of us under the bus to save you."

"How dare you say that?" Zoey crossed to him and shoved a finger in his solid chest. "He died for the cause. You're still here, spending each day with your lovely mate, while Mitchell's nothing but ashes."

Tears burned the backs of her eyes, but she refused to let her dear friend see her cry.

"Stryke isn't Mitchell," Demetrius said softly. "We don't even know how much of what he says is true. You've saved me with your blood and I didn't taste brimstone like I did when Calli was bonded."

"Stryke's brimstone isn't overpowering in the first place." She sounded like a petulant child. Her blood hunger roared back as she recalled his addictive taste.

A contemplative gleam entered Demetrius's eyes. "He admitted as much."

She shrugged. "Must be an energy thing. But I can't cut ties with him while he's in Hypna's control. She'll keep coming after us. At least since he's convinced he's in love with me, he can help us fight her. Who knows, maybe he'll realize that once he's free, he's not interested." Her heart constricted, threatened to cut off her breathing.

It was the stupid bond. She wasn't going to risk everything for a demon, no matter how well he kissed.

"Take Creed."

She cut Demetrius a sharp look.

Demetrius sighed. "Yes, I know about the thing you two had going, but I trust him not to be impulsive as far as the demon's concerned. Rourke's going, too, because I need a level head with you two. We get Stryke, we sever the bond, and we get him away from us."

"Agreed," she said before the bonded part of her could argue.

Chapter Seven

Zoey peered through night-vision goggles. She was planted in a snowbank, stretched out on her belly, wearing her standard black garb. The cloud cover over the nighttime sky cast shadows over their surroundings, concealing her better than moonlight.

Unfortunately, none of it would help with infiltrating the prime dwelling she surveyed.

A stretch of midnight-blue water sat between her and the house.

A private island. On a lake. Owned by a female named Yancy de Mornay, who had set up no-flashing wards over the entire island. The wards ebbed out over the shoreline and made Zoey's skin itch.

One of the things Zoey loved the most about her job was that the primes' money couldn't protect them from her and her team. It couldn't protect them from the Synod. However, money *could* build an island with the equivalent of a damn moat.

She stared through the goggles while Creed swore next to her. A hulking, dark monstrosity of a house had been plunked in the middle of the waterlocked landmass. Raggedy trees that had lost their leaves for winter, but wouldn't look much better with them, filled the perimeter between the building and the water's edge.

"How the hell do we get to that?" Creed dropped his goggles but stayed positioned in the snow.

Rourke shook his head. "We get wet."

Zoey had come to the same conclusion. Boats couldn't sneak up on the place. Cold water was an effective barrier for humans. But for vampires, it'd just be a frigid swim. Slightly less pleasant than lying in snow in the middle of the night. Could she pack a couple of Gatorades to guzzle after the trip? The energy of keeping herself warm, even as a creature who couldn't be killed by cold, could mortally deplete her. She would come out the other side, lie down for a nap, and not wake up until someone shoved a bleeding wrist in her mouth.

She hadn't packed her juice, had been in too big of a hurry to leave once the sun set. Most of the time, she didn't need much replenishment in the field, only in cases of extreme blood loss. Hopefully, this was one of those nights.

"Our guns might not survive the water." Zoey glared at the ice stretched over half the lake. The water was going to be more of an obstacle than she'd first thought. Swaths of ice and snowpack plugged most of the shoreline. "Are we going to take on vamps, possibly some possessed humans, and a demon?"

Stryke might be compelled to fight. She didn't think he'd do it otherwise. He was, literally, the lesser of two evils right now.

"We have enough blades between us," Rourke said. "We'll have the element of surprise and we can pilfer guns from our kills."

Creed snorted, his blue eyes flashing in the dark. "If we don't have the element of surprise as we're shivering our asses off, then what?"

"Then we cut a swath a mile wide," Rourke said, his face as placid as the half-frozen lake. "And rip that band off the demon so he can go all underworld on the rest of them."

"How do I know he won't go all underworld on me?" Creed pursed his lips as if he'd relish the opportunity to take on Stryke. "He's obsessed with Zoey and sees me as competition, though she's made it clear I'm not."

Zoey suppressed a sigh. Awkward. Nearly the whole time she and Creed had been sleeping together, they'd hidden it from their team. A month since she'd been with him, and it was being brought up constantly.

Thanks to that demon.

She couldn't summon as much anger as she wanted.

Zoey pointed to the right. "If we enter the water there, we won't have as much ice to bust through. The less noise the better. I'm sure it's monitored. Then," she swung her arm to the left to indicate the far shoreline, "we get out of the water there. The ice is thicker and if we can find a section to haul ourselves on, then we can flatten ourselves and slither to shore."

Creed nodded. "We'd still be noticeable, three black figures on white, but the overcast night helps."

Rourke cocked his finger toward the opposite end of the island. "I'll come out there. We have a better chance of one of us getting by their security if we split up. I'll also find a separate entry point."

Creed dropped his forehead in the snow. "Sometimes this job sucks." He lifted himself into a crouch and crept toward the agreed-upon entry point.

Zoey followed and Rourke split off in the opposite direction.

She crunched through the layer of ice rimming the shore. Old reeds crackled and the sound carried like a hammer through the night, but there wasn't much else to do. She could run and leap, but the splash and ripples might create more of a ruckus.

She picked her way behind Creed, using the path he'd already broken to help minimize sound. Ice water seeped through her boots and wicked up her pants. Yep, her energy took a downturn.

Could she ask Creed for a sip since she had no juice? Hell, she didn't want to ask…because she didn't want to drink from him. Before, it'd been a physically pleasant experience, but her emotions just hadn't been invested. What would it be like tonight?

Smooth and easy, Creed lunged into the water with a shallow dive. Inky water swallowed him and Zoey waited a heartbeat for him to swim clear before she dove.

The shock of the cold induced an instant ice-cream headache. She sucked in a mouthful of water but managed not to inhale it as the water froze the roof of her mouth. She fought the urge to surface and clamber to shore.

She'd heard humans became paralyzed from the cold when they fell through the ice, and she risked the same reaction. As her body fought the cold, her electrolytes would diminish until she couldn't heal herself as thoroughly as a healthy vampire.

Gritting her teeth and blowing out her mouthful of lake water, she used broad strokes to propel her along. Every minute, she and Creed rose to take a breath and ducked back under.

She sighted her objective with each breath and recalculated her direction. Supernatural senses were only slightly better than a human's in the frigid darkness of the water.

She bobbed with her head exposed to just under her nostrils as Creed tested the sturdiness of the ice layer. It was the middle of winter in Freemont, but this year, temps fluctuated enough to make ice cover sporadic and thinner than usual.

Fatigue weighed on her. She wanted to float for a while, let her eyelids drift shut, but her waterlogged clothing and heavy boots would drag her to the bottom.

She'd need a solid few pulls of Stryke's blood.

Creed's! Hellfire, *Creed's* blood.

She forced her lids wide as Creed jetted out of the water with as much power as he could muster and skittered like a starfish across the surface. He slowed, then abruptly stopped. He had to pry himself off as his clothing had frozen to the top.

His teeth chattered almost as loudly as when he and Zoey had crashed through the ice.

Zoey followed suit, but the shivers in her muscles made her grip rubbery. She hauled herself onto the ice only to slide back in.

Scrambling, she clawed and lost a fingernail or two to keep herself from submerging. She only felt the tug and rip of her nails; the cold had numbed the rest of her.

Creed grabbed the back of her shirt and hauled her flat next to him.

Her lower jaw had a life of its own as she shook and shivered.

"L-let's go." Creed dragged himself forward, gaining momentum the more he moved.

Zoey wasn't as lucky. Her body wasn't generating heat like it should. Her midnight swim was letting her disorder flourish.

"I need...your blood." Her lips barely moved. She hoped he understood what she'd said.

He nodded and cool relief flooded her. They were almost to the end.

A crack resonated from beneath her.

Oh shit. Cracks spread out in a radius all around her.

"Move, Zoey." Creed's panicked words were the last thing she heard as she plunged through jagged shards of collapsing ice.

Freezing water surrounded her once again and the surface floated farther away. Her feet touched the uneven bottom. There, just above her head, she could make out the difference between cloudy ice and clear water.

Just push off, her brain commanded, but her body couldn't follow.

Her muscles twitched, no longer shivering. The twitches were from her trying to move, but she remained as still as an ice sculpture rooted to the lake bottom.

A hand punched into the water.

Creed. Safety. The two words were the only thing she was conscious of.

She didn't want to die; she had a job to do. Her job had saved her after Mitchell died, and it'd save her again. Stryke's violet gaze flashed through her mind. Yes. He was her duty. That was why he was going to be the last thing she thought about before she lost consciousness.

No. She had to finish her damn job.

Raise. Your. Hand.

Creed was waving his arm, grasping for her. He must be able to see her. Could he see she hadn't moved?

Her right arm jerked.

Move.

Ever so slowly, her arm drifted up in front of her eyes. She kept ordering it to go higher until her marbled skin brushed Creed's fingers.

He reacted instantly, circling her wrist and yanking her up and onto the ice next to him.

Lacking all stealth, he rushed her to shore. Ice cracked under them, but they moved too fast to fall in again.

They got to shore and Zoey barely noticed it wasn't any warmer.

His face pale, his mouth set in a line, Creed raised his wrist and bit down.

Zoey was as motionless as she'd been in the lake.

He slapped his wrist to her mouth and cool blood spilled in. She swallowed and a tiny amount of strength bloomed. As Creed healed, his blood warmed and so did Zoey.

There was nothing sensual or pleasant about the feeding. It was pure survival.

A male's roar shook the night. Zoey recoiled from Creed, flinging his wrist back at him. "He's coming."

***

He felt Zoey drink another male's blood.

Rage, hot and fierce, speared his logical mind.

Hypna's calculating chuckle, cloaked in Yancy's voice, broke through his fog of fury. Her back was to Stryke as she monitored the shoreline. "Look at that. She's drinking him dry. I guess you won't resist when I tell you to kill her. Kill her. Kill him. Don't stop until they're dead."

He stormed off. Any gratefulness he'd experienced at his female's arrival had dissipated.

As soon as the vampires had neared the lake, Hypna's lackeys had manned the windows to watch. Hypna had abandoned her efforts to seduce him, which she found a whole lot more challenging without stabbing him with her horns and poisoning him.

Stryke charged through the manor. His horns straightened past his hair as he banged out the door.

The three possessed humans that had survived the attack on Demetrius's compound scattered out of Stryke's way.

His eyes probably glowed with the energy coursing through him.

His female. Had drunk someone else's blood.

His female. Lips on someone else.

It was one thing when she hadn't known he existed. Now, it was intolerable.

Hypna's command raged through him. Kill them. Kill them all.

He brandished his claws and crossed the expanse of the lawn to where Zoey was wobbling to her feet. Creed was helping her. A fleeting moment of concern was quashed by ire.

Creed's hands. Were on her.

Kill them. Kill them all.

"Stryke." Zoey staggered back out of Creed's reach and wiped her mouth.

Stryke's lips curled back into a snarl, his fangs dripping with bloodlust. Someone else's blood stained her lips.

How long had he watched her from within her mate? How long had he kept his hands to himself to let her process the loss of her mate? For *five years*, he'd wasted time in the underworld to give her time to heal, to figure out a way to reveal his connection to her without her burying a knife in his chest.

For what?

She'd sucked on Creed's vein right under his nose!

There had to be a reason. There was always a reason with Zoey.

Hypna's commands beat around his skull, pounding his common sense to dust. What had he just been thinking?

Metal glinted in Creed's hands and fueled Stryke's killing haze.

Stryke's gaze locked on him and he charged.

Creed leaped and met him halfway. Stryke lowered his head and skewered Creed in the shoulder. Pain blazed in Stryke's side. Creed must've stabbed him, but Stryke's adrenaline was running too high for the blow to register. Creed shoved him away and ducked under the reach of his horns to plunge his bloodied knife back into him. Stryke wrapped his arms around Creed and flipped him to the ground.

Creed's head bounced on the frozen soil, leaving him dazed. Stryke bared his fangs and lunged, aiming for his throat.

A force tackled him from behind. Zoey's scent enveloped him, calming him only slightly.

Kill her.

He shook his head as he tried dislodging her.

She bashed her elbow into the crook of his neck. The power drove him to his knees, but he surged back up.

"I thought you didn't want to hurt me." She sounded breathless from the struggle, but she managed to hook an arm around his throat and squeeze.

"I don't," he huffed. No, that wasn't right. "I do."

He'd used up the last of his air. He bent and twisted to fling her over his shoulder, but she wrapped her legs around his waist.

Wasn't there a time he would've killed for this contact?

Kill her.

No, that wasn't right either.

Her arm was a vice, cutting off his air. He'd recover, but she was going to incapacitate him.

Creed rolled off the ground to his feet. He crouched and hovered around them, waiting for an opening. Stryke swelled with fury, seeing the male. He reached back, grabbed Zoey's damp head, and yanked her over his freshly healed shoulder.

She wasn't strong enough for him and her grip loosened. Stryke tossed her and caught her, putting her flush against him, her back to his chest. This time, he anchored his arms around her and his fangs hovered at her neck.

"I hope you enjoyed drinking from your boy-friend," he growled. Unfamiliar rage slammed at his skull, demanding he hurt her.

She clawed at his arms and he let an evil smile cross his face.

Then his smile faded.

Zoey was in his arms and he was supposed to kill her. But he didn't want to. Did he?

His fangs were poised over her jugular. Would she taste like Creed? Stryke spit to the side and returned to her neck.

Kill her.

No.

"I would've died if I hadn't," she said.

He blinked. He didn't want her to die. But he was supposed to kill her. Why again?

He gave his head a strong shake. He was never confused. The movement stirred up her scent, an action that should've enraged him, but instead he sniffed.

He detected the other male, but brushed it aside to get to Zoey's scent. She smelled…sick… No. Not completely healthy was a better way to describe it. Had he always brushed aside that aspect of her scent before? Zoey's strength and confidence didn't convey illness.

His grip loosened just as Zoey snapped something at his wrist.

Clarity rushed back, but he didn't drop Zoey in shock, he hugged her closer.

Sweet brimstone, he'd been trying to kill her.

Creed froze, eying him warily. When his gaze flicked ever so slightly over Stryke's shoulder, Stryke pushed Zoey away.

Before he could spin, something lodged into his back and he dropped, blinding pain spread over his torso.

His face buried in the snow-packed ground, he coughed. A knife lodged next to his heart made breathing excruciating.

"Aw, man." Zoey's voice echoed like his brain was a tin can. "I just got the bracelet off him."

"I didn't know if he was going to stop trying to kill you." Was that Rourke?

"Should I shoot him in the head to incapacitate him while we search the island?" Creed would likely do it anyway.

"One of us should stay with him while the others look for Yancy," Zoey said. "She must've been the cloaked figure in the woods."

Yes, it was. Stryke couldn't talk. He was stuck in a state of constant healing from what would've been a fatal wound in a human.

"I'll stay." Dammit. Rourke.

In his periphery, boots crunched away. Zoey and Creed were paired up. Anger and frustration clouded out the pain.

Rourke squatted next to him. Stryke turned his head as much as he could to look into the serious, dark gaze of the male.

"I'm gonna keep you there until they get back. Savvy?"

Yep, he most definitely understood. Stryke moved his head a millimeter in an attempt to nod.

"Are they going to find anyone?"

"Yes." It came out as a croak.

The farther away Zoey got with another male, the more adrenaline flooded Stryke. He twitched his shoulders. Fucking hurt, but he could move if he had to. He'd need to refuel with some serious beef and ice cream after this.

"The prime?" Rourke asked.

"Plus her second-tiers. Three left."

Rourke rose. "Then we wait."

Stryke relaxed, reserving his energy. Zoey and Creed were skilled enough to take care of everything on the island. It's not like Hypna had had enough time to booby-trap any of it. She wouldn't stick around and risk her host getting killed, but Zoey and her team would probably let Yancy live to interrogate her.

If you asked him, staking her would be the best thing in Stryke's opinion, or Hypna would keep using her. But no one was going to ask him.

Chapter Eight

Zoey crept through the mansion. She sensed a vampire and human hosts but not as much brimstone as she'd expected.

Had the demons fled, leaving their hosts to deal with the fallout?

She snorted softly. Probably. Cowards.

At least strength poured through her veins, thanks to Creed's generosity.

Stryke had been so volatile. How much of his murderous rage was due to the band she'd snapped off him? Not all of it, and that was a problem. If he was so territorial of her he'd hurt her or her friends, well, this thing wouldn't work out between them.

She stalled and Creed frowned over his shoulder at her.

She waved off his concern and increased her pace. Why in the world was she thinking in terms of a relationship? Must be brain fog from the ice water.

Totally the reason.

But she'd have to watch herself around him. His alleged connection to Mitchell could weaken her resolve.

The scent of sulfur and rich vampire blood grew thicker. She didn't bother with her gun but pulled a six-inch knife out of a thigh holster. Its cold bit into her hand, but she was confident it'd work better than a waterlogged, half-frozen gun.

A bulky form darted out from behind her with no stealth whatsoever. Zoey spun and buried the blade in the person's gut.

The man's face pulled back with shock and pain. The wooden stake he clutched tumbled with a clatter to the floor. Zoey withdrew her blade and he landed in a heap.

His eyes had been clear. The demon that had been inside him had left. They were no longer just recruiting humans as hosts, but as body-guards.

A scuffle caught her attention and she spun toward Creed. He had another man slammed against the wall, the man's arm in a vice grip above his head. This human fisted a stake like the human Zoey had killed.

Creed bared his fangs and struck. The man's cry drowned to a gurgle until he died. Creed withdrew his fangs, let the man drop, and wiped his mouth on his shirt.

"Yuck." He spit mouthfuls of blood on the body. "Like sucking on a book of matches."

But Stryke's blood wasn't. He had the sub-tlest tang of brimstone…

Zoey cut off that thought. That male scram-bled her brains.

"We might find one more human and Yancy." Creed crept forward. He'd also drawn a knife. Capturing a prime would take more than fangs.

They wove through hallways. The mansion was dank and lifeless. No wonder Yancy had offered herself up as a host. She must be going bat-shit crazy, alone on this island.

Zoey didn't know her personally. They'd gone to school around the same time, but the female had always kept to herself. She'd always reminded Zoey of the vampire version of Wednesday Addams. Straight black hair, big eyes, and a creepy vibe a mile wide.

Yancy's scent grew stronger as they neared the far end of the house. They could find no basement in the place. The lack of light came from blackout shades on every window. A few were raised. The guards must've been watching for them.

Creed broke to the left of the closed door at the end of the hall. Zoey took the right.

Loud blasts rocked the walls, and wood from the door fragmented outward. Creed and Zoey ducked while bullets flew overhead.

Zoey grunted as two rounds struck her.

Shit! Fire burned in her thigh and from a long graze over her back.

The scent of Creed's blood mingled with hers. He'd been hit, too. She crouched lower and caught his eye.

His shook his head to convey that his wounds were minor, nothing to worry about.

Zoey embraced the pain. It warmed her, even as blood leaked out, taking precious electrolytes with it.

The gunfire died down. She and Creed maintained eye contact. She nodded and they both spun toward the door. Little remained for her to kick down. She stomped through, letting the agony in her thigh propel her through the door.

A woman reared up and Zoey flung her knife. It landed with a *thunk*, buried to the hilt in the woman's chest. She cartwheeled backward, dropping her machine gun. Zoey didn't have to keep watching to know that the woman had been dead when she'd hit the floor.

She and Creed spread through the room. Zoey had expected a bedroom, but it was a huge sitting room. Antique, upholstered chairs dotted the floor. It was easy to see that no one hid around the furniture.

Zoey looked toward Creed. He motioned to the walls.

Right. Yancy's scent was strong. She was in here, but there wasn't adequate hiding in the rest of the room.

The prime had to have a bolt-hole.

Zoey rolled her eyes. A hidden room. Real original, and a favorite among vampires.

They swept the room, looking for knobs and levers disguised as everyday items.

Zoey spotted three possibilities. A bookshelf with perfectly lined books. A random picture hanging by itself on a section of wall several feet from the bookshelf. A fireplace poker alone in a stand next to the opening. The fireplace itself was spotless.

If she were a vampire who suddenly had a need to hide her brimstone-tainted scent, which place would she choose? Zoey drifted closer to the fireplace.

Creed inclined his head and stationed himself between the picture and the bookshelf. If the poker was a fluke, Creed would pick one of the others to try, and Zoey would dive for the third.

She jiggled the poker, moving it around like the clutch of a stick-shift vehicle.

Stone scraping against stone shrieked through the room. The entire section of wall that held the fireplace swung out. Zoey jumped back and busted the poker out of the stand. She brandished it like a baseball bat. Yancy came flying out of the opening, fangs flashing and claws extended, hollering a shrill battle cry.

Zoey swung. Yancy's head recoiled backward and her body followed. She landed with a thump, her eyes dazed as she blinked at the ceiling.

Zoey stood over her. Yancy's eyes were mud brown, free of demonic influence. Zoey inhaled. The brimstone tinge was fading. Hypna must've abandoned her.

"Yancy de Mornay," Zoey lifted the poker for another swing, "you're coming with us."

Yancy's eyes flashed with rage and intent, but before she could react, Zoey put her poker into motion. She whacked the prime hard enough to knock her out.

Creed came up beside her. "I don't feel like carrying her. How about we hog-tie her and drag her out?"

Zoey shrugged. "Sounds good. At least now we can use her boat to get back to shore."

***

Rourke, the sadistic bastard, had kept the blade in Stryke's back until they reached the manor. "Better than cuffs," the asshole had said.

Creed came out dragging Yancy, who was unconscious, a poorly healing red welt on the side of her head.

Stryke rose to his knees and swayed. They should've killed her. And he told them so as he examined Zoey. He smelled her blood, but she walked like she'd healed already.

"We don't kill indiscriminately," Creed said with an arrogant tilt to his brows. Zoey stood next to him. Several strands of hair had escaped her severe bun, but damn, it'd held up well through the swim and their struggle. He smelled human blood on her and assumed they'd taken care of the hosts.

In her hands were a stack of papers and a thumb drive. Her expression was more stoic than normal.

"Hypna's a sneaky bitch," Stryke wheezed, hating himself for appearing weak in front of Zoey. "Ask yourself: Why didn't she make another attempt to kill Zoey? Why not sacrifice the host?"

Creed's eyes glinted with dislike. "Maybe hosts are hard to come by."

Stryke barked a laugh and *fuck*, that hurt. "I think it's getting easier. You lot aren't as popular as you'd like to think. A ton of vampires don't want to be ruled by a government that includes shifters, or their half-spawn." He shook his head, only to freeze mid move. It jiggled the blade in his back.

"I'm afraid he might be onto something."

Stryke shot a surprised look toward Zoey.

She tapped Yancy's skull to make sure she was still out. "Hypna had a reason for leaving her. She could've been counting on us throwing Yancy in our prison so Hypna could inhabit her there."

"Where she'd be in prison," Rourke pointed out.

"But closer to me, and him." Zoey tipped her head toward Stryke. "Better odds of getting to us. We need to hold her somewhere else."

Creed made a disgusted sound. "I just towed her ass all the way out here. Fine. Where should we hold her? Here?"

Zoey shook her head. "Only if it's the last option. We don't know who knows about this place. And you can't flash from here. Plus, we have these." She waved the documents. "Hypna's targeting anyone who's close to us who—"

"Grace's family?" The urgency coming off Rourke was the most emotion Stryke had witnessed from him.

Creed nodded, his solemn expression increasing the anxiety emanating from Rourke. "Melody and the boys, too. Demetrius's parents." He toed his unconscious load. "I hate to say it, but the demon is right. If we bring our loved ones to the compound for safety, we can't have this monster under the same roof."

"Where the fuck do we put her?" Rourke eyed Yancy like he'd rather stake her and forget about her.

A wave of dizziness crashed into Stryke and he swayed on his feet.

Zoey's incensed words broke through. "Rourke, did you leave the knife buried in him?"

Rourke shrugged, his mask of calm back in place.

"A minor nuisance." Stryke held himself rigid, not wanting Zoey's pity.

"It looks like more than that," she said.

"I was talking about Rourke."

Zoey snorted a laugh, then her shoulders went rigid. She turned to Creed. "We're running out of night. I hate to leave her here, but our kind is safer with her on this island. Can you rig up a surveillance system that'll trigger if someone gets on the island?"

"I have some items in the vehicle. I'll go put her back." He walked away, grumbling, "I might knock her head against a few more doorframes and walls."

"Be my guest." Zoey faced Rourke. "I trust you can restrain her so there's no way she'll go anywhere?"

"I won't make it comfortable."

Zoey's mouth twitched, then she turned serious. "I'll head back with the demon."

Rourke's black gaze flicked to Stryke and back.

Zoey arched a brow in challenge. Was she waiting for Rourke to offer Creed's chaperoning capabilities?

Rourke merely nodded and strode toward the mansion.

"Two things." Stryke held up two fingers in defiance of the nausea punching him in the gut. Bile rose in his throat, conjuring fantasies of removing the blade and jamming it hilt deep into Rourke's gut. "I need the knife out of me, and I need to get my things from Lee's place."

She made no move to help him with the knife situation. "You have things?"

"As of yesterday morning."

"You just tried to kill me a couple of hours ago."

He scowled at the reminder of helpless confusion and murderous rage. Never again. "You're alive, aren't you? And I've had a knife buried in my back for two hours." He scanned the ground around him. "Where's that damned bracelet anyway?"

Why hadn't he been obsessed with finding it before? It might've busted off him, but its power was probably still intact. He shuddered. She who wielded the bracelet, wielded him.

"In my pocket."

He narrowed his eyes at her but couldn't discern her thoughts.

"Destroy it." He should say please. But he was a demon and the bracelet was worse than the blade.

"No."

"No?"

"You bonded to me without permission. I'm keeping the bracelet."

"To turn over to Demetrius?"

"No."

"To give to the Synod?"

"No."

They stared at each other.

Her tone offered no negotiation, but at least she wasn't handing it over to anyone else.

She broke the silence. "Turn around."

He did. Presenting his back to another being wasn't a natural action, but someone had already stabbed him in it anyway.

Without warning, she yanked the knife free. He released a shout, partly from shock, but *dayum*, it was like being stabbed all over again.

Relief flooded his tight muscles and he dropped his head back. Warm blood seeped down his back and he welcomed it. Sweet brimstone, the constant pain was gone.

"We gotta take the boat back." Zoey was already several yards away, moving swiftly and efficiently.

He jogged up to her and matched her stride. "About the choke hold earlier…"

"Yeah."

The words "I'm sorry" hovered on the tip of his tongue, but verbalizing it was so foreign. Zoey was a smart female and she'd know the circumstances. Apology averted. "You said that if you hadn't fed from Creed, you'd have died."

Her pace slowed for a beat, then resumed. "And you bought it and didn't kill me. Sounds like it worked."

"Your poker face is superb, but I know you're lying."

"Why else would I say it? I needed to warm up after the freezing water and Creed has been my blood source for a while now."

"Not any longer," Stryke growled. "Besides, he'd just gotten out of the water, too."

"And?"

Stubborn female. He worked another approach. "Let me ask you this. If you'd had Creed on the left and a crate of Gatorade on the right, which would you have chosen?"

They neared the boathouse, a small, square structure that housed a second fishing boat. The dock stretched into the water about twenty feet and the boat Stryke had arrived on was tied off at the end. A third boat would be sitting at the dock on the far shore. The no-flashing wards were a pain in the ass, but effective.

Zoey gave him a sidelong look. "My choice is my business."

"Humor me."

"I am by answering. I don't need to say a damn thing. By the way, you're welcome for saving your ass."

Touché.

She stepped off the snowy path and onto the dock, her steps light and sure. "We'll stop by Lee's, get your shit, and go back to the compound. Think you can behave?"

Not where you're concerned.

The boat rocked as they boarded. Zoey froze and inched slowly to the driver's seat.

"Worried about being dumped in the cold water?" he teased.

She glared at him before firing up the motor as if she handled fishing boats on a daily basis.

They didn't talk on the way across the lake. He watched her strong profile. Long, straight nose. Strands of brown hair framed her patrician features, her doe-brown eyes monitoring the boat's progress.

When they docked, he let his evil side flare and shook the boat extra hard as he jumped out.

Zoey yelped and flashed onto shore next to him.

Laughter bubbled up within Stryke.

"Asshole," she muttered and flashed.

He followed her energy signature, a comforting weave through the spectrum, easy for him to trail.

He appeared next to her outside the back of Lee's house. Tension radiated off her and he snapped his gaze toward the house.

Lee's scent was suffocating. That only happened when—

No.

Stryke sped toward the house. The back door hung askew. Sulfur mingled with Lee's blood. Stryke dreaded what he'd find as he charged through the busted door. He ripped it off the rest of the way, tossed it aside, and skidded to a halt.

The mudroom was a bloody mess. Lee was spread-eagled in the doorway, fully clothed, but they hung off him in tatters, shredded by claws and fangs. The kid's throat had been ripped out.

Stryke shoved his hands into his hair, his horns straightening in rage.

"Oh no…" Zoey was behind him.

Stryke hadn't heard her come in. He couldn't take his eyes off Lee. "He was just a fucking kid."

He let his hands fall to his sides. He rubbed his chest. The ache in his back was nothing to the unidentifiable, dull throb he felt now.

"You cared for him."

"Of course not—he was just…a host." Stryke swallowed hard. The energy he kept tucked away, coiled into a ball at his disposal, unfurled. Lee was so young. He'd been so lost, dependent on Stryke.

So young… Lee was as close to an innocent as Stryke had ever met. And that demon bitch had *killed* him.

Stryke splayed his hands wide. Lines of energy danced between his fingertips. He ordered himself to get it under control, but energy zipped through him from head to toe. Any lights that Lee

had left on before he died blew out, glass shatter-
ing. It went dark and shadows fell across Lee's
body.

Ball it up! But he couldn't. He couldn't tell
himself Lee was just a host. He and Lee had gone
fucking *shopping.*

If he didn't release some energy, he was going to fry the neighborhood. He dropped to his
knees and bellowed.

Chapter Nine

Zoey covered her ears as electric shrieks coursed through the tiny room. She squeezed her eyes shut against the arrows of light zinging all over. Were they coming from Stryke?

Pain filled his deep voice as he hollered. The lights must be making the shrill noise.

She should be used to this. When the compound's industrial fire alarms went off, much more frequently now that Fyra was in residence, they shriveled her eardrums. Her sensitive vampire hearing could be out of whack for hours after they shut off. But this felt like Zoey was standing in a small room with ten of those alarms, plus twelve disco balls.

She dropped to her knees and curled into herself, her mouth open in a soundless cry.

Abruptly, it stopped.

Silence. Her ragged breaths were as loud as crashing ocean waves. She released her ears and tentatively opened her eyes.

Stryke's back was to her. She crawled toward him and placed a hand on his shoulder.

He jerked his head to the side, his shoulders heaved, his expression stricken. "I need to bury him before we go."

"Wait."

When he winced, she realized she'd shouted because she couldn't hear a damn thing. So she pointed.

He followed her finger to the bare wall to their right. What had once been a closet was hanging open, all the coats flung down. Blood was smeared in stark contrast to the white wall.

You belong to me and no one else.

"She will die." Stryke popped up and bent toward Lee. He hefted the body into his arms and cradled him like a child.

Was that what Lee had been like? Not like a child, but someone Stryke felt responsible for, a lost soul he'd helped find a place in the world.

Only days ago, when she'd come awake in the guest room, Stryke had hidden Lee from her. She'd thought he had ulterior motives, but protection had been the only one.

Lee dripped blood as Stryke carefully carried him outside.

Zoey gave Stryke some space to figure out what to do with the body. The ground would be too frozen to dig a hole. They could do it with their combined strength, but the chunks wouldn't settle well over Lee's body.

She inspected the room Lee had been killed in and the surrounding rooms. The entire house had been trashed. She located shopping bags that had been left untouched. Stryke's?

Grabbing those, she finished her search. She found no other messages, written in blood or otherwise.

Her nose tickled. The smell of charred flesh floated through the house, but she detected an odd odor to the scent. She peeked out the window to see Stryke with a hand splayed over the prone form. He was using his energy to cremate Lee, leaving behind the smell of burning electrical wire.

His back was to her, but she imagined the look on his face. His violet eyes would be empty, or simmering with rage. His mouth set and his square jaw rigid. The male was capable of great emotion, a trait she hadn't expected from a demon. She saw hints in Fyra, but Bishop was probably the sole witness to the depth of them.

When Lee had been reduced to nothing but ashes, Stryke fisted his hand and let it drop to his side. Zoey tightened her grip on the bags and went out to meet him.

"Do you need anything more than these?"

He shook his head without looking at what she held.

Zoey waited a few more moments, unsure what to say. Dawn was soon approaching. Stryke wouldn't be bothered, but she'd depleted her resources once already tonight. Healing from the weak morning rays of the sun wouldn't be smart.

But she couldn't prod Stryke before he was ready. After Mitchell had died, she'd wanted to drag a sleeping mat to the spot he'd perished and camp, just to be close to him. Stryke had lost…

what? A friend? A mentee? Whatever Lee had been, Stryke needed another minute.

"I'm sorry," she finally said, "about Lee."

"He was young and stupid." Stryke's rough voice was thick. "His parents are still alive and I have no idea when they'll figure out their son is missing. They'll probably just be dismayed that they have no one to watch the house. Or relieved that they no longer need to deal with a son they never wanted." He barked a sarcastic laugh. "Yet I'm the evil one."

Zoey's forehead wrinkled with surprise. Fyra had made similar comments. Before her, Zoey had functioned under the assumption that all demons need to die. But Stryke was right.

"He didn't invite me in." Stryke's hands were balled into fists. "He was such a sad sack that it was easy to walk into him. It made sense to keep using him as a host, and he listened." Stryke shook his head. "And he didn't freak out when he saw me or learned what I was. Just soaked up everything I said. I should've left him alone."

Stryke rubbed his chest.

Was he feeling...guilty?

Zoey cleared her throat, which was suddenly thick with emotion. "Nothing will ease the pain of loss but time. But, from what you've said, I don't know that Lee would've changed anything."

Stryke spun on her with an incredulous look. "The pain of loss? I'm angry that she took something that was mine!" He pivoted back, grief clear in his features. "I'm not...sad."

Uh-huh. The light show earlier was not just him being pissed. "We need to get back. The sky is already brightening."

He turned back to her. "Yes, I wouldn't want you to burn yourself and turn to Creed for comfort."

"Dude." She shoved his belongings into his chest. He was hurt and angry, and it was okay if he directed cutting comments at her to hide his pain, but she had to get one thing straight. "Mating me against my will doesn't give you authority over me."

She flashed back to the compound. The drab, gray exterior softened her anger.

Stryke arrived a second later. "It's not you and Creed—"

She rolled her eyes toward him.

"Okay, yes. It is. But I'm more perturbed that you won't tell me what's wrong that you weaken after such exertion."

He'd lost Lee and now her condition was likely bugging him more. She accessed the building and let him in. The door swung shut behind them and she led him to her room.

She hadn't informed Demetrius, or anyone else, that she was bringing him back here, didn't want to face another charged conversation. After Lee's brutal murder, she couldn't leave Stryke at his place. If Stryke was the okay-ish demon he claimed to be, then making him find refuge in the underworld where the Circle wanted to breed him didn't make sense. Not because she didn't want anything bad to happen. If they succeeded, what would the power from Stryke's young give them?

So she asked.

Stryke's expression remained placid. "It's just Hypna's plan. In a cruel twist of fate I'd enjoy watching, the new Circle member has been after her. I don't know why, probably to control her in some way."

Zoey stopped in front of her door. "That's awful."

He shrugged. "Power and control are her only priorities. I could've been sacrificed, too, but both my parents already had energy abilities. It would've been a waste of effort." There was a trace of bitterness in his tone. "There's so few of us, and most are in hiding."

"Why?"

He hesitated before answering. "I'm kind of the poster child for why. Desired servant of each one of the thirteen, enslaved for my seed. That's the norm down there anyway. It's just worse if you possess a coveted ability."

What a shitty existence. She let him into her apartment, the act so natural it should disturb her. Stryke was in her home. A stark warrior with exotic eyes roaming her plain, unadorned place.

"But your parents raised you?" Zoey asked.

"Parent, not the plural." Stryke set his bags down and started removing garments and meticulously folding them. Dark clothing was stacked neatly in a pile as he talked. "My sire bonded my mother and stashed her away so she couldn't be found and killed. That way he couldn't be used for breeding, either, you see, but still fuck around. My sire was a renegade of sorts."

Zoey detected no pride from Stryke, just acceptance.

Stryke straightened. One bag he'd left untouched, but in his arms was a set of flannel pajamas with cartoon skunks and red lips.

Her gut tied in a knot. Did he know her secret obsession was cartoons? Of course he did, he'd essentially lived with her when he'd been in Mitchell.

He caught her coveting his pants and his lips twitched. "I'm going to shower."

Make yourself at home. The thought was supposed to be sarcastic but came off as genuine. Snorting to herself in disgust, she went to the kitchen to prepare some food.

She couldn't deny she'd missed having a tall, dark male roam her home. But she'd missed *her* male, and Stryke wasn't hers, no matter what he claimed.

Picturing Mitchell in her tiny apartment didn't come naturally. He would've scoffed at such a small dwelling. The kitchen was only big enough for one person to work in at a time, not that Mitchell had ever cooked so much as toast. Zoey had no table. She either propped a hip at the counter while holding her plate or sat on the loveseat and watched the morning news. Her living room was tiny compared to her old digs.

Zoey preferred her new way of life to how she'd grown up. Now she could walk through the halls and offer standard greetings to those she passed. No bowing and scraping because her grandmother had been on the Vampire Council.

Her grandmother. Zoey paused as she gathered food from the fridge. Some guilt festered. Her grandmother had walked into the sun after the council had been dissolved.

Zoey resumed meal prep, browning the sausage, going on with her life now like she had then. Her father had died when she was younger and her mother wanted nothing to do with her, Zoey's role in the takedown of their former government unforgivable.

Her team was her new family, had been for decades. Zoey was a hundred and five years old and didn't miss the old ways at all. The only thing she'd missed was her mate, but her duty saw her through the worst of her loss.

Piling sausage high on her plate, she chewed her bottom lip. Should she prepare a second plate?

The shower kicked off.

She grabbed another dish. Filling two plates felt as natural as before, when she'd been mated. Next, she scrambled a dozen eggs and added diced veggies. Would Stryke say anything about her choice of food?

Eating like she always did, she leaned against the counter by the sink. She downed a Gatorade when she was done.

Stryke didn't show. She couldn't hear him moving around.

Rubbing her pocket where she held the band she'd broken off him, she pondered what she'd

do with it. She'd report back to Demetrius.
Would she tell the Synod that she had a device in
her possession capable of controlling a demon?

They might want it. But Zoey was on the
Synod, so technically, they had it.

Where was Stryke?

She dropped her dish in the sink and went to
the bathroom. Empty.

She peeked in her spare room, which was her
weapons room. Nothing.

Facing her bedroom, she gulped. Her bed
was around the corner, not visible. She padded
inside, harboring a small fear that a naked, six-
foot-five demon was going to jump her. Or
worse, a partially clothed demon with cartoon de-
signs on his flannel pants.

When her eyes landed on him, she froze.

He was sprawled on her bed, but not on the
side she slept on. Her side was left empty, like an
invitation for her to crawl in. He'd thrown one
arm over his eyes and his other over his stomach.

She crept closer. His chest rose and fell
evenly, his soft lips were parted. His swarthy skin
was nearly lost in the shadows of the room on her
plain, taupe bedding.

Wet hair was slicked off his forehead and
over his horns. Her fingers itched to stroke them.
Would they be warm, like the rest of his body?
Would they be hard, with a smooth finish? Their
color blended seamlessly with his coffee-brown
hair.

She'd always wanted to be a coffee drinker; the smell was divine. But she could never risk the depletion to her electrolytes with a diuretic.

Her gaze wandered leisurely down his body. Demons healed as completely as vampires. His skin wasn't marred by scars and it emanated a soft sulfur odor. She would've thought brimstone in any quantity would be undesirable. Ever since the invention of electricity, vampires had ditched most things fiery. Flammable creatures much preferred to flip a light switch rather than toy with one of the few methods that could permanently destroy them.

She jumped when his rumble filled the silence. "Are you going to stand there all day or come to bed?"

**

"I thought you were sleeping," she said.

He bit back a smug grin at her flustered reply. "I was dozing."

Sweeping the arm off his face, he pinned her with his violet stare.

Her clothes were tattered and dirty from her midnight swim, but she would always be as beautiful as a summer day to him. After the dream he'd had—he'd lied, he'd done more than doze—waking to her over him destroyed any restraint he had. In his sleep, his sire and Lee had taunted him, telling him he was a waste of demon blood and had failed everyone in his life.

Stryke should have his demon card revoked just for having nightmares like that, for even giving a shit that one of his hosts had died terribly because of him.

Stryke kneaded his chest. Sometimes, it was like a tiny flame ignited behind his heart and heated it until Stryke wanted to tear it out of his chest.

What was it about Lee that bothered Stryke so much? He'd been in and out of hosts without much regard whether they lived or died. Maybe a little more concern than a true demon should have. So he'd shown Lee that the kid could better himself, could be more than the loser his parents thought he was.

Stryke wasn't going to psychoanalyze the situation. It's not like Lee had reminded him of… himself or anything. The kid whose parents didn't want him, thought him unworthy. The kid who'd finally realized his potential and had been working toward it. Stryke had hoped to see the man he'd turn out to be.

Silly demon. Only humans had weak emotions like that. Stryke had built himself an admirable reputation in the underworld, had even lived to see the tables turned on his sire.

"You're thinking about him again." Zoey hadn't moved.

Humiliation burned through Stryke. She wasn't supposed to witness this weakness, the part of him that mourned life unnecessarily taken. *He* protected *her*.

"I was thinking about a lot of things." He swung his legs down and sat up. "I don't like this place, Zoey."

Her walls went up immediately, the reaction he wanted. Because he planned to bust them down. "I didn't design it with you in mind."

"You didn't design it with you in mind, either."

She crossed her arms and cocked a hip out.

He wanted to smile. He'd gotten to her.

"And what do you know about me?" Oh, the challenge in her eyes.

"I know that you like bright colors. You like everything you weren't growing up. You like pants; you'll never be caught dead in a dress or a ball gown. You like shooting guns and throwing knives better than sewing an inch of ripped seam. I know you resented your family and the role they played victimizing others of your kind, and shifters, even humans. But as for your dwelling, where's your contemporary art? Where's your shower curtain with clown fish?" He swept his hand toward the bare wall next to her bed. "Not one Garfield picture. Where's your portrait of the large, orange, cartoon cat?"

"Mitchell hated them."

"He tolerated them for you. Why are they gone?"

"How I decorate is none of your business." Her features were pinched. She was upset with him.

"Do you even sleep in fun pajamas anymore?"

Her jaw fell open, but she recovered quickly. "How I sleep is—"

"None of my business, I get it." He rose and stalked her. "I saw you in my sleep the other night. You sleep as plainly as you live."

Her eyes went wide and her cheeks flamed. Embarrassed or angry, or both?

"Does your personal invasion know no bounds?" From her mutinous glare, she was ready for a fight.

He loomed over her. "You've been nothing but your job for five years. You've shoved everything away in your grief, even yourself. You feel guilty. You got rid of anything that was a point of contention between you and your mate. I'm even surprised you live in such small square footage. You know how much he hated anything less than a palatial expanse of marble and fine art."

She slapped him across the face.

He reeled back. It was no light slap by an incensed woman. She'd put her strength into it, wanted him to hurt.

She reared up, her finger jabbing his chest. "You think because you were a passenger in my mate that gives you a right to judge me and interpret anything of what I do. I have a job. I work. That's all I need to worry about."

He closed his fist around her finger. She tugged, but he didn't let go. "I was right. You hate living here because you know he'd hate it, and you're punishing yourself because of it."

Her other arm flew up, but he caught it before it made contact. Bingo. He'd just decoded her. Had she even known she was doing it?

He held onto her, their arms crossed. He yanked her close and let go of one of her hands to wrap his arm around her waist. "You don't have to make yourself suffer anymore."

He crashed his mouth down on hers.

Her lips had been open, probably for some angry retort, and he used it to his advantage. He tasted her. Sweet and savory. She'd just eaten and his stomach reminded him that he hadn't yet, but food could wait. In his arms was all he needed for nourishment.

A whimper escaped her and he released her other hand. He wound his hand around her neck and tipped her head back.

She held onto his shoulders as if she was unsure whether to shove him away or hold him close.

He tightened his grip and dined on her, wanting so badly to take that damn bun out of her hair. It was secured so well he'd likely rip half her hair out and kill the mood.

He couldn't risk it. He had his vampire in his arms, in her place, where no one could bother them. No one knew he was here. A spark of self-satisfaction welled up. Had she not told anyone because she wanted him here, too?

She kissed him back, their tongues clashing, their bodies aligned. She had to feel how much he desired her. Flannel sweats were shit at holding back erections. If she moved away from him, his shaft would follow her like a divining rod.

His warmth seeped into her. She'd healed from her frigid swim, but her temperature would always be lower than his, thanks to his origins. For an extra dose of heat, he infused his energy into her.

She shivered and melted into him.

Was this really going to happen? He'd essentially watched her for months, then monitored her for years from afar. Would she give herself to him, if only physically at first?

A growl rattled his chest. Just having her physically wasn't good enough. Then he'd be no more to her than Creed. Stryke wanted her acceptance of him, of them. He wanted her dedicated, like he'd been to her.

Her hands crept around his neck and she rose to her tiptoes. A sense of victory surged through him. He placed his hands at her waist and released her weapon belt. It thudded to the floor and he tugged her shirt out of her waistband.

Her breath quickened. He felt it both through her kiss and through his hands. As he skimmed his fingers over her soft, satiny skin, she threaded hers through his hair.

He tensed as she closed in on his horns. Would they frighten her? Would she be disgusted and run?

Her fingertips bumped a horn on each side. Their kiss slowed, but they remained fused together as she explored his head.

The sensation was more than pleasant for him, and she seemed more than curious. Her hands rubbed and massaged his scalp and horns. Did they feel good to her?

Reassured that she wasn't going to run off in disgust because she was making out with a demon, he continued his exploration upward. He reached her rib cage, only a few more inches to the soft globes he'd been dying to sink his fangs into.

He took the chance at breaking their kiss to nibble his way down her neck. Her head tipped back, opening herself to him. Should he bite?

He wanted to. Instead, he stayed his lips over her fluttering pulse and rocked his hips into her.

If his eyes weren't closed, they would've crossed. He'd rather be inside of her, but he was so close, his imagination at how good she'd feel was going to kill him.

Her body echoed his rhythm. She wanted him, too.

He abandoned her torso and glided his hands down to the clasp of her pants. He had to put some distance between them and he mourned the loss of her proximity.

A loud pounding at the front door stalled his hand.

Zoey moaned and fisted her hands in his hair.

He ignored the door and prepared to rip her pants open.

The knocking continued.

With a frustrated hiss, Zoey broke contact with Stryke. Her eyes were glazed, her cheeks flushed, and her chest heaving. She blinked at him a few times, her mouth slowly turning down into a frown.

She put a hand to her forehead, spun, and lurched her way to the front door.

Stryke took a step to follow, but glanced down at the tent his cock had formed in his pants. What a sight he'd make. His cheeks were probably red from desire, his eyes crazed, and his horns straightened to pierce the one who dared disturb him.

Zoey's face when she'd left... Stunned regret.

Stryke fisted his hands, yearning to punch a hole in something, but he went to stand by the door and eavesdrop instead.

Chapter Ten

"I'm coming!" she shouted at the door. She could've been—almost was. Until someone had saved her from her traitorous body. What was it about Stryke that had her abandoning duties left and right? "Just stop the damn knocking."

The pounding finally quieted. She sensed Creed on the other side.

She inhaled and held it for a second to steel herself for a whopper of a lecture. A demon. In her place. Having a damn sleepover.

She ripped the door open. "Creed."

He backed up at the ferocity of her greeting.

"Just checking in. You haven't called or reported to Demetrius."

Oh shit, she hadn't.

Creed narrowed his eyes. This time, she stepped back. Did he suspect she'd just been intimate?

"Is Stryke in there? *With you?*"

"It's as good a place as any." What a dumb answer.

He crossed his arms. She often forgot what an opposing figure he could be when he wanted.

He usually avoided drawing attention to himself unless it was for his supposedly lackadaisical persona. But he was still in his black tactical gear, his hair swept off his forehead. A stunning male, just not one she was attracted to.

"We have a prison."

As if she hadn't thought of that. Thankfully, she had. "One with an electronic lock. And electric lights. He could stroll out anytime he wanted with the touch of a finger."

Creed scowled.

"And there's nowhere else to stash him without one of us babysitting him."

"What about the host's place you reported to us about?" He shot her a look like he'd busted her flimsy excuse.

"Hypna knew about it." She checked over her shoulder. No sign of Stryke, but he was probably listening. It's what she would do. "The host was killed," she said quietly.

He shook his head, his expression flashing anger. "That demon is dangerous. He can't be allowed to stay here. Not when we're bringing in Grace's family…and Melody."

Zoey considered Creed. Genuine worry glimmered in his eyes. Creed didn't want Grace's family at risk, but he also wasn't admitting that Melody's safety was just as important to him.

Her guilt at stringing him along until she'd broken things off diminished. But she couldn't rejoice. Melody was human, and while her celebrity crush on Creed was sweet and humorous, there was no chance for a serious romance. Long-term to a human meant a forty-year marriage, not a five-hundred-year mating.

And Creed was right. If they were bringing people here to protect, having Stryke under the same roof was bad planning.

"We'll be gone by nightfall." Maybe they'd need to get out of Freemont altogether. Where would they go? It had to be away from people Hypna could hurt.

Creed's eyes flew wide. "We?"

"Hypna's after me as much as she's after him. We'll both go together and distract Hypna until you can get Grace's family and D's parents to safety."

Creed opened his mouth, then snapped it shut. Like Zoey, he couldn't think of a better plan. "Be safe."

"Always."

She let the door close. When she turned around, Stryke was leaning against her bedroom doorframe, blending into the shadows. His broad shoulders filled her doorway and his head came close to touching the top. Those stupid pants of his were cute as hell on his hard body and her arousal irritated her.

She steeled herself and walked toward him, only to veer off into her weapons room. She went to take off her tactical belt, but her fingers swiped air. With a burn of humiliation, she recalled Stryke had taken off the equipment during their make-out session.

Her core ignited with the anticipation the memory brought. She bent down, unhooked the knife holsters on her legs, and flung them aside. Disappointment with herself raged hot, displacing her desire.

The reasons why she couldn't get close to Stryke kept piling up. He was an unknown, for one. Could they trust him? He'd tricked her into bonding with him. What if Mitchell had lived? It's not like she and Mitchell would've just invited him into the mating. And so many people were threatened by Hypna's obsession with the male. Grace's parents, their two little boys, and Melody. Demetrius's parents. Ophelia was out there, working undercover. Could Zoey even count her? Hypna and her worker bees would likely go for the easy targets.

Zoey stared at the grains in the hardwood floor. She should clean up. During her shower, she could figure out where she was going to sleep. Entering her bedroom again was a bad idea. She could wait until he was asleep and get some clean clothes. Maybe he'd lie down and pass out while she was in the bathroom so she didn't have to put her crusty lake clothes back on.

She crossed the hall into the bathroom. Stryke had remained in the same spot, not saying a word. She slammed the door and methodically stripped down.

The room smelled like Stryke. His towel hung on the rack next to the shower. She glowered at it as she took the pins out of her bun.

The demon in her shower, using her towels, made him seem, *made it all seem*, so damn normal. The more he was around, the more he ingrained himself into her world and the more natural it felt. The more she wondered how empty her life would be without him.

No, she wasn't a lonely, desperate female. She'd never been that girl. She'd grown up chafing in the dresses that were so common for females of her time and station. Even human women at the time had worn trousers, which had made it worse for her kind. She'd fallen in with Demetrius, and the idea of true mates hadn't been for her, she'd had a job. She'd kept that job even when she'd found her unlikely true mate, and that job had saved her from heart-wrenching insanity when he'd passed.

Throwing her job away for a male wasn't in her DNA. Not at all.

She stepped under the warm spray. The memory of the icy lake water rose, but she quashed it. She wasn't cold anymore. She was well fueled with Creed's blood and her electrolyte juice. That was all she needed. The void inside her was something she'd grown used to after her mate had died and she'd get used to it again.

Suds piled up as she massaged shampoo into her tresses. The weight of her hair was pleasant, a sensation she didn't often feel since she was always working.

Rinsing the soap out of her hair, she froze when the door opened with a whoosh of cool air that snaked into the shower.

The door clicked shut, but she sensed his presence. His hulking form now leaned against the wall outside of the shower.

"What the hell are you doing?"

"No barriers." He was infuriatingly calm.

No barriers? Was he fucking naked, too?

"I want to talk," he continued. "Just you and me."

"We can do that when I'm done with my shower," she said between clenched teeth. And she had no intention of talking with him, or being in the same room. They'd have to leave together, but she'd be occupied with evasive tactics.

"After you'd finished in there, you would've gotten out, dried off, twisted that glorious hair of yours into another bun, and walked out with your armor in place. Your weapons might be stored away, but I know where your real strength is."

She quit hiding behind the curtain and whipped it open, an angry retort on the tip of her tongue. His hungry gaze licked a path down her body and leisurely made its way back up. He still wore those ridiculous pants.

"You're beautiful."

The sincerity in those two words robbed her of breath. Most vampires didn't draw the short straw in the looks department, but she wasn't as voluptuous or as ethereal as many other females, especially prime females, who were supposedly raised with the best of the best. Many considered Zoey plain by vampire standards. Zoey had always considered herself adequate and above the notions of superficial creatures.

Until Stryke told her she was beautiful with both words and hungry looks.

Facing him without clothing was a bad idea. "Get out."

He shrugged. "I'm here. Might as well chat."

She shut the water off and reached for a towel, dismayed to find that she'd forgotten to grab a fresh one and the one he'd used was the only one available. Better than nothing. She wrapped it around herself and stepped out. His smoky scent lingered on the fabric and teased her. She stayed on the opposite side of her small bathroom, but he was blocking the exit.

"Just what do you want to chat about?"

"Why you're stopping yourself from enjoying how good it can be between us."

What had she expected—that he'd wanted to discuss the weather? Their plan to stop Hypna from targeting her friends' families?

She squared her shoulders and met his violet gaze. "I've already done the mutually pleasurable thing and it didn't work out. And I'm not jumping into bed with you because of the bond."

His gaze turned smug. "You and I would be more than 'mutually pleasurable,' and the bond isn't why you want me."

She crossed her arms. "Why do I want you then?"

He crowded her. Out of self-preservation she backed up, but her butt hit the sink counter. "Because you're starting to feel like you can be yourself around me." His hot finger tapped her chest over her heart, making her body tingle.

"Because deep down, you know I know you and you've seen how badly I want you and you like it."

Indignation bubbled but faded as his heat seeped into her. "You don't know anything."

A sad smile touched his lips and kept her gaze riveted on his full mouth. "I know you."

He wedged himself between her legs and she didn't resist. The flannel was soft against her thighs and she craved the touch of his skin. He feathered his hand over her wet hair. "I can't wait until this dries. Your hair has given me many long, painfully hard nights."

Her legs spread wider. If he kept spilling sweet nothings, he wouldn't have to move. She'd do all the work.

He leaned his head down closer. "I want to kiss you again, but I need to taste the rest of you."

Her already loose towel fell away with little effort on his part. He closed a large hand around a breast and she arched into him. Addictive. All of him. His deep voice murmuring all the things he desired about her. His hot skin stroking hers. His hard erection pressing into her.

His other hand skimmed down her belly to her center. Damn her legs, they had a mind of their own. Her reasonable brain had shut off and she was nothing but a pleasure center waiting for ultimate satisfaction.

A calloused finger parted her folds and she released a needy moan and rocked into his hand.

He wore a cocky grin as he descended on the other breast. When he closed his lips around her nipple, she cried out. He lapped her with his tongue as his finger found her clit and began circling. She gripped the sides of the vanity for stability, her knuckles white. Part of her wanted to close her eyes and drown in the ecstasy, but his hard head with the tips of his horns peeking out was erotic as fuck. His hand disappeared between their bodies and stroked her to a fast release.

She matched him, rolling her hips almost frantically, her orgasm rising rapidly.

She never came this fast and he was barely trying. Humiliation took a backseat to the impending climax. There'd be time enough to berate herself for her reaction afterward, but she wanted this. She wanted something for herself.

He shoved his pants down and his cock bobbed against her leg. He removed his hand and placed himself at her entrance but didn't press in. Releasing her nipple with a smack of his lips, he rose and met her gaze. The smoldering intensity only stoked her climax.

"I want to watch you when you come." He shoved in halfway. She sucked in a breath at how the fullness felt so right. He backed out and she rocked into him as he surged forward.

Once he was fully seated and coated in her juices, they paused. She didn't see a demon in front of her, but a very aroused male that enjoyed pleasuring his female. His female.

She almost embraced him but kept her hands planted, as if keeping part of herself away from him. He couldn't have all of her. This was just an orgasm.

He began thrusting, fast and hard.

Not just any orgasm. It coiled inside her, tighter than other previous experiences. She hitched her legs up and he lifted them over his shoulders. Her breathing came in pants and the vanity shook with the force of their coupling.

"I want to feel you fall apart around me."

She tightened her grip. The orgasm just grew, promising to demolish her when it hit. It didn't help that his voice reverberated through his cock until she dissolved completely. She was putty, his for the taking, and he took her. Hard.

"Stryke!" Who was that needy female calling his name?

She bowed, needing to find her release. Her peak slammed into her and she tensed briefly before she shook in her climax.

He growled and went rigid as his pumps shortened and he spilled his release inside of her.

She cried out as wave after wave crashed into her and she clenched her inner muscles to milk every second of it. She jerked with the force and nailed her head on the mirror over the sink. The sounds of breaking glass filled the bathroom, but she didn't care. She needed to finish her orgasm, needed to feel him as long as possible, more than she needed her next breath.

"Oh shit, Zoey." His words came in breathless huffs as his climax waned. "Are you okay?"

Okay? She went limp. Only the shattered glass behind her and her legs on his shoulders kept her from rolling off the vanity.

Finger by finger, she released her grip on the counter. Dazed, she looked down to see it had fractured under the force.

Stryke gently lowered her legs and eased himself out of her. Instantly, she mourned the loss of him inside of her. Could they do this again? Those types of orgasms had to be once in a lifetime.

He gathered the towel from behind her as he drew her toward him. "You're bleeding. Shit, are you hurt?"

She cautiously touched the back of her head. Warm, sticky blood covered her hand. She twisted around, still in his arms. The glass was more than spider-webbed. Shards had loosened where her head had ground into it.

Damn it, she'd probably given herself a ton of lacerations.

Stryke bunched the towel to the back of her head. "You're really bleeding."

Scalp wounds did that. She batted his hand away and put pressure on the towel.

Time for that berating.

She'd just started to ask herself what she'd been thinking when Stryke lifted her down and shuttled her toward the shower. He had a fresh towel in his hand.

"What are you—" Her question drifted off as he shucked his pants.

He wasn't flaccid. He could take her again, and she'd let him. But instead, he helped her into the shower and rinsed the blood off them both.

Vulnerability wasn't an emotion she felt in front of many people, but it was raging now. Only she also felt safe. She felt taken care of.

Why did she want to run?

***

Stryke rinsed them off and wrapped the towel around her. Her movements were hesitant as she exited the shower. The minor wounds in her head had already mended shut. Stryke expected her to bolt and shut herself in her bedroom. Her stubborn streak was probably to thank for that—she had to see where he was going with his actions.

But his only plans were to keep her in his arms all day.

He snagged his sweats off the floor and ushered her toward the door. He didn't steer her toward her bedroom when they left the bathroom, but to the main area where he'd left his bags.

She waited with her eyes narrowed on him as he retrieved a bag and dug through it. He handed her a couple of garments to sleep in.

"What the hell are these?"

He bristled at her harsh tone, but it wasn't unexpected. He stepped into his pants and jutted his chin toward the pile in her arms. "Matching pajamas."

Her expression said *You've got to be kidding me* when she looked over the boy shorts with lip prints all over them. He'd chosen them because they came with a white tank that would outline Zoey's breasts beautifully. And because the red lip smacks all over the short shorts matched his pants.

"If you like them so much, then why don't we trade?" A touch of honey dripped from her words and he smiled.

"I'm all right if you just wear my bottoms and no top."

She glowered at him before she turned and shimmied into the clothes. Adjusting her towel as she dressed, she managed to remain covered. As if he hadn't seen every glorious inch as she was coming and screaming his name. *His* name.

She tossed the towel over the back of a chair and started for the kitchen. He beat her there and stood in front of the fridge.

"Hungry?" she snapped.

Propping one arm on the fridge and the other on his hip, he smirked. She was trying to distract him—she was after her juice. She'd fed from— He couldn't go there or he'd take her again on a different countertop. She'd eaten while he cleaned up, but a bloody spell had happened and now she was after her drink.

"Thirsty?"

"I'm not going to apologize for what I drink." She shoved him, her hands digging into his bare chest.

He didn't move but admired her effort. "Good try."

The calculating gleam in her eye worried him. Would he get a knee to the groin? An experience that'd be incredibly painful since his shaft was still hard and throbbing for her.

He opened the fridge door, swung it wide. "Let's see... A rainbow of flavors." He shot her an amused look. "I'm surprised your blood was actually red. Oh, look. Sausage. Bacon. Pickles. Bone broth. And..." He abandoned the fridge to slide his hand along the counter, naming the foods he passed. "Chips. Saltines. Pretzels."

When she didn't say anything, he turned toward her. Color leeched from her features, and she glanced from the fridge to the food and back.

"Zoey," he kept his voice gentle, "I know vampires are born disgustingly healthy, but I've heard rumors of the occasional anomaly. You need this type of food to live, don't you?"

Her guarded expression didn't change. "We all need food to survive."

"Do you just need salt or all the electrolytes?"

"Don't be stupid. Whoever heard of such a thing." She lacked conviction.

"Does anyone know? Did Mitchell know?"

Guilt flashed through her features. Finally she sighed and her shoulders sagged. "No. I never told him. He had enough to worry about when he made my quest his."

Yes, if Mitchell had known, he would've yanked her to safety much earlier than he'd been planning. Yet Mitchell was clueless enough to not have noticed? Stryke had known the male's inner thoughts and he'd never suspected Zoey's disorder, whatever it was.

Zoey pushed a hand through her drying hair, spreading it across her shoulders like a heavy cloak. The movement spread her top snug over her chest and gave Stryke an amazing eyeful.

"The humans have a condition that results in low sodium levels. It's called hyponatremia. That's the closest thing I've found to what I suffer from."

She'd told him. Stryke couldn't speak for a moment. She'd been smart enough to know she was busted, but he hadn't expected a real confession.

"What'd you do before Gatorade?"

She shrugged and folded her arms again. "Not much different than what you saw in the fridge. Pickle juice. Homemade bone broth. Growing up, I just noticed I felt better when I had those things." A wry smile twisted her lips. "Thankfully I was born during the era of mass food preservation and salt was everywhere. Anyway, my parents' blood was enough until I was an adult and had to find blood on my own. Then I ate more of what gave me energy until I was drinking several jars of pickle juice a week."

Would her blood have tasted like brine during those days?

"When I was mated, it was easier to hide." Her smile turned sad. "A steady blood supply helps."

"Wait—your team doesn't know?"

Her shoulders tensed. "I don't need to be coddled."

"What if you're mortally wounded?"

She was back to warrior Zoey. Hard and no-nonsense. "I've been mortally wounded before and survived. I don't want them treating me differently and risking themselves."

And he thought demons kept secrets. She hadn't told her mate of eight years, or friends she'd fought beside for decades?

Stubborn.

Cautious.

He moved toward her until he was in front of her. This time, she didn't back up.

"And what about my blood?" he asked.

"Blood is blood," she said flatly and sidled around him to dive into the fridge and grab a bottle full of purple juice.

She sauntered to the loveseat in her living room and plopped down. He settled next to her. A TV that took up half the wall hung across from them. She flipped it on and a daytime talk show filled the screen.

"Demon blood is not just any blood." Did she really watch this stuff? She never used to.

Using the remote, she flipped through channels, but her thousand-yard stare wasn't focused on the TV. "I won't need to test it."

"Just saying. *Electro*lytes are called that for a reason. And I'm an energy demon. My blood may be what you need." He didn't know much about vampire biochemistry, but it was a reasonable assumption.

She snorted. Sweet brimstone, he'd always found that adorable. "I doubt that." The remote clanked when she dropped it on the end table after leaving the TV on a morning news show. Now that was a little more like Zoey. She faced him, her eyes full of challenge. "You know something about me no one else does. Tell me something about you no one knows."

Spill his secrets? He didn't have many. What could he tell her that would help her trust him?

"My sire…" *Was a hateful bastard that I adored and followed around like a puppy. Oh, and he didn't want me.* Okay, he wouldn't go there. "My sire was a member of the Circle, but I was raised by my mother. She was one of the last female energy demons."

Zoey frowned. "Don't you guys procreate?"

"I should amend—purebred energy demons."

He realized his unintentional revelation when Zoey asked, "But you're second-tier. Both of your parents couldn't be purebred."

"Right."

"But your sire was on the Circle."

"Right."

She sipped her Gatorade and waited for him to continue. He didn't want to spread his family shame out for her to see.

"He was strong, had many of the exaggerated demon features you'd expect—horns, fangs, claws." His father had towered above him, lorded his size over him. "Several members of the Circle and other purebred females wanted to breed with him, build energy into their genetics. But if they succeeded, imagine their surprise when a second-tier was birthed. Father couldn't take the chance. He bonded my mother and managed to lock her away deep in the underworld."

"And bonding does what for energy demons?"

"We can control our seed being spilled."

Understanding dawned in her features. "So when Hypna forced you to…"

"When she didn't get pregnant, despite using her venom on me, she knew." Sympathy shimmered in her eyes and Stryke didn't mind. "The worst part was fearing for your safety."

Zoey looked away and set her drink down. "She figured out it was me when she determined it was you who saved me from Morgana."

Stryke nodded. "Fyra and I worked together and didn't hate each other like the Circle would've preferred. Hypna naturally figured out it was me who helped her by helping you."

Only he hadn't been helping Fyra. Stryke's only concern that day had been Zoey's safety.

Zoey still wasn't meeting his gaze. She curled her legs under her and stared at the TV while two newscasters talked over each other. "You still have to tell me something no one else knows. The whole underworld probably knows your story."

Stryke had to take his gaze off her, too. Most days it felt like the entire underworld had witnessed his shame. It hadn't been his humiliation per se, but his sire's. Stryke had managed to elude any more attention. He'd become a second-tier, done his job for decades, and coasted through life until he'd landed in Mitchell.

Zoey focused on him, the intensity burning a hole in the side of his face. He clenched his jaw and let his biggest secret spill.

What would she think?

"I had a brother."

Zoey's eyes flew wide. "What? Where?"

"I never met him. I was imprisoned for my first twenty years before my sire deemed me useful to him. I guess my brother was born sometime after." His jaw tightened. Likely right after Stryke had been freed. When his father had "dealt" with his mother. "Mother hid him from Father," *protected him, unlike me*, "but when he went down to end her for good, when the secret of his genetics was in danger of being revealed, he killed them both."

"How old would he have been?" Zoey was filled with way more compassion than Stryke. He'd never gotten to know his sibling but had walked in on his sire's rage-filled tantrum and gotten the gist of what, or who, had been found.

"If he had lived, he would have been fifty-eight. When he was killed, he was probably only thirty." In captivity longer than Stryke had been.

What lies had his mother spread about him? Chalk up another family member who probably had hated Stryke and cursed his birth.

Her mouth dropped open. "You're seventy-eight? I'm older than you, too?" She shook her head, then gathered her hair over one shoulder.

He wanted to shove his hands through all that hair and smash his mouth onto hers.

"Was your mother awful?"

Ripping his gaze off Zoey's long locks, he forced himself to meet her stare. "Yes."

"That's why you left her there and went with your sire. What was his name?"

Stryke sank back into the cushions with a sigh, his eyes on the ceiling. "I never knew his real name, but he called himself Burhn. Anyway, I was proof my mother wasn't clever enough to best my sire, who was a mere second-tier who had not only posed as a pure-blood but had also attained Circle status. I was proof that my sire wasn't purebred. Imagine being imprisoned with a parent who wishes you were never born. No, if she had been freed, she'd have tried to kill me as a start to reestablishing her strength."

Then he'd have had to kill his own mother. It was bad enough he'd done nothing to end his sire's humiliation.

When his sire had come by, throwing them food and supplies, Stryke had been stupidly en-amored with the powerful male. Had copied every movement. Once he'd been freed, he'd taken on every mission his sire had favored. Like eradicating vampires.

Until he'd laid eyes on Zoey.

"Family, huh?" Her dry chuckle held no humor.

He rolled to the side and slid off the couch to his knees. Zoey pressed into the couch but didn't run.

Was she as emotionally raw as he was? Their explosion together in the bathroom was a sign he hadn't been wrong about them. They had chemistry and they'd just shared personal stories.

Now he needed to share her body.

Her breathing hitched.

"No mirrors out here," he said.

Her gaze darted around as he crept closer. He was mere inches away; she licked her lips.

A smile curved his mouth. She wanted him again, too.

"I don't think we should…"

"Probably not." Agreeing would put her at ease; otherwise she'd think of reasons to object. He was only thinking of the ecstasy his body could bring her.

He rolled up her flimsy top and dipped his head down. She sucked in a breath as soon as his lips landed on her stomach. A sizzle of energy coursed between them.

Zoey squirmed under him as if she were trying to get closer. He kissed his way up to a breast and captured a nipple.

Her hands dug into his hair. Like him, she needed to feel good. To be taken away from debilitating disorders, lost mates, and crummy families.

Busying his hands with wrestling her shorts off, he was hit with the scent of her arousal. Sweet and fruity, like the juice she'd just drunk.

He had to taste.

Releasing her, he shoved himself down between her long legs. Her hands were still buried in his hair and they fisted as soon as he found her clit with his tongue.

Brimstone and tinder, she tasted like dessert. He settled in for a full meal, licking and sucking until she dripped. Feet pressed into his shoulders, she moaned with each lap of his tongue. He glanced up. Her head was thrown back, her eyes closed, her mouth open with her moans. Part of him knew that she'd shut her thinking self off, that she allowed her body to feel good but refused to consider Stryke. He was more than a vibrator to her, but he didn't fool himself. Just because they'd each shared a secret didn't mean she would hand herself over to him. Not his loyal Zoey. She'd had a true mate, and while Stryke no longer had to hide within Mitchell, it'd take an inhuman effort to step out of his shadow.

"Yes." Her hips bucked, and he redoubled his efforts, wanting to be at the apex of her release, responsible for it, like he had been earlier.

Her hands landed on his head. She threaded her fingers under and around his horns to ride his face.

He'd grin if he could, but his tongue was busy. As a starving male, he'd take any sign that she was willing to let him all the way in, eventually. All restraint was fading and a zing of electricity curled between them.

She gave a sharp cry and shuddered. Stryke sent another small shock. Her juices coated him and she cried his name.

His name.

He reared up, shoved his sweats down, and impaled her with his shaft. It vibrated with his energy and she tried to spread her legs wider to accommodate him, but she couldn't. Her legs had draped over his shoulders when he'd risen from her center. Planting his arms on either side of her, he began to ruthlessly thrust, each re-entry more forceful, filled with more of his energy than ever before.

Zoey collapsed back. Tremors shook her body as his energy rippled through her. In the back of his mind, he entertained the concern that his energy flow would disrupt her, deplete her resources. But he'd take care of her. He'd always take care of her.

Her channel was still rippling from her recent orgasm and he was stoking another climax. Fingers curled into his biceps and he swooped down to capture her mouth.

Her eyes flew open, then shut again as she relaxed into him so he could dominate her. Always a strong female, he was humbled she let him take full control of her body.

Sending energy into his kiss, it connected where they were connected, at their sexes.

Zoey tensed, her nails digging into his flesh. She tried to distance herself and scrape closer to him at the same time, but he refused to let her budge an inch away.

A primal snarl ripped from her throat and he swallowed it into himself. With their mouths smashed against each other, she couldn't cry or holler her ecstasy, but she tried. Her orgasm suspended her in his arms and he soaked all of her in.

Stryke's strokes shortened as his release exploded, encompassed by Zoey's welcome heat.

Urgent grunts and groans escaped him, but they converged into one, holding on as if their lives depended on it.

He went still and so did Zoey, and they supported each other. Breaking their desperate kiss, he nibbled his way down to her neck.

She sucked in a gusty breath and tensed to squirm away, but he nipped her neck.

Her sex convulsed and he chuckled, his hot breath wafting over her until she shivered.

"I'm not done yet, Zoey." Her hips rocked and his softened shaft hardened to granite. One time with Zoey was more than enough to get him through another five years. Two times was a fantasy. Three times was going to be reality.

"We shouldn't…" she tried again. Her rational self was returning and he much preferred making her mindless.

"We already have." He sank his fangs into a delicate vein.

Her hands were back in his hair and he was beginning to think she had a thing for his locks. "You can't drink from me," she murmured.

Did she fear he'd take too much and she'd need a Gatorade after sex? Releasing her only to say, "I'll give back what I take," he bit her again as he rocked his pelvis.

Her wet heat answered by gripping him with the strength he associated with her.

Yes, she needed this as much as he did. Wanted it as much—a startling realization for him. By now, she couldn't fool herself that he'd taken her body for his own.

He lost himself as she breathed his name, lowered her legs from his shoulders, and wrapped them around him.

***

Creed scowled at the solid wood entry door and gave it a couple of hard knocks. Rourke waited with him. They'd been assigned to bring Grace's family to the compound for safety. They'd gone back and forth. Bring them in where they'd all be in one pot for the demons, or set up surveillance to watch their place? But they didn't have the manpower to be spread out, so they were here to bring the family in.

The door swung open and Creed cringed. Melody's gaze landed on him and stuck, the beam of infatuation at full strength. Ever since they'd rescued her from Rourke's brother, she seemed to think Creed had hung the moon and stars just for her.

He hoped it'd fade the longer she was around. The nanny position had been created just for her. They couldn't send a human who knew all about them back into the human world. Her sunshine-filled personality, and the fact that she was all alone with no family, had endeared her to the rest of the team. But time had not faded her raging crush.

"Creed, what a surprise!" Her smile was wide and while it was a nice one, full of white teeth and no fangs, strong enough to light up an entire room, Creed dreaded it being aimed at him. Didn't the poor girl realize that there could be nothing between them—even if he'd been interested? Which he wasn't.

Her grin warmed as she turned to greet Rourke. "Hey, Rourke. Ari and Xavier will love to see you."

The corner of Rourke's mouth twitched. For him, it was a warm smile. "We don't have time to stay and chat. Are you all packed?"

His friend had been the one to make the call to the Blanchettes. The orders had received no resistance. The Blanchettes had thought Grace had been slaughtered as a baby, only reconnecting months ago. They were taking no chances with their family's safety.

"Yes, I'm packed," Melody answered. Her cheeks were stained with the bright red blush she usually developed around Creed. He stifled his sigh. He was no one's superhero and wished she'd direct her desire elsewhere. A human had no business lusting after him.

"Their bags are loaded," she continued. "Grace's parents are in the den, waiting for you guys. I was just finishing packing when I heard you knock." She glanced at Creed and her blush deepened.

Rourke inclined his head. "I'll load up the rest. Creed, help Melody with her bags."

Creed slid an incredulous glare toward Rourke. The male was normally levelheaded. Why in the world would he fan the flames of Melody's crush?

Rourke strode into the den, ignoring him. Cold bastard.

Creed forced a pleasant smile and when her smile increased in wattage, he immediately regretted it.

She turned to trot upstairs to her quarters. He stayed on her heels and she jabbered the whole way.

"I just have to throw a few things in. I mean, I'm done, but if I can have another minute, I can throw more stuff in." When they reached the top of the stairs, she spun and walked backward while talking, her hands flying with each word. "I don't need help, but I really appreciate it. I bet a guy like you has better things to do than carry luggage."

Creed grunted his reply. She darted into her room, but he waited outside. Curiosity propelled him toward the opening.

And she was still jabbering about what she'd bring, what she'd decided to leave behind, and what'd she fucking packed for the children.

Creed didn't bother smiling and nodding. He caught every word and couldn't help but think her name fit her. Her voice wasn't shrill or annoying, but a pleasing sound that he only minded listening to because she had a major thing for him.

He examined her room. He had expected bubble-gum pink and frills, and it was…if he counted her pink-camo bedspread.

He cut into her next sentence about choosing which toys to bring for the boys. "Is that antler rack real?"

Without missing a beat, she explained, "It was my dad's. He was an avid hunter and that was the biggest buck he'd ever tagged. In storage, I have all of the wild game he hunted and preserved before I was born." She fell quiet, her expression introspective. Creed hadn't known she had a serious side. "I've been thinking about finding a museum to donate them all to. I know what some people think about hunting and hunters, but he really loved and respected nature. Do you need a bearskin rug?"

Creed's gaze had wandered to the mounted fish hanging above her bed, but it ricocheted back to her. *"What?"*

"That's a nice trout, am I right?" She grinned, her baby-blue eyes twinkling. "I caught that one and I love a good fish fillet, especially the way my dad fried it, but I was only, like, eight and it was so pretty that I started crying when my dad went to fillet it. He had it mounted and gave it to me one Christmas. The bearskin is really nice. My dad was so proud of it. It was the biggest game he'd hunted." She giggled, a sound like musical bells. "The tale of his bear hunt was always part of my bedtime stories. No princesses for me, no sir."

"Ah… I must decline. My thanks for the offer."

She slanted him a humorous look with her mouth quirked. "You become very formal at times."

"Is your bag ready?" Creed didn't mean to sound short, but being busted acting like the prime male he'd been born as by the little pixie chatterbox caught him off guard.

Her eyes were as round as saucers. "Yes, sorry." She zipped the suitcase and dragged it off the bed. "So sorry. I really…that was out of line. I didn't mean to offend you."

While her attention was on struggling with the heavy luggage, Creed rolled his eyes to the ceiling. He stepped in her path and secured the suitcase, easily hefting it. He marched out and down the stairs as she gushed her thanks behind him.

Creed went straight for the garage to load her bag, and to his relief, she veered off to help the Blanchettes gather the boys.

Rourke was in the garage, arranging items in the trunk of a teal sedan. "I'll drive Grace's parents and the boys. You flash back with Melody and get her settled."

"You can't be serious." Creed shoved the suitcase on top of the rest and frowned. Melody had actually packed less for herself than the others.

Rourke paused in his task. "Why not?"

"She's human. She won't take the flash well." Creed had flashed with her once before and she'd passed out. He'd caught her and added another level to the pedestal she'd put him on.

"She'll recover; she always does. You'll cover her and if we run into any problems, we can flash quickly with the kids without worrying about Melody's safety." Creed's expression must've reflected the dismay he was feeling because irritation flared in Rourke's dark eyes. "What the fuck is wrong with the plan?"

"The plan has me in charge of Melody. You know how she is about me. I don't need to encourage her—we all know nothing can happen between us." He tapped a hard rhythm on the side of the vehicle. "She's got this hero worship or something and it's ridiculous. I'm a vampire from a wealthy family and she's a fucking human we'll forget not long after her short life ends."

A soft gasp echoed in the silence after Creed's tirade. Rushed footsteps faded into the house.

He closed his eyes. That did *not* just happen. "Fuck. That was her."

"Yes," Rourke said quietly. "She's gotten good at sneaking up on the boys. I didn't hear her until you were finishing your prime-vampire rhetoric."

Creed opened his eyes to glare at his friend. "Fuck off, Rourke. You know I'm not like that."

Rourke arched a brow.

Of course his friend was a commoner, so what Creed had said sounded as bad to Rourke as it had to Melody.

"Fuck!" Creed spun and stomped after Melody.

He found her waiting by the front door, her back to him, her shoulders hunched.

A hundred things ran through his mind to say. All sounded inane compared to saying she was nothing compared to him. He settled on, "I'm sorry."

She straightened with a sniffle. "Apology accepted."

Her words were lifeless and Creed felt like a heaping pile of old manure. She refused to meet his gaze and he missed the life in her eyes, missed it directed at him.

He opened the door and stepped out. She did the same, and when he held out his hand, she accepted, her face set, staring straight ahead.

"Ready?" he asked. The flash would give her a raging case of vertigo.

She nodded without looking at him, her touch cold, light.

He flashed them outside of the compound. Melody surged into him with the landing and he

went to wrap his arms around her to steady her.
She shoved herself away, swaying and weaving
toward the door, one hand on her stomach.

Her humanity had always been a detriment
to him, but now that she'd shut herself down in
front of him, he found he missed it.

Chapter Eleven

Zoey checked her messages while Stryke dug through the records Lee's parents kept in the house. The office was as out of date as the rest of the house, with cornflower-blue-plaid curtains and faded, threadbare carpet. The smell of death didn't cling to this room as much as the rest of the house. She'd worried Stryke would lose it again coming back here, but he maintained the calm focus that seemed to be his default. It'd been his idea to come here in the first place. Since Lee's family had seemed to avoid him, it made sense that they had a lake cabin or property close by.

Darkness knows, they hadn't spent their money on their son.

Zoey had found Lee's phone, but there were no missed calls. She checked the call history. "Mom and Dad" only showed up once in the last two months and it was all of a thirty-second call.

Before Zoey had totally demolished her family ties, she'd kept in touch regularly. When Zoey ran across her mother in her work, they were civil to each other. Zoey suspected that she'd been granted some leeway after losing Mitchell. Not in her right mind and all that.

What would they think now—but Zoey didn't care what they thought, and hadn't since they'd presented her with her first starched dress.

She raised her eyes to where Stryke tapped at an old desktop computer, looking like an extremely attractive thug businessman. He wore a black, long-sleeved turtleneck and black cargo pants, his wavy brown hair slicked off his face and hiding those horns. Her belly rippled. It's not that the horns turned her on. They reminded her that Stryke wasn't an ordinary male, and *that* turned her on.

Was he what it took to get her out of her funk from the loss of her mate? Her walk on the wild and irresponsible side? She couldn't deny that his single-minded attraction to her was an aphrodisiac. She hadn't experienced that in a long time.

Or ever, if she were to be honest. Mitchell had loved her, cared deeply for her well-being. He'd just been more "them" minded.

If Zoey announced she wanted to feast on a Chicago-style pizza and dance all night long, she suspected Stryke would drop whatever he was doing and use his energy transit system, or whatever it was called, to haul her ass to Chicago and steal the closest radio.

Turning away to rummage through the file cabinet, she hid her self-disgust from both him and herself. She'd prided herself on her independence since she was birthed. No good came from that level of devotion from a male.

"Here's something."

Her insides warmed at his voice, desire flooding her sex. The previous day should've worn her out, chafed her nethers, but leave it to Stryke to take care of that, too, always ensuring she was wet and ready. They'd fucked in so many positions, the variety kept her body on a fine edge of readiness for him.

She sifted through the papers in the cabinet, afraid that if she turned around, she'd walk right into his lap and ride him fully clothed. "Oh yeah? You found something?"

"Yep. A lake cabin, north of town." He whistled. "Look at the specs on this thing."

If it impressed Stryke, she had to see. Her traitorous body planted itself next to him within seconds.

"A six-thousand-square-foot *cabin*. I think eight of my caverns could fit into that thing."

Her gaze cut to him. His ease in the human world made her forget that he had been raised in the underworld and his home was a cave. Bishop had been in the underworld and he'd described it as dark, dismal, dank, and disgusting—and Bishop wasn't a high-maintenance guy. But that was Stryke's home. The cell he'd been imprisoned in was probably worse.

Stryke could be lying to gain her sympathies, but she didn't think so. She sensed no lie or deceit.

She checked her messages. Nothing from Creed or Demetrius that they'd secured their loved ones. "Can you get us there or will we have to drive?"

"I could maybe find it, but you still couldn't flash there and I can't transport you."

"Do you basically flash?"

He nodded. "It's similar and both are likely based on energy. Probably something that stayed from my ancestors." Pushing back from the desk, he stood and she despised herself for how excitement coursed through her when those broad shoulders hovered close. "Lee has a truck we can use. It looks like the cabin is just a couple hours away."

"I…" She frowned. For once in her life, she didn't have the drive to ingest salt. At one point during the day, he'd cradled her head to his neck and she'd drunk her fill. So rich, so salty, so full of the energy her body craved.

She glanced up at Stryke. His violet eyes shone with interest and the constant simmer of sexual heat.

"I need to stock up on juice." Heat flooded her cheeks. "I should have it in case I can't drink from you."

Desire flared. His gaze swept over her until she felt as naked as when she'd woke snuggled into his body. He inclined his head. "Better safe than sorry."

There it was again, his concern for her overriding his male ego. Her disorder craved him and him only, but her safety was his priority. If they were separated, he wanted her prepared.

They were alike, only her dedication was to her work. She hadn't faulted Mitchell for thinking about himself, or them, instead of her solely. Because her work comprised 100 percent of her concern. And Mitchell had understood. She considered Stryke. Did he understand? Could he accept it?

What was she thinking? There was no her and Stryke. The bond between them flowed one way, but she needed him to annihilate Hypna. With the demoness after her, Zoey couldn't do her job. Her job was protecting the species in this realm, and sometimes the underworld interfered with that.

So did her disorder, and that was another place Stryke came in handy. If she didn't have to rely on food and drink to replenish her electrolytes, she could fight more ruthlessly. The next time Hypna came for them, Zoey would be stronger from Stryke's blood.

Once Hypna was dealt with then, well, Zoey would have to deal with Stryke. When it came down to it, she wasn't losing her job over a male.

Zoey peered around. Stars littered the sky, millions more than she could see in the city. Nothing but trees, water, and a few roads this far out from town.

This area was the human equivalent of a prime neighborhood. Sprawling mansions disguised as cabins dotted the lakeside. The lake,

Canary Waters, wasn't cheap to build on. Canaryville was the only city nearby, and when they'd stopped there for a few more supplies before hunkering down at the cabin, Zoey had learned they offered high-end grocery and catering services. The rich people that "camped" out here spent enough money to justify the services. Zoey had choked when she'd bought her juice and some snacks. Never had she had to spend three digits to buy junk food.

The cabin came into view, a real-life version of the blueprints they'd seen. Two stories high, it had an alpine roof with floor-to-ceiling windows that faced the water, an attached garage—because that's roughing it—and a deck that spanned its width.

"I wonder if Lee ever came here." Anger infused his words as Stryke glared at the structure.

His attachment to Lee made sense after hearing the story about his brother. Purebred demons were cunning, cruel monsters that cared only about themselves. But as they'd procreated with "lesser" species like humans and vampires, they hadn't been able to breed out emotions. Stryke had cared that his parents were hateful creatures and he'd cared that he'd been too late to save a brother. Lee had been the human version of his brother, a boy forgotten and destroyed by his parents.

Zoey pursed her lips. She didn't need to empathize with Stryke. It was hard enough to keep her distance physically. She couldn't fall for his caring nature.

He jumped out and punched in the garage door code that had been attached to the cabin's records. Pulling inside, Zoey gathered their things and got out.

The same code let them into the house.

Eyes wide, she studied her surroundings. The deeper they went into the place, the more opulent it was. Quality logs comprised the walls, and the peaked ceilings were lined with beams. The glass shimmered with moonlight and this high up on shore, the expanse of midnight-blue water created an image more beautiful than any artwork.

Plush furniture lined each room and Zoey noted marble countertops, ceramic flooring, and wall art, all in warm colors and comforting hues. This house was the stark opposite of Lee's place. Zoey hadn't met his parents, but she knew they'd put more effort into designing this house than they had raising him.

For the first time ever, she wished to kill humans she'd never met.

"I hope Hypna finds us here," Stryke said with the same uneasy expression Zoey must have. "I'll gladly trash this place, turn it all to unusable ash."

"I say we do it anyway."

He flashed her a smile with a hint of fang and her insides went liquid.

She found the kitchen. The power wasn't on and the fridge was warm, so she spread their groceries on the counter. Her skin tingled as Stryke came up behind her.

"Whatever should we do while waiting for some demons?"

Keeping her back to him, she continued organizing her chips and pretzels and juice bottles. Strength coursed through her veins, no sense of encroaching fatigue. She hadn't felt this whole since her time with Mitchell. Which made sense; she'd never told him about her condition, and he'd drunk his fill from her. She'd peppered him with salty food and gotten him to drink Gatorade to mask the lingering effects her blood had on him.

But Stryke had only sipped enough to create a maximally erotic experience. Since she hadn't had to worry about making up for her electrolyte-deficient blood, she'd been more uninhibited than normal.

To be sexually free with Stryke wasn't enough to make up for all she'd lose. Fyra had been incorporated into their world and she'd proven herself an asset. The demoness had had to prove herself before she'd been allowed to live with them. But Fyra wasn't Demetrius's mate, who sat on the Synod. She was Bishop's. And Zoey sat on the board.

Could Zoey give up her position on the Synod? Who else could take her place? Creed and Ophelia had refused. The Synod couldn't risk putting someone they didn't trust in a place of leadership. The primes were too infested with demonic activity and while Demetrius had trashed their previous government, he and Zoey were primes and therefore more likely to be accepted with grudging regard. Throwing a non-prime on the Synod just wasn't a situation her people were ready for.

Why was Zoey even considering stepping down? She was with Stryke because she had to be to destroy Hypna, and terminating another member of the thirteen was always a goal. Keep them disrupted. Rancor's death had upset the Circle, as evidenced by Hypna's impulsive and blatant attacks. Zoey and her team could deal with obvious demonic activity; it was the insidious undermining they were behind the curve on.

Another reason why Zoey needed to retain her position, to keep their government strong.

But as Stryke curled a loose tendril of hair behind her ear and his warmth seeped into her, the song of his blood promising to fulfill her needs, it was harder to convince herself that she could keep the relationship between them "just sex."

Again, a sexual relationship with a demon. She was crazy! She wasn't this irresponsible girl. The last five years, she'd worked hard to rid herself of any frivolity. But sex with Stryke was way more than Saturday-morning cartoons and lip prints on her pajamas.

Her eyelids fluttered closed when he pressed a kiss to her nape and his hands landed on her hips. She sank back into him. This felt too good, too right.

But it was so wrong, and she had to find a way to free herself.

Free herself. As if she were here with her arms tied, pleading with Stryke to let her go. She exhaled slowly to ease her mind. It was a conscious decision, not a matter of the heart.

Just sex. Their bond made it phenomenal. That was it. She could maintain distance between them if she kept telling herself that.

Chapter Twelve

Zoey snored softly next to him. Stryke cradled her in his arms, stared at the log ceiling, listened to her like he had so many years ago. No one else would guess that under her stern exterior, she made the silly sounds she did. In Mitchell, he'd learned that she snorted when she laughed or found something absurd, and when she was exhausted, she made the cutest little snores. She wore nothing now, but on the night stand were the most immature pajamas. They were littered with tiny, white kittens. Zoey would be adorably sexy in them.

The bed was as plush as the rest of the house, but restless energy pulsed through Stryke. He couldn't lie on the feather-stuffed lavender and taupe duvet for much longer. A side effect of his years spent on a cold dirt floor. Often he'd camp on the floor, and the marble floor in the bathroom looked pretty inviting. It'd be uncomfortably hard and cold and Stryke would probably wake up, expecting his mother to hurl feces at him.

He winced at the memory. As a kid, he'd thought shit fights were a game until he'd realized they were symbolic of how she'd felt about him. He'd been well into adulthood before he'd had food without dirt and crap smashed into it. It'd even taken a while for his taste buds to adjust.

He hugged Zoey tighter. Then he'd tasted her sweet blood, dulled by Mitchell's senses, but bursting with clean flavor nonetheless.

Slipping his arm from under Zoey, he deftly rolled off the bed and snatched a pair of sweats. These had mistletoes imprinted on the dark fabric with a giant one planted over the crotch. He padded into the hallway.

Why was he plagued with memories? His mother was gone, his captivity over. Demetrius and the others might not trust him, but they didn't want Hypna breeding with Stryke either. The only way Stryke would go back to the underworld was as a rotted corpse. Anything more usable and he'd be nothing but breeding stock, inseminating females to produce an army of powerful second-tiers. Or worse, purebred females would follow Hypna's lead and sacrifice the babies for power.

How did Hypna think she was going to get away with that?

He pushed a hand through his hair to get it off his face. If humans wouldn't freak out when they saw his horns, he would give himself a buzz cut. Although, in this day and age, he could probably grow himself quite a following flashing his horns. Besides, the wavy hair and odd eye color helped opponents underestimate him.

Jogging lightly down the stairs, he went to the kitchen first to grab a Gatorade, having developed a taste for it the longer he was with Zoey.

Entering the living room, he let his gaze drift over the architecture. A lot of time and money had gone into this cabin. Funny how all species placed their priorities on so many other things besides their loved ones—until they became unloved ones.

Stryke should be drawn more to a place like this. It was everything he hadn't had growing up, but he could do without it all. Except modern bathrooms. He was admittedly a fastidious demon about basic needs.

Tingles raced up and down his skin. He frowned and screwed the cap on his bottle.

Electrical pulses zapped his spine and exploded behind his eyes. Stryke squeezed his eyes shut and when he opened them, a male stood fifteen feet away. His eyes were the light-purple color of the bedspread Zoey currently slept on. He towered almost seven feet tall, with a mouthful of ragged teeth. A floor-length robe swept the hardwood but couldn't disguise his massive shoulder span. His horns pointed to the ceiling and were the color of a summer sunset. He was hunched on one side and the sleeves of his robe hung past his fingers, but the tips of his claws stuck out.

The male attempted to whistle around the mouthful of misshapen fangs. "Nice digs. I didn't expect this of you, Stryke." His voice was deep and sounded like he gargled with rusty nails every morning. Given the predilections of many demons, the male might.

Stryke narrowed his gaze at him. Alarms were going off in his head, but he didn't sense immediate danger—and he should with an unfamiliar demon standing in the place. But a subtle transparency overlaid the demon, wavering at times. He was an image.

Stryke had been imprisoned as Hypna's tortured love bunny when the newest member of the Circle had been appointed, but he recognized the scent that sometimes had tainted Hypna after a scuffle with the demon.

"Quution."

The male smiled, and Stryke was struck with the feeling like he should recognize Quution beyond the fact that he was one of Stryke's leaders.

It was the grin. Like the male was in on a joke and Stryke was clueless about the punch line. His mother had looked at him like that. *What would you do if you got out of here? You think your father wants you? You are nothing but the pet of all the creatures down here.*

Stryke hated Quution just for reminding him of his mother. But he wouldn't act rashly. A demon who could make Hypna scramble and panic earned his attention, couldn't be underestimated.

"Stryke. I'm surprised you're here, but I shouldn't be shocked you ran from Hypna. You seem to be good at fleeing."

Stryke bristled at the insult. Even by underworld standards, he wasn't weak. He always faced challenges, but protecting Zoey wasn't about his pride.

"Well, I'm not the one sending an apparition to do my dirty work."

A gravelly chuckle came out of the male. "It's more of a hologram. I followed your energy signature. Had to meet the infamous Stryke, the second-tier coveted by every member of the Circle. The lowly demon who was servicing Hypna. Did you both get what you wanted?"

"Why am I of any concern to you?" The thirteen wanted Stryke because there were so few energy demons and he could help their plans for the earthly realm come to fruition much more easily than the less civilized demons. But Quution obviously had his own energy abilities; the rest would likely covet Stryke more because of it.

All expression left Quution's face except for roiling anger. "Because you deserve to suffer. Here on Earth, protecting a *vampire*."

Stryke's brows drew together. Quution's accusations came across as personal, but this was the first time they'd met.

"I have no ties to the underworld." Never had, but it'd taken a few years before he'd figured out he meant almost nothing to his sire.

The male cocked his head. "Don't you?" He tapped his chin with a jagged claw, leaving a spot of blood from where he cut himself. "Haven't you left a tie with Hypna?"

"That bitch will never get my seed."

Approval rippled through Quution's face. "No ties, then. Indeed?"

Stryke was pondering what in all hells Quution meant when Zoey's scent wrapped around him. He tensed, loosening his coil of power.

Quution's gaze darted to the top of the stairs where Zoey stood at the banister. She wore the kitty top and bottoms, thankfully. Stryke would've ripped out Quution's holographic eye-balls if she'd still been naked. Her hair billowed around her, and as a hologram, Quution couldn't scent what she and Stryke had done, but she looked as sexed up as she'd been.

"Look who we have here." The male's sinister laugh sent prickles of dread racing through Stryke.

The male was an image. What danger could he be? But energy flowed through Stryke as he studied the male's energy signature.

So damn familiar. Stryke knew the patterns he detected…but he didn't. Quution's energy signature was absolutely new to him.

"We have company." Zoey's arm was behind her back, probably holding a gun. She'd have figured out by now it was useless.

"Zoey, meet Quution. Newest member of the Circle."

"The one who has the crush on Hypna?" she asked lightly. Her gaze was glued to Quution. "You should know, I don't think she's into you."

Quution lifted his droopy shoulder in a shrug. "She doesn't have to be. Her obsession with Stryke made her a weak link."

Stryke's brows shot up and so did Zoey's. Quution was after other members of the Circle? Why?

Quution calmly eyed them in return. "The Circle cannot tolerate a weak link. We kill her and replace her, or we kill you." He juggled his hands like he was weighing the two options. "I'm not picky, but she obviously disagrees. Surprisingly strongly. I must admit, I'm more than happy to see what she resorts to when she's pushed too far. But even if I disposed of her, there'd still be you," he spat.

The demon's form thickened until Stryke worried he'd be able to cross the realm, that Quution had pulled a, well, Stryke and secretly bonded to someone to roam in his true form.

Quution raised an arm that crackled with power. An orb of pure energy sizzled at his fingertips. He aimed for Zoey and let loose. Stryke lunged, flinging his hands up. He jumped and caught the orb, immediately lobbing it back at Quution.

The male's eyes widened and he ducked. The energy caught the tip of Quution's horn and jerked his head backward, but he quickly recovered and absorbed the blast. His form grew even more solid.

Stryke prowled around him. The male was partially in this realm, not in body, but in energy.

And the other demon wasn't used to fighting another energetic being. But neither was Stryke.

Separating his power until a ball flickered at
each fingertip, he bowled all of them toward
Quution.

"What the—" Quution danced back, his
heavy boots not making a sound, confirming that
his corporeal body was still in the underworld.

He almost teetered over, but at the last second he twisted and tossed two balls of energy
toward the stairs.

Fuck. Stryke zapped one out of the air, but
the second one blasted the railing. Zoey dove
down the stairs, rolling as strategically as possible. The smell of burnt wires filled the room and
smoke tendrils rose from the seared wood.

"We'll kill Hypna, and we'll kill you,"
Stryke snarled.

Quution ripped his attention off Zoey to
growl at Stryke. "Are you sure you don't want
someone else to do it for you? You seem to be
good at it."

Stryke's arm was cocked back, ready to whip
a ball of light at Quution's face, but he paused.
"What the hell are you talking about?"

The form shimmered, his energy draining
from fighting and maintaining his form in this
realm. "You *know*."

No, Stryke didn't, but there was no time for
words.

Quution left the realm with a boom that
shook the cabin and flung Stryke back. He let
himself land where he may and focused on the

energy trail Quution had left behind. Stryke sent a burst of energy along the path, ensuring Quution would receive a wicked shock in two seconds. Then Stryke shredded the energy patterns so Quution couldn't pop back right away, if he had enough energy to do so.

Silence fell around him. Stryke was on his back, blinking at the wood ceiling.

***

Zoey gave herself a quick once-over. No broken bones. More than a few bruises. She rushed to Stryke's side. He was splayed on his back, his strong body still, but she didn't smell any of his rich, salty blood.

Dropping to her knees, she meant to cradle his head but stopped when she saw his eyes open, a frown on his face.

"I feel like I should know him."

She sat back on her heels. "You haven't met Quution before this?"

Stryke shook his head, his empty gaze glued to the ceiling. "Hypna kept me…busy. I was using the distraction he caused when he was anointed to properly heal."

"What was it like?" Zoey clamped her lips down. Had she seriously just asked that? If his time with Hypna was the most traumatic experience he'd ever had, would she feel better? What if it was the opposite, how would she feel?

He swiveled his head to look at her, his expression serious. "About like you'd expect sex with a purebred demon to be. Painful, disgusting, and demeaning—just how they like it." Stryke groaned and sat up. He propped an arm on a knee. "Hypna might be a female, and not a sight that'd make my eyes bleed, just throb a bit, but sex with her wasn't an erotic experience. She has poison in her horns to get her males aroused, but it's not a natural arousal. Not even close. And she might have, uh…the parts…but they're not…" He shuddered. "I think my dick would've shriveled without her venom."

"I'm sorry."

His face crinkled in confusion. "For what? Why would you apologize?"

She shrugged. "Because you went through that."

"Life in the underworld." His tone was cavalier as he jumped up.

Her nose was even with his crotch, and she knew what was underneath that mistletoe. Her belly fluttered. Stryke's hand was out to help her up, but he'd noticed where her gaze had landed and wore a smirk.

Scowling at him as she stood, her mind turned to Quution.

Black scorch marks marred the floor where he'd been.

"How'd Quution do what he did? All energy?"

Stryke's features tightened and he glowered at the place they'd faced off with Quution. "Yes. I'd always heard there weren't many of us left, but I've never come across another energy demon besides my parents. I knew I wasn't the last one, just that the others made themselves scarce—for good reason."

Zoey nodded. Stryke was a perfect example. The Circle and any other demon with a healthy dose of ambition would try to breed them. Quution's image popped into her head. Except for his deformities, some of his features were similar to Stryke's, like his unusual eyes, strong jaws, and dark, wavy hair. "He reminds me a little of you. Maybe you all look alike."

Stryke's brows drew together. "Maybe."

"What would your brother have looked like?"

Stryke cocked his head to the side, considering her question. "Probably like me. Not as big and misshapen as Quution, but he's pure, obviously. Otherwise he wouldn't be one of the thirteen."

"But your sire was one of the thirteen."

"Out of deception. Once the others discovered his betrayal, they dealt with him quickly—and brutally."

She studied his reaction. Calm, his words simple.

How would she have felt? Her father had passed when she was little. She was estranged from her mother. Mitchell's death had almost brought them closer, until her mother had discovered the reason behind the circumstances. The rebellion and the coup. Then after Grandmother had walked into the sun… No, for Zoey and her mother, it was as if one of them were dead. But if her mother was captured, tortured, and killed, Zoey would track down whodunit and execute them.

Stryke pinned her with his violet gaze. "I can feel you thinking."

"I was wondering how your sire's death went over with you."

"He was too ashamed to claim me as his own, was using me for his benefit only, and would've killed me in an instant to protect himself."

"Right. But how did *you* feel?"

He didn't speak. A muscle jumped in his jaw. She had given up on a response, moving onto the next issue to deal with, when he spoke. "I had quit feeling by then. I did my job. I was good at it. Burhn's death tied off any loose ends emotionally. I was transferred to Rancor and he was so erratically focused on destruction that none of his missions made sense and that was just fine with me. I could find a host and roam this realm and fight and fuck and…be a loser."

Zoey couldn't envision Stryke as an aimless loser. "What changed?"

"You," he said softly.

She stepped back, like physical distance would help with her internal struggle. "What do you mean?"

"I wasn't susceptible to my host's emotions. I thought I was above them." A derisive laugh left him. "Or below them. But… I'd never felt the strength of a true mate's bond. It was staggering, his devotion to you. It caught my attention to say the least and I paid more attention to you. Then to your team."

So it wasn't just her. A weight lifted from her shoulders. Being someone's everything was a heavy burden to bear.

"You were all so patient, methodical." Stryke's introspection suspended her breath. Learning about herself through someone else's eyes was a surreal experience. He'd had an inside view to plans *no one* but her team had known. And Mitchell had only been a part of their team because he'd been her mate. "Hidden messages, false personas—you all lived as the bad guys, big picture in mind. So unlike home. They have a big picture, to take over and rule Earth. But they're demons and can't work together for shit." A smile lit Stryke's eyes and he twined a lock of her hair around his finger. "But not you guys. Completely in sync. Completely on board with your mission."

A shadow flitted across his face, but he covered it. Her brain moved onto working out another problem.

"Then why Mitchell? He didn't invite you in?" She ended on a higher pitch, making it sound more like a question. Doubts about Mitchell crept back in. Toward the end, he'd been almost despondent. Making fervent love to her, then falling into melancholy silence.

"I can manipulate the energy required. A loophole. The world's full of them."

No. There was something else. She narrowed her eyes on him. "What kind of loophole?"

He shoved a hand through his hair and spun around to stalk the perimeter of the room. No clues would be found, Quution hadn't been there for real, and Stryke was avoiding her question.

"It's different for everyone."

She trailed him. "Give me an example. What was different for Lee?"

Stryke glanced at her over his shoulder. "Lee was a mess. The kid had zero self-esteem and mommy and daddy issues. He was a lost soul. Those are the best kind."

Mitchell had been raised in a good family. And with his looks and prowess in bed, self-esteem hadn't been an issue. Her gaze dropped to the floor. Was that the reason? He'd been a fish out of water with her team. Mitchell had been unused to deception, and working to upend everything his family had stood for had taken its toll, but he'd remained by her side. Was that the opening Stryke had capitalized on?

Stryke turned and she drew up short. He clamped his hands on her shoulders. "I don't always know what figurative demons are chasing a person, I just know I can use them to get inside."

"But once inside them, you're privy to all their inner thoughts. It can't be long before you know."

His voice dropped to a caress. "Zoey, the dedication between you two was intoxicating." He moved closer, lowered his head, his lips hovering above hers. "It was the first thing I felt when I got into him. Then I saw you that first time. You were in bed, your hair spread around

you like a halo—and I fucking hate halos." She
smiled and their lips brushed together. "You were
a vampire. And I hated them, too." He kissed her,
a light press of his lips. "But you opened your
eyes and those red lips curled into a smile and…
I never wanted to leave your side."

Their lips met again. She relaxed and his
hands landed on her waist. Her shorts were
shucked off and she was lifted onto a china cabinet. Glass ornaments and knickknacks clattered
to the floor, but neither of them cared. She spread
her legs and he was at her entrance, his sweats already pushed out of the way.

He thrust in and took her hard. She gasped
with the intensity and turned herself over to his
strong embrace. He wasn't so out of his mind
with lust to not ensure her climax.

Her body tightened, then uncoiled as her orgasm rolled through her. His hot release inside of
her sent ringlets of energy curling through her
veins.

As he finished shuddering through his peak,
he murmured, "Let's go back to bed."

She nodded and two thoughts bombarded
her. One, she couldn't sleep because she had to
report Quution to Demetrius and the Synod. And
two, he'd fucked her to avoid answering her
question.

Chapter Thirteen

Nightfall was near. Zoey tapped her fingers continuously on top of the mahogany dining-room table. All she had was her phone, but she'd set up a makeshift workstation at the head of the table.

She and Stryke had gone back to sleep for a few hours, but she'd risen by early evening to begin the calls for arranging a meeting with the Synod. Stryke had prepared her food while she'd talked and negotiated Stryke's presence at the meeting place even farther north than the cabin.

That had spurred hemming and hawing over whether Stryke would reveal the location to the underworld. Zoey ignored Stryke's droll eye roll, and both she and Demetrius argued that the shifters had had their government in that location for centuries and that the prime vampires had known about it. With so much demonic meddling in the prime families, the underworld also had to be aware and were either worming their way in or planning to. If Hypna wanted to take on the colony surrounding Synod headquarters, it was her funeral. Shifters were too inherently good; most demons had a natural aversion to them, preferring to meddle with vampires instead.

Ultimately, Zoey would bet curiosity about the energy demon had won out when the rest of the Synod acquiesced to his presence.

As if Stryke would stay behind. He'd follow Zoey's energy trail and either barge right in or, more his style, monitor the process from the shadows.

Hellfire, why'd that turn her on? She liked his methodical, meticulous, calm personality. A hothead had never been attractive to her, which made her bond with Mitchell odd. They had still worked together, and it had gone well most of the time. There'd been some arguments and she'd had concerns over how he'd take certain info, like when they were relocated to work under-cover. But she was used to maneuvering spoiled prime families and Mitchell had been no differ-ent. As much as she'd loved him, he had been prime to the bone. He'd made up for his defi-ciency with self-righteousness.

Stryke lurked, watched, considered all angles before he reacted. Habits that increased his sex appeal off the charts.

But she couldn't forget that he'd avoided her questions about the emotional opening he'd used to get into Mitchell.

She also couldn't forget that it didn't bother her that Stryke had been spying on her for months. During her most intimate moments, dur-ing heart-to-heart conversations with her mate, Stryke had been watching, eavesdropping. For darkness's sakes, he'd even bonded to her without her knowledge, or her permission. Only the latter elicited any kind of feeling, and even then, it was just irritation. Not fury, not despair. Try as she might, she couldn't muster the level of anger she should against Stryke's intrusions.

It was done. And honestly, he hadn't stolen any time away from her and her mate. If he had, Zoey would find his actions unforgivable, a deep violation for a male who proclaimed the level of compassion for her that he did—that he showed.

A plate of nachos slid in front of her and a Gatorade was positioned on her right.

He'd just served her a meal. She stared at the food. A meal hadn't been prepared or presented to her since she's been a youngster. Once she'd left home, she'd been on her own, her dietary needs too important to trust with a near stranger, so specific that she hadn't turned over the duty to her mate.

This demon was catering to her needs—literally.

She flashed him a smile and continued texting meeting arrangements with Demetrius while her mind whirled over her sudden conflicting urges. On the one hand, who wouldn't want a large, sexy male who could stroke her to ecstasy to wait on her? But he was the demon who'd tricked her into a bond and who was still keeping secrets.

Would he keep her secret? Or would he be offered a better deal from the underworld to kill her?

No, not as long as she was his everything. She wanted to tell him to get a hobby. That kind of single-mindedness never ended well.

With silent precision, Stryke sat in a chair to her right and dug into his food. She munched on her salty fare as she finalized plans through messages but didn't speak. Stryke would have to know them eventually, but sitting over a shared meal, idly chatting about a mission, was more intimate than when he was inside of her. Disengaging her logical mind wasn't an option when they were fully clothed.

"We leave after this?" Stryke asked around a mouthful.

She swallowed, more for a delay than a necessary function. Since when had she avoided anything hard in her life? She could talk shop with him and not lose her heart. She could forget about how he'd saved her from Hypna and getting sucked into the portal. His distraught reaction over Lee's death was a little harder to dismiss, and she'd never been one to fawn over a male because he looked like a walking immortal fantasy.

Clearing her throat, she used her most brusque tone. "The meeting is set for ten p.m. Demetrius will get there first and go in instead of waiting for us so it doesn't look like an us-versus-them thing. He'll wait to share his opinions," she rolled her eyes toward the demon, "which won't be totally flattering."

Stryke lifted a shoulder and wiped the crumbs off his fingers. "I wouldn't believe him either if he professed to be my newest admirer. Tell me about the Synod."

She paused and instantly guilt flooded her. She couldn't spill details on people who might not be her closest friends but who she trusted with the rule of her people.

"Zoey," Stryke chided, "I wouldn't believe you either if you suddenly trusted me with every asset of your job. Tell me what I'd learn just by being there. Names, species, whatever you're comfortable with. But I don't wish to attend an inquisition at a complete disadvantage."

He was right. She had no reason to feel guilty, and he was smart enough to figure out much about the others within minutes of meeting them. Again, his reaction unsettled her. How could he be so calm and accepting? Because his default was to be unwanted and untrusted?

How shitty had his upbringing been to turn him against everything the underworld stood for?

"D and I are the vampire representatives. The shifter reps are Demke and Sylva. Demke was on the previous council for the shifters and he's a good guy. Mellow and even-tempered, a rare trait for a shifter male who's willing to rule. Sylva has a chip on her shoulder, but it makes her a powerful advocate for the overlooked members of her kind. And my kind."

"Ah, because *she* was an overlooked member."

She dipped her head even though it was a statement. "Then there's the hybrid, John. He's our unspoken leader."

Stryke's lips quirked. "And the others would admit that?"

"I think so. It's hard for five strong personalities to work together without a top dog." She chuckled. "Or wolf-vampire mix. He's reasonable and was raised away from both of our worlds. It gives him enough of a distance to be objective when we can't."

She considered Stryke as he nodded in understanding and attacked the rest of his food. Perhaps that was the reason he was an oddity. Raised away from the crux of his realm, with a cruel mother and little outside interference. He'd idolized his sire but had experienced the burn of betrayal and, with no way out, had coasted through life. Until, like he said, he'd met her.

A spark of trust ignited. The feeling hadn't been totally absent. Almost like she'd grown to trust him with her, but she now felt secure with him. Just him.

The others on the Synod would never accept him. Nor would they accept her with him. The more her fondness for Stryke grew, the more the foundation of her life lost stability.

Could she trade her duty for Stryke? Could she be like Bishop and Fyra and battle the demon influence in the realm? No one but her team trusted Fyra and if it wasn't for her and Demetrius's influence, Fyra might've been turned over to the Synod and the Guardians, the police force of their kind.

Without Zoey on the Synod, supporting her friend, would Bishop lose his happiness? It was easier to think she would be letting down her people, but the generalized version was much better than knowing she'd let down her friends. Would her successor allow Zoey's team the free rein she and Demetrius had been able to secure?

She squeezed her phone in one hand and grabbed her plate with the other. A portion of her meal remained, but she'd lost her appetite.

"Zoey?" Stryke didn't too speak loudly.

"I must ready for the day." She winced at her formal tone. How quickly she reverted to the pampered girl her mother had tried to make her into.

Get the Synod meeting over with, then she could figure the rest out.

***

His meal finished, Stryke frowned at the scorch marks on the floor, but he wasn't pondering the problem of Quution. Zoey's abrupt departure at the table made him suspect she was having an internal struggle. He ran through the conversation but failed to pinpoint a specific cause for her turmoil.

Must just be him in general. He brushed his hair off his face. Briefly, he'd considered using the gel he'd found in the bathroom to style his locks to stay over his horns. The Synod might work with him better if he didn't display his obvious demonic traits.

He was good at concealment, but the Synod would have to deal with him as is. Just like they'd had to accept that his friend, Fyra, wasn't an atrocious beast. Not many from his home were decent beings, but some weren't nightmarish creatures, just beings left with no choice of locale, who lacked the power to change their circumstances. Their realms were slowly melding and it was up to the vampires to limit the intrusion. Because demons being demons, they'd naturally want to take over and enslave everyone. If the Synod refused Stryke's assistance, they were only hurting themselves. And Zoey. If they forbade his relationship with his bonded... Well, he wasn't sure. All the cards lay in Zoey's grip. And despite their time between the sheets, and on the couch, and the bathroom counter, Stryke still wasn't confident in them. She was so tied to her damn duty that if she abandoned what simmered between them, he wouldn't be shocked.

At the same time, if she ever unearthed the circumstances behind Mitchell's death, it might be their only saving grace.

But she wouldn't find out. She'd just have to accept that Mitchell's stress about how her team was undermining the government was the opening Stryke had needed. It wasn't an untruth.

He turned at footsteps on the stairs. She swept down them, her bun so tight that no hair dared escape. They hadn't cleaned the banister debris, and bits of wood crunched under her black boots.

In full tactical gear, she was a vision. The weapons belt only enhanced the curve of her hips. The holster strapped around her chest framed her breasts. Her clothing was formfitting and he'd love to strip it from her lanky frame bit by bit.

She stopped at the bottom. "Ready?"

He closed the distance between them and cupped her elbow. He'd rather not showcase his ability to follow flash-energy trails.

Her gaze lifted to the ceiling, then lowered to the walls. "If we stay here any longer, we'll have to ward the place against flashing." A smile danced over her pink lips. "But it's a nice treat to flash in and out of a building instead of stepping outside."

He'd been thinking the same. She could take care of protecting the cabin against vampire invasion, and Stryke would lay down the spells he could to keep demons out. Quution's ability might be a little harder for Stryke to ward around, but he'd find a way to keep the male from popping in. Hopefully the demon needed a solid recovery after their encounter. Humans stopping by or, worse, Lee's parents returning were the easiest problems to deal with. A little entrancing from Zoey and they'd drive away, their minds like butter, easily molded.

Zoey flashed. A sizzle of disorientation dissipated quickly as Stryke blinked at his new surroundings.

Trees. Evergreens as far as the eye could see. Stryke studied the energy patterns around him, and much like the underworld, there was a steady buzz interspersed with differing energy signatures. Dwellings. A colony surrounded the Synod headquarters. A large structure, with more personality than the vampires' compound, loomed in front of him. Built with concrete like the compound, this place also had wood accents and windows. Lots of windows, since it'd been the shifters' place of governance for centuries. Vampires could travel long distances faster than shifters, and powerful vampires like his bonded could flash long distances. The area must've made sense to all to keep it.

If demons cared enough to get out here, they'd raze the wilderness. Surprisingly, they were smarter than that, meticulously, if somewhat distractedly, targeting the prime vampires.

The Circle would succeed, too, if the Synod didn't learn to harvest what knowledge and assistance they could from Stryke and Fyra.

Of course, Stryke understood why they wouldn't. He couldn't care less about anyone in the underworld, and Fyra only cared more about Bishop than herself, but the Synod would choose caution.

He glanced at Zoey's profile. Her jaw was set, her gaze grim, her shoulders squared, but her hands twitched at her sides. She was ready for battle. But over him or her future?

She briefly met his gaze, then looked back to the front door. With an audible inhale, she marched toward the entrance.

Falling in next to her, he examined his surroundings as they went through the doorway.

Very anticlimactic. The inside wasn't as plain as the exterior, but it was close. The stone

floor lent it some character, and it was nicer than
the dirt Stryke was accustomed to. The walls
were a mixture of drywall and painted masonry.
The chamber Zoey led him into resembled the
courtrooms he'd seen on TV. Large, open, and
circular, seating surrounded the outer edges for
public meetings. A carved, wooden table dressed
the front of the room. The five chairs present
could rim the table or line one side for when they
addressed individuals—or when they tried a
criminal.

Today, the chairs flanked one side of the table. And there were only four.

Was Zoey on trial, too?

Demetrius was positioned in the chair far-
thest right, wearing a pensive expression. A male
sat next to him, his gaze contemplative. Then it
was a woman, Sylva, and the last male. The female evaluated him with disdain plain across her
face and the two other males seemed more curious than anything, their gazes flicking between
Zoey and the top of his head, where his horns
weren't completely covered.

Zoey stopped in the middle of the clearing
two steps lower than the table. She radiated tension and subtle anger. She wouldn't like the
slight of only four chairs when she was supposedly on equal footing.

"Zohana," the male next to Demetrius spoke.
He had lighter brown hair than the vampire.
Stryke's senses weren't as powerful as a vampire's, but the male's energy signature was a
blend of several Stryke had come across before.

Ah, he was the hybrid John.

She inclined her head as a curt greeting. "Have you decided already, then?"

"You must understand—" Sylva said.

"I understand just fine," Zoey snapped. "I called you together to present new information, but it looks like I'm on trial. Have you already decided that I've traded my priorities and removed me from the Synod?"

"No." John crossed his arms and reclined as much as he could. "But like you said, you understand that your relationship with the demon affects your standing."

Stryke bristled at the male's words. They were professional, almost courteous, but he'd used Zoey's words against her. A quality not only demons excelled at, apparently.

"What. Relationship." Zoey's rigid posture vibrated with anger. Stryke couldn't fault her for denying him. He'd known it'd be an uphill battle when he'd bonded her.

The shifter's nostrils flared as if to inform her they smelled Stryke on her and they knew it wasn't from proximity.

The second male, Demke, steepled his fingers together and leaned forward. "We made an educated leap of faith when Demetrius concealed critical information from us to protect Callista. But she was his mate. We've been cautiously guarded about Bishop Laurent's relationship with a demon, but she's proven herself useful to our cause—and Bishop's not on the Synod." He hesitated, the corners of his eyes pinched. "Zohana, we know you've lost your true mate, otherwise we would've allowed more time and understanding. But our people, this realm, is under attack— by *his* people." Demke switched his gaze to Stryke. "Have you, or have you not, carried out underworld missions against our people?"

"Yes." Stryke didn't feel the need to elaborate. They wouldn't trust him. Stryke would abandon his home—had already—and this place. He'd leave everyone. Fuck them all. Stryke's only concern was what Zoey thought about him. But where he lacked the willingness to muster compassion and caring, it was part of her identity.

Sylva's mouth pulled down and the males' energy swirled with distrust, even Demetrius's.

"So that's it. I'm out?" Zoey demanded. "Tell me so I can quit wasting my time here."

John waved her words away. "No one's made a motion to remove you—yet. But Zohana, your seat is precarious. We can't have," he glanced at Stryke's horns, "outside influence among us when our people are being corrupted from the inside."

"I agree." Zoey relaxed slightly, a bad sign for Stryke. Would she toss him for this crew? "Like it or not, I am a target and anyone close to me is, too. The Circle seeks to use Stryke to get to us and bolster their own power. Whether he's with us or working against us, we can't let Hypna or the others breed him."

"This Quution," Sylva interjected, "what are his plans for Stryke?"

Stryke repressed a snort. "Death."

"Kill him or kill Hypna," Zoey added. "According to Quution, he's not picky."

The panel fell quiet and studied Stryke.

"Can you fight Quution?" John asked.

"Yes." Again, Stryke wanted to scoff. *I already have.* "But he won't take his full form in this realm. I'd have to go to the underworld, where I'm at a severe disadvantage since, you know, it's me against everyone down there."

Sylva waved off their conversation. "I want to know about the bond."

Icy tendrils spread along Stryke's veins. Dammit, not them, too.

"I agree." Demke pinned him with his sharp gaze. "We aren't going to work with you until we know your motivations."

"My only motivation is Zoey's safety," Stryke said tightly.

"But," Sylva was a damn dog with a bone, "you're a second-tier, yet you possessed a prime. It's my understanding your level of demon couldn't do that even with the host's permission. Were we mistaken?"

"No." Tension mounted in Stryke as foreboding swept through him. Zoey had taken a step back, wanting the same answers he'd refused to give her. He still refused, couldn't hurt her like that. "I can capitalize on a host's weakened mental state, attach myself to the openings in their energy, and get inside. I often don't take over the host but ride as a passenger to gather information."

That would have to be enough.

"Mitchell and I were tight. How'd you possess him?" Demetrius asked as if he was afraid to know the answer. He should be, and Stryke was going to avoid telling him.

Stryke answered calmly. "He was fraught about his mate's safety. The conflict between your mission and his family obligations wasn't an easy one for him to overcome."

Demetrius's eyes gleamed with empathy. The male felt responsible for the demise of Zoey's mate. That made two of them.

"Did you have anything to do with Mitchell's death?" Sylva's question snapped like a whip.

Zoey's attention was fixed on him. Part of him wanted to be upset that she would think he would do such a thing to her, but the rest of him knew the truth. The longer he took to answer, the more hurt and suspicion built in her gaze.

Bile rose in Stryke's throat. "No."

A breath of relief passed through Zoey's expression and it gutted Stryke. It was for her own good. She couldn't know what had really happened. It'd ruin everything for him, for them.

The shifters adjusted in their seats and they exchanged glances. Stryke's stomach plummeted. No, dammit. *No.*

"You lie," Sylva said. "I can smell it."

Zoey's audible inhale cut through him. Forget getting tortured by Hypna, this was Stryke's worst nightmare. Since he'd fallen for Zoey, his one goal had been to protect her. His life was dedicated to her and her alone. If she found out, it'd kill him—or she would.

They all watched him. He didn't speak.

"Well?" Sylva demanded.

Stryke fantasized about ripping through her jugular with a horn, but the point of this trip was to get Zoey and her team to trust him. His mind spun for a suitable answer.

"Mitchell's death was not something I could've prevented." There. That was absolute truth.

The two shifters' nostrils flared and Stryke held his gaze steady.

The quieter male, Demke, spoke. "Tell us what happened. In detail."

Zoey went rigid. Sweet brimstone, this had to be hard on her. If he didn't talk, they wouldn't trust him and he'd lose Zoey. Inside, he screamed with frustration. Literally no good could come from the truth. The damage was done. Zoey thought Mitchell had died for his dedication and she was beginning to trust him. All of that would be undone if the Synod insisted on this course.

Five pairs of eyes watched him. Stryke might not have shifter senses, but even he could sense their patience was growing thin.

"Stryke," Zoey said softly, "what really happened when he died?"

He would've risked imprisonment, but the way she asked...he couldn't stay quiet.

He clenched his jaw. "Mitchell was locked in the room with the fire."

"The lock had been busted," Demetrius pointed out. "We thought it was from him fighting to get free."

Stryke couldn't bring himself to look into Zoey's anguish-laden gaze. She was waiting for him to say more. Maybe he could still talk his way out of this. "The door wouldn't open due to the heat of the fire."

"Another lie." Satisfaction glittered in Sylva's gaze. Stryke's mouth twitched to bare his fangs, but the hurt pouring off Zoey in waves took priority.

They'd gotten to the root of Stryke's true interference, where he went from watcher to total takeover. He couldn't say anything more beyond this point without either spilling the entire truth or spewing lies that he'd get called on.

But he couldn't bring himself to reveal his ultimate deception. "Mitchell planned to escape with Zoey, and to hell with overthrowing the Vampire Council."

Zoey recoiled, her hand flying to her chest. "What?" She shook her head. "No, he wouldn't do that to me."

Little did she know how often her mate had contemplated it, or that he'd done so since the very beginning. "He would've, but when he killed the two Vampire Council informants and tried to burn their bodies, his haste made him sloppy."

"And the—" She swallowed. "And the lock. Are you telling me he could've escaped?"

Stryke finally met her eyes and they shredded what was left of his resistance. He'd tried to protect her from her mate's deception. Letting all of his love for her shine through, he let the story roll out. "He killed the informants. They were onto you and he planned to squirrel you away and throw Demetrius under the bus. But he was too frantic and had no stake to ash them, so he tried burning them. The fire raged out of his control. If that door had opened, you would've been caught in the fireball, and Mitchell was going out of his mind with his survival instinct." Stryke's heart tore in two at the tears that shimmered in her eyes. "I pushed his conscience aside and locked the door, then smashed it." Stryke almost choked on the next words because they'd rip Zoey apart. "Then I receded so you could say good-bye through the window."

Her mouth dropped in horror. *I watched him die.*

Stryke took a step toward her. His stomach churned; he never felt sick like this. "You would've died, too. He was desperate to get to you, didn't understand the danger he was putting you in."

"I wanted to die with him." She choked back a sob and pressed a hand to her temples. "Oh my... You killed him?"

Everyone in the room had long since faded; Stryke's only focus was his bonded. She'd gone pale and her hands shook. Disbelief stained her features, but realization was taking over.

His arms ached to hold her. It'd been tough enough when Mitchell had died and he'd gotten sucked back into the underworld. He'd had to leave her during her darkest moment. "Zoey, I know this is—"

"You don't know anything," she hissed and backed away from him. "You've taken *everything* from me. You stole my mate's life, then you stole him from me." She swept her hand toward the silent members of the Synod. "Now you've taken everything I worked for. I *hate* you." She breathed heavily, her chest rising and falling, until she visibly calmed herself and straightened. "Release me from the bond."

The world went still. Did she know what she was asking? There were no take-backs after removing a bond. "Zoey, I can't—"

She moved too fast for him to track. A warm object snapped around his wrist. He looked down and cool air wafted over his face as the blood drained from it. The bracelet. Zoey had kept it and used it against him.

He could snap it off. His other hand twitched to do so. But as much as his insides were crumbling apart, he'd already done enough. If Zoey wanted to turn him over to the Synod, he'd respect her wishes. It was the least he could do. It'd be a long crawl back into her heart.

Her expression resolute, her body ramrod straight. "Remove. The bond."

He couldn't resist the compulsion, but he forced a few words out. "Once it's broken, it can't be remade."

Her eyes narrowed, her resolve unwavering. "Do it."

The undoing words spilled from his mouth as his brain screamed at him to shut the hell up and his heart cracked in two. He retrieved a knife from his belt, ignoring the guns suddenly pointed at him from the others. With slow precision, he sliced his hand to seal the spell.

Red drops plopped on the floor, the only sound in the room. Deep down within him, an empty hole formed. He was just a second-tier demon again, with no purpose but to be used by those over him. And without Zoey, he didn't care. He'd had no purpose in his life before her. She was the reason he'd stopped coasting through life, uncaring of what went on around him, uncaring of everyone else.

A muscle jumped in her jaw and her throat worked as she tried to swallow. They were the only signs that crept past the hatred in her gaze. Her hate tore him apart.

His hold on the realm weakened as their bond dissolved. Zoey's eyes widened slightly. She must've noticed his fading essence.

With a snarl that might've been half sob, she spun around and stormed to the exit. No one on the Synod said a word. Stryke prepared to go after her with all the energy he had left.

"Don't," was all Demetrius said.

As Zoey disappeared from the chamber, Stryke vanished from the realm.

Chapter Fourteen

Zoey stormed out of the Synod's head-quarters, and once fresh air brushed her face, she flashed back to the cabin's kitchen.

Son of a bitch. Why had she flashed here?

Because the compound had too many people. They'd see her tearstained cheeks, get hit by the waves of fury and remorse cascading off her, and start asking questions.

She'd been too damn hard at work to have any other place to grab a little solitude. It was a good thing Stryke couldn't follow her here. She hoped he had a bumpy trip back to the under-world.

A sob echoed in the room and she folded to her knees, unable to hold herself up.

She'd stayed until Mitchell's last breath, un-til his body had crumpled and his ashes had been caught up in the storm of flames. The building's sprinkler system had come on but couldn't handle the inferno in the concrete room. She had been getting drenched while her mate had burned alive.

All because he couldn't leave the room. Be-cause he'd been locked in.

Save me, my ass. Zoey rocked back to her butt and put her head in her hands. Tears streaked down her face to hit the wooden floor. If Stryke had been so damn obsessed with her, he could've very well killed Mitchell on purpose. How did she know Stryke hadn't set the fire?

A faint buzz feathered over her skin. She sniffed and looked up.

A sight that would've flipped her insides only left her seething with loathing and confusion—and melancholy. Stryke stood only as a hologram behind her. He must've used Quution's trick to project himself here.

"Get out," she snarled. "Go back to hell."

Lines etched his face, his violet eyes filled with anguish. They probably matched her own.

When he didn't leave, she glanced at his wrist. The bracelet was gone. He wouldn't have to listen to her anymore.

Stryke followed her gaze. "You didn't command me not to take it off. I ground it to dust."

The logical part of her that was still functioning knew it was for the best. Whoever controlled that damn bracelet controlled Stryke, and in the game they played, that'd be dangerous. She glared at him.

She'd trusted him. And he'd deceived her all along.

"I'm sorry, Zoey."

She snorted a laugh lacking all humor. "Now you finally apologize about something? Should I feel like it's monumental and forgive you? Get. Out."

His expression grew more haggard, his strong body almost withered, as if he lacked the will to keep his energy at the proper levels. "I don't expect you to forgive me. Perhaps one day. It truly was the only way to save you."

"What about opening the damn door and letting him out?"

"Introducing oxygen to that kind of blaze would've killed him immediately and allowed the fire to spread." Stryke squatted before her. Too bad she'd only cut through air if she attacked him. "One of the informants had been possessed and had abilities similar to Fyra's, although much weaker, and fueled the blaze unnaturally. Mitchell might've won the fight, but he'd lost the battle."

Zoey's hostility faded, but not much. She didn't want to hear what Stryke had to say because he made too much sense. Her words had been honest. She'd wanted to die at the time, and for a long time after.

"I had to save you."

She sighed and her shoulders sagged. Rolling her neck back, she glared at the beamed ceiling, bitterness rising. "I guess you two have—had—that in common. It's all about how devoted you are to me, but you both don't—didn't—don't, whatever— You don't see it's just as selfish. How many have been put at risk because of me? First Demetrius and the rest of the team. Now it's Grace's family, Demetrius's family, hell, even Lee's death could be pinned on your single-mindedness."

"How many others would be in danger without you here to protect them?"

Touché, bastard. Still didn't make it right. Mitchell and Stryke had both decided to put her before others. Neither had asked her. How many had Stryke hurt to keep her "safe"?

"I'm not yours, Stryke. I never was."

"I'm not giving up."

She jumped up and stabbed her finger toward him. "I'm not losing my seat because of this mess Mitchell started and you finished." Stryke straightened and gazed down at her, his eyes bleak. "Through all of this, nothing has changed. I'm not giving up until your kind is under control."

"You will never get demons under control. It's in their nature to deceive and take over."

"I know," she yelled. "Their nature is your nature."

He winced at the truth in her statement and his image wavered. "I don't care about my kind. I don't work for them anymore."

With a grunt of frustration, she stormed around him toward the stairs. "If you follow me around, haunting me, I guarantee I will find a way into the underworld and destroy you."

He was on her heels, his energy dogging her. "I wouldn't be able to get you back to this realm. When you forced me to break our link, it destroyed the bond."

"Good!" She whipped around and her heart fractured at the hurt shining in Stryke's eyes. She opened her mouth to… What? She didn't know,

but his reaffirmation that their bond was well and truly destroyed…bothered her. But she had no time for words. A blast of hot wind slammed her against the wall. She kept her feet on the ground, but her brain rattled from the impact.

A deep chuckle resonated through the cabin. "Did I interrupt a lover's spat?"

Quution was at the top of the stairs. Zoey frowned as she reached for her gun. She fisted her hand. The bullets would be totally fucking useless against Quution's apparition. How could he be here when Stryke had fried the pathway behind him? But then, Stryke was here, so he must've forged another.

No wonder energy demons were on the underworld's most coveted list.

"I'm just that strong." Quution's sinister laugh boomed again with her stunned expression. "Relax, strumpet. I don't read minds. Your face and his see-through image say it all."

Stryke crowded in front of her, blocking her from another blast. He didn't need his corporeal form. His energy spread in front of her like a wall. Sparks crackled along Quution's jagged-claw-tipped fingers. Stryke's shoulders formed a shield as energy sizzled off him.

Was Quution planning an attack or trying to intimidate them?

Quution disappeared. Zoey spun around. That couldn't be it. The male had to have more up his holographic sleeve.

And he did. He appeared in front of them, but as soon as he formed, Stryke's hands flew up.

A sizzling blast crashed into the force field around Stryke. Zoey stepped away before she had to recover from an electrocution, but her progress stalled as she watched the energy get absorbed by Stryke.

Hellfire. Could he really do that?

Quution's eye twitched and he straightened, almost seemed to catch himself, and slumped again.

Couldn't he hold an upright position without slouching?

Quution smiled, his jagged fangs protruding. "Good trick. Try me."

Zoey froze. Would Stryke lob an energy orb just to let Quution try and absorb it? Could Quution do it when he wasn't physically here?

Stryke didn't move, but the soles of her feet tingled. Energy flowed through the floor.

She scrambled farther back as a line of light burned through the hardwood from Stryke's feet toward Quution. The demon disappeared just as the blast reached him. A yelp echoed off the walls and Quution reappeared at the bottom of the stairs. A heat wave reached Zoey a millisecond before she was zapped.

Her breath whooshed out and she flew backward, hitting a wall. No air returned to her lungs. Gaping like a fish, she writhed and twisted as she slid to the floor. Burning energy coursed through her body, robbing it of natural function.

A snarl ripped from Stryke. Zoey blinked, tried forcing herself to relax.

Another ball of light zoomed in her direction. She arched to roll out of the way before she passed out. Stryke intercepted the blast, diving in front of her and sending the object back toward Quution. But Quution had lobbed a second energy grenade.

Zoey's body calmed as the energy dissipated, and she dragged in a ragged breath, then another. Her heart beat erratically, threatening to disrupt her breathing. The air around her crackled and tasted like seared wiring. She might be dazed, but she registered that Stryke had saved her more than once, even after her adamant rejection.

"S-s-s—" She couldn't get his name out and he couldn't hear her over the energy sizzling in the room. If her hair had been out of her bun, it'd be standing on end.

The battle raged, each catching and throwing balls of destruction. Quution tried to get his strikes around Stryke to attack Zoey, but Stryke was a formidable wall.

Why did he keep protecting her? She should be glad to see his ass get kicked, should root for Quution to destroy him.

Should.

Every blast of searing wind toward Stryke sent a surge of adrenaline flooding her veins. Was she scared for him, or for herself? She wasn't one to fear death, especially not after losing her true mate. How could she be worried for Stryke after what he'd done?

The floor burned and sputtered, but Zoey didn't move from behind Stryke's protection. She'd never felt more useless since the day she'd watched Mitchell burn to death. Inch by inch, Stryke closed the distance between him and Quution.

Fear clawed up her throat. If their two forms connected, what would happen? Could their collision destroy Stryke in the underworld?

"Get out of here, Zoey." Stryke lunged, a wall of energy, his arms flung wide.

What was he doing?

But when he met Quution's image, they both shimmered and disappeared, the deafening bang like a large firework going off by her ear.

"No!" Her voice echoed through the empty cabin.

Her ears rang and her heart was thudding. She waited. Were they going to come back?

She swallowed and tested all of her limbs. Stiff, they worked on command, but she'd have to guzzle some Gatorade. If she hadn't fed from Stryke as much as she had, the attack would've depleted her completely.

She stared at the spot the males had disappeared from. Stryke was gone.

Her breathing slowed and she rolled to her hands and knees and groaned as she pulled herself up. She limped to the kitchen and wrestled open a juice. Propping herself against the fridge, she sipped.

He was gone. Was either one going to come back?

Zoey chugged the rest and tossed the bottle. Wait here or head back to the compound?

She checked her phone but couldn't get anything beyond a black screen.

Super. Her phone had been fried in the fight. Not her fight, though. She'd been so fucking useless and if it hadn't been for Stryke... Well, none of this would've happened. Not Quution, not Hypna...not Mitchell.

She screwed her face up. No. She'd been there and Mitchell's chances had been slim to none.

Had her mate really been planning to turn on their entire team? He'd been so moody those last few months before his death. She'd assumed it was the stress, had no idea... Mitchell had to have known she wouldn't have left.

Tears welled as she recalled how he'd tugged and banged on his side of the door while she'd frantically pounded her side while her skin burned each time she touched the sweltering door. But the door had been constructed for creatures with their strength and it had held.

Stryke was right. If Mitchell could've gotten out, he would've, and he hadn't been thinking about anyone else's safety. Who could blame him? Zoey wouldn't fault him for reacting to the most basic instinct of survival. If he had gotten out and she had gotten hurt, it would've destroyed him.

Hot tears rolled down her cheeks and her anger toward Stryke ebbed. The irony was that Stryke had done exactly what Mitchell would've wanted to be done if he'd been in his right mind and not in full-panic mode.

She snatched a bag of potato chips and ripped it open. As she munched, she lost hope that Stryke was coming back.

Why would he? She'd forced him to break the bond. She'd chosen her work over him. And he was gone.

Had he survived Quution? Of course. He had to have.

Had he?

Enough about Stryke. What about her team? No fucking phone. She had to find out what was going on and daylight was coming soon. The cabin was no longer safe.

She eyed the destroyed living room. It looked like fireworks had gone off. Scorch marks marred the floor, walls, and ceiling. Furniture had been destroyed or overturned. A haze lingered behind the electrical battle. Her gaze swung toward the banister, to the gap left behind Quution's first attack when she'd somersaulted down the stairs.

The owners of this place were going to shit themselves when they returned. Zoey's mouth quirked. If she didn't have such an aversion to fire, she'd burn it to the ground. Instead, she packed her items and gathered Stryke's few belongings and stepped outside. Dawn lightened the horizon with pink and orange. Salt infused her body, but fatigue weighed on her. She doubted

there'd be time to rest when she got home. Up-
dates had to be made, and she had to find out if
her presence put her friends in jeopardy.

***

Stryke entered the underworld. The charged
air between his hands filled with clothing and
muscle as he faced Quution in living color.
Stryke was still in his chamber, but Quution was
here. Had he tracked Stryke down, then followed
him to the cabin?

Stryke summoned all his anger—at the
Synod for demanding Zoey choose, at Hypna for
forcing his hand before he was ready to reveal
himself, at himself for not handling the Mitchell
situation differently, and…at Zoey for using that
damn bracelet because she'd wanted away from
him so badly.

With a roar, he gripped Quution's shoulders
and spun him into a choke hold.

Quution's claws speared his arm and Stryke
gritted his teeth against the pain. Winding back as
far as he could, he punched Quution in the kid-
neys, or whatever organ was in the middle of his
back. He never knew with the full-blooded
crowd. His hit glanced off Quution as he twisted
and dropped, loosening Stryke's hold. Stryke
dropped with him and his arm slipped. His limb
screamed with agony, and when he rolled back to
kick Quution in the trunk, he stalled.

The claws that had been buried in his arm were still there and no longer attached to Quution.

Quution grunted and flipped over, sending waves of energy meant for harm toward Stryke. He absorbed each tendril and stared at the gap in Quution's ratty clothing. Detachable claws, but a normal torso with rippling abs?

"What the fuck are you?" He was on his butt, should be on the offensive, should at least be ready to defend himself.

Quution paused and glanced down at himself. "Oh, demon balls." He snapped his robes together.

Stryke's goal shifted from destroying Quution to uncovering what he was hiding.

He crouched to leap to his feet, but Quution slammed a booted foot into his knee. Bone crunched and Stryke gritted his teeth against the agony. Quution reared his leg back for another kick and Stryke waited. He hadn't noticed how odd the boots looked before, but with the jagged pant leg hitched up, the thick sole was revealed— at least three inches thick. Stryke couldn't risk the distraction to inspect Quution's other foot, but if both boots were platforms, it'd bring the male closer to Stryke's height.

Quution's leg extended, but the male lacked extraordinary speed and Stryke was ready to seize the opportunity. He caught the boot and wrapped his legs around Quution's, giving him a good punt in the groin. From Quution's squeal, his dick was in the standard spot.

The boot had laces. Stryke wiggled his fingers under them and tore as many as he could in one shot, then he yanked the boot off.

A normal foot. With a sock even.

"What the hell are you doing?" Quution couldn't holler; he was still wheezing from the direct hit to his underworld jewels.

Normal torso. Fake claws. Regular humanoid foot. Was Quution compensating for a more demon-like extremity, like a cloven hoof?

Stryke pitched the footwear at Quution's head and wrestled the male's other foot into his grip. By the time the second boot came off, Quution was raining fists onto Stryke's shoulders, weakly because of the odd angle. No hooves, but a matching athletic sock. Since when did one of the Circle shop at department stores?

The way his knee throbbed, Stryke needed to keep the fight on the dirt floor or he'd be at a major disadvantage standing. He unwrapped his legs and tossed Quution's limbs in the opposite direction. The other male recovered quickly and flipped over onto Stryke. He attempted to pin Stryke but couldn't gain a good hold. Stryke twisted and jabbed fists, trying to gain his own handhold.

Quution hissed, his jagged teeth and fangs dripping saliva onto Stryke's chest. Stryke aimed a punch at the male's ugly teeth. His fist connected, and teeth tore into his flesh before they dislodged and went flying.

Quution's eyes flared and he touched a hand to his mouth. Stryke expected blood to be welling through the male's hand. He'd just gotten his teeth knocked out! Instead, the male grimaced, flashing sparkly white chompers and a normal set of fangs.

"What the fuck are you?" Stryke asked again.

Quution's gaze turned black and he hammered his fists into Stryke's chest.

Easily batting his arms away, information clicked into place. Concealing clothing, hidden platform boots, fake teeth—Quution was a fraud. He'd gone to great lengths to create the appearance of a pure-blooded demon.

Stryke snagged one of Quution's fists in his hand. "You're not a full-blood."

"Aren't you the smart one." Quution ripped his hand out of Stryke's grip and jumped off. Stryke scrambled up, favoring the knee that was slowly mending itself.

Without the boots, or the teeth, Quution wasn't as fearsome as before. Stryke prowled around him, covering his limp as much as possible.

"How'd you fool them all?" He couldn't keep the awe out of his voice. His father had fooled the Circle, but he'd genuinely looked the part. Quution was as humanoid as Stryke, with horns that could be concealed by his hair and minimal fangs. The male's hair was a few shades lighter than Stryke's. His horns were the unique color of the sunset, but hell, maybe he polished those a different color, too.

"It's not hard. Humans have been using costumes for years."

Stryke cocked his head. Quution sounded different. The male's real voice was smooth, not harsh and garbled like before, but then talking around prosthetic fangs couldn't have been easy.

"Temporarily in costume." Stryke stopped his movement, gave his leg a rest. The throbbing cleared his head, pushed the memories of Zoey abandoning him away. "You must've been living in that getup."

Quution nodded, the hostility in his eyes at a low simmer. "Had to be done."

"Why?"

"I'm not going to be another slave to the Circle." The glimmer in his lilac eyes turned to hatred. "I'm not going to be locked away until I'm useful, only to be disposed of at a moment's notice."

Stryke's brow creased. Everything he said sounded so familiar. Quution had always seemed familiar to him, but Stryke had assumed it was because he was also an energy demon. Then there was the personal hostility Stryke had felt during their first encounter.

Puzzle pieces fell into place until an idea formed that seemed impossible. Yet, they were demons. Wasn't trickery and deception part of their very being?

But it all made perfect sense. Stryke straightened and drew his shoulders back. He'd only heard the story of his mother's demise from his sire, had never seen the evidence. That was his mistake. "You're my brother."

Displeasure and satisfaction undulated over Quution's expression. "I guess you're not as stupid as I thought you were."

"And you hate me. I get it."

"Do you?" Quution sneered. "While you were gallivanting around with our sire, I was locked away. Told every day how useless I was, how my birth was a waste of time. How my *conception* was the worst thing that had ever happened to her."

Stryke chuckled, but it lacked all humor. "Ah, the nurturing of a pure-blood mother. It was the same for me. Until our sire found a use for me, and it certainly wasn't to claim me as his own."

Disbelief shimmered in Quution's gaze. "Of course you'd say that. But our sire didn't try to kill you, did he? It took me months to recover." Quution spit in disgust. "The only good thing Mother did for me was die. I used her for fuel while I healed."

A sour taste filled Stryke's mouth and he swallowed. The nightmare Quution must've endured... "I didn't know you existed until our sire said he'd killed you and her."

"And you believed him?" Quution's lip curled.

"I had no reason not to believe he'd slaughter his own mate and son. I was only alive to aid in his ruse."

I would've saved you should've spilled from Stryke's lips, but he'd been a different male then. Too eager to please their sire. Sweet brimstone, what would he have done had he known Quution not only existed, but survived? Pleased his sire, or taken mercy on his brother?

The answer was instant. As much misplaced hero worship as he had for his sire, he'd been raised—neglected and abused—by his mother. He would've gone for Quution. Even if he hadn't had the demon balls to stand up to his sire, Stryke would've squirreled his brother away to heal.

"I would've saved you." His voice rang with truth. All his life, Stryke had wanted a connection. His mother had been beyond useless, his sire a lesson in futility. Lee had paid with his life. Zoey—his chest constricted.

Quution glared at him, then rubbed his face, like he was suddenly tired. He shuffled to his boots and stomped his feet into them. "You don't bother checking on my mortality, but you'll defy the underworld for that female."

Fair enough. "Is that why you want her dead? Out of resentment?"

Quution nodded as he straightened his clothing. "You helped our sire, you helped the vampires, but you left me rotting in a dank cell."

For the second time, Stryke found himself saying, "I'm sorry."

His brother glanced sharply at him, his expression probing. "Me, too… I guess."

"Now what?" Stryke asked.

"Isn't that the million-dollar question. If you plan on telling anyone about me, I'll have to kill you."

"Cuz you've done such a good job of that so far."

Quution scowled at him, then went in search of his teeth. Stryke turned his arm over and plucked the claws from the skin that had healed around it, wincing each time.

He waited until his brother brushed the dirt off his teeth and fitted them back in his mouth. "I've got a deal for you."

"I'm sure it benefits you greatly."

Of course. "Both of us. Make me your second-tier and I'll help you keep your secret. Together, we make sure the rest of the Circle quits tampering in the human realm. I know they think they can rule both realms, but all it'll do is expose us and turn things into a massive witch hunt. The numbers aren't on our side."

Quution shuddered. "And who wants to live under the thirteen's power? The human realm is the only place to get away from them. No one but them wants to change that."

Stryke had the exact same thought. All of the second-tiers relished the ability to escape to the human realm. "We deal with Hypna."

"How do you know I won't kill you after I help you kill her?"

"Because you're as curious about me as I am about you."

Quution's mouth screwed up. "What does that even mean?"

Stryke shrugged. "We both wanted some sort of connection to our parents and they more than disappointed. Now we have each other."

"You have Zoey." Quution rolled his eyes toward Stryke but paused. "Wait. You *don't* have Zoey. Am I like your rebound? Your plan B?"

Stryke ground his jaw. What else was he going to do? Zoey had spelled it out clearly that they were done and it wasn't in Stryke to roll over and die. But he had a brother now. One who wanted Hypna dead. Stryke would have an easier time figuring out the rest of his life if he didn't have Hypna after his seed. He wasn't fool enough to think that if Quution backed off of her, she'd give up. She saw the power, craved it.

Quution narrowed his eyes and straightened, then caught himself and hunched again. "What if Zoey comes running back, throws herself into your outstretched arms, and begs you to take her back? Do you tell her everything about me? Report to her team? Draw a picture of what I really look like?"

"I still don't know how you really look, only that you're not as god-awful fugly as you are now."

"Aw, Stryke. Are you jealous you're not the only one that got the looks?"

Well, one of them had a healthy dose of arrogance. Was hubris Quution's driving force? If so, Stryke would have to tread carefully. He'd learned the hard way, watching his sire's demise. Brotherly love wasn't strong between the two of them, but Stryke had no wish to see Quution accept their sire's fate. He didn't even trust Quution, but they were bonded by blood and that had to count for something. Chasing after the male blindly, like he had with Zoey, wouldn't happen.

"Your secret is safe with me, Q." Stryke ran a fang over his palm to open a narrow wound and held it out to Quution.

Quution recoiled, his mouth drawn down. "Are we bonding?"

"Just making a deal. I help you get rid of Hypna, you make me your second-tier."

Suspicion hadn't left Quution's gaze. "And you protect my position?"

"We watch each other's backs. It's what brothers do… I guess."

Blood dripped from Stryke's palm, but Quution still didn't hold his hand out. "Why? I tried to kill you and your female."

His female. Sounded right but was oh so wrong. Stryke took a breath to figure out his response. He went with honesty. "What else am I going to do?"

"Ah, desperation." Quution sliced his fang into his palm and smacked it against Stryke's. "That's something I can work with, but I must tell you, power's not the reason I'm doing this. Come, I'll show you."

His brother limped out of his cavern and Stryke eyed him. If not power, why? He trailed after Quution's ridiculous swagger. Whatever influenced his brother would now influence him.

He shook his head. Had history just repeated itself?

Chapter Fifteen

Zoey finished her report. Demetrius leaned against the wall of the garage bay. Rourke, Bishop, and Creed surrounded her. Zoey hadn't bothered to call a meeting, just popped in and announced to the camera that everyone needed to convene in the garage.

"So, what's going on here?" She tried to keep her tone light but sounded dismal nonetheless.

"Zoey…" Demetrius started and from the pity in his voice, she didn't want to hear it.

She held her hand up. "What's going on here?"

"The Blanchettes and Melody are in house," Creed filled in. "D's parents aren't going to stay here, but they're on guard and will flash here as soon as they feel threatened."

Creed spoke so matter-of-factly, like he was so over her. She hadn't come back hoping to rekindle anything, hadn't planned to feed her ego on Creed pining after her. But damn, he was done with her.

Would Stryke move on that quickly? Whatever. If he did, it was none of her business.

She was such a liar.

Steeling herself, she eased her mind back to work. That was what she'd betrayed Stryke for.

No, she hadn't betrayed him. She hadn't asked for the damn bond in the first place.

Yeah, keep telling yourself that. Would she believe it one day?

The only way to redeem herself to…well, herself, was to dive back into work.

"Zoey?" Demetrius pushed off the wall and walked slowly toward her, like she was a skittish colt.

Way to come back, roaring to prove yourself competent. Space out within ten minutes.

"Are you okay?" Bishop asked. "Really okay?"

Bitterness crashed into her. The guy who got to keep his demon asked if she was okay.

Don't think like that! She wasn't Stryke's, dammit. She had her purpose and it wasn't to turn over her life's work for a male.

She'd thrown the bracelet on Stryke and demanded he release her so she could feel in control again. Nothing about this moment felt like she had any control, and she struggled to find a way to give the power back to herself.

"I have a blood disorder." As soon the words left her mouth, she wanted to swallow them back up. Her way to take the reins back was to blurt her major secret and weakness? But only Stryke had known and she couldn't leave it at that.

The males all stared at her.

"Is this new?" Rourke asked in his typical dry manner.

Zoey could've hugged him. He was just Rourke. This was her team and they should know a variable about her that could be life-threatening for them. They relied on each other in the field. "It's why I drink Gatorade all the time, eat processed foods—I'm naturally low on electrolytes."

Demetrius's face twisted. "Uck, your thing with the pickles and bone broth?" He shuddered. "And here I thought those days were done. All right. Give us the details."

Her mouth twitched. She'd been terribly selfish to keep a secret like this from these guys. "I need to constantly replenish myself, even with a steady blood supply."

Bishop crossed his arms. "Blood doesn't satisfy your disorder?"

Zoey shook her head. "Only—" She clamped her mouth shut and bowed her head.

"Stryke's," Demetrius finished. "He supplied the energy you lacked."

She nodded, couldn't speak past the tightness in her throat.

Bishop slapped a meaty paw on her shoulder. "Well, that sucks."

She snorted and patted his hand. Her thoughts exactly.

"But, Zoey," he leaned down and spoke gently, "he held too much power over you with the bond and his blood. A relationship must be equal."

Hellfire, Bishop could nail the undercurrent of an emotion. Blinking back the burn of tears, she refused to cry in front of anyone. "Anyway, I don't think he's a threat to us. He's the most ambivalent creature I've ever met."

"A male like that won't lay down and die," Demetrius said. "He'll find another cause to stroll behind until things aren't looking his way again."

The way Bishop and Demetrius spoke painted Stryke in a whole new light, but it'd confirmed to Zoey that she'd done the right thing. She couldn't be Stryke's everything, and he couldn't be hers.

Zoey cleared her throat to keep her voice from cracking. "So that's done. I guess I should ask if I should find another place to stay."

"Why? Like I'm going to kick you off the team for that after we've worked together for decades." Demetrius shook his head. "Fuck, Zoey. No. Okay, here's the update. Hypna's tried to hit us once here, she'll do it again. Her vampire host, Yancy, slipped out of her restraints and was gone by the time we went back for her. Probably had more humans helping her, or Hypna sent her second-tiers to free her. Who the hell knows, but she's gone. Creed's already put up some surprises in the trees and a couple of extra cameras."

Creed pinched the bridge of his nose. "Those kids, though. Melody's gotta watch them better."

Zoey's brows shot up. Never had she heard so much censure from him.

A muscle tensed in Rourke's jaw. "Melody and Grace's parents are watching them every second."

"Obviously not." Creed's voice rose and he closed his eyes briefly before resuming. "They've gotten out twice already, and the way Melody rushes out after them gives me a damn heart attack."

"Yeah," Rourke's right eye twitched, "and you yelling at her totally helped."

Creed threw his hands up. "Instead of two kids to worry about, now I have to corral a frantic human. Meanwhile, the kids are flashing to their home and all over the fucking woods to play hide and seek."

Zoey listened to the two bicker about Creed's treatment of Melody. Had she only been gone two nights? She'd come back and the dynamics had changed. Rourke and Creed were butting heads. Creed and Melody had drama, apparently.

Demetrius and Bishop exchanged looks like this argument was getting old.

Zoey sighed and squared her shoulders. "All right. D, you and I need to notify the rest of the Synod and update them. I'm staying." The words left an acrid stain on her taste buds. "Creed, afterward, I need to be updated on the changes." She spun on her heel to head to her apartment. "I need fifteen minutes, D, and I'll meet you in your office. Rourke, maybe Grace should have her brother over for a fun sleepover, then the next night, have Ari over. That way, you can divide and conquer the kids. Bishop, stay cool."

Bishop coughed a laugh. She wasn't used to being the one cracking jokes, either, not anymore. As she breezed into the empty hallway, her smile faded. She was going to her empty apartment.

How had she never noticed how empty her life was before? Work had fulfilled her as much as it could in her widowed state. And it had. Just not anymore.

She charged into her apartment and slammed the door. In her bedroom, she dropped to her knees and wrestled a plastic tub out from under the bed. Ripping the top off, she tensed, ready for the memories to assault her.

On the top of the clothing packed away was her favorite nightshirt. Mitchell had joked about petting her pussy whenever she wore it. On the front was an outline of a fancy, white cat. The image was filled with downy soft fur that was fluffier than the rest of the fleece material. Sleep was heaven in that thing.

She ruffled through the rest of her items and gave up. Heaving them out of the box, she plopped them on the bed, then sorted each item into piles. Finding space in her drawers wasn't hard. She chuffed quietly to herself. Like the rest of her life, her furniture was empty, too.

Once the task was done, she stared at her dresser for a few minutes. What had she been expecting—a profound change in her mentality?

Disgusted with herself, she stomped into the bathroom. At least her appearance wasn't as ghastly as she'd feared. Most of her hair was secured in the bun and she had a few smudges of black on her face. All the damage had been on the inside, in so many ways.

She washed her hands and watched the water carry the grime away, swirling down the drain. The water ran clear for several seconds before she switched off the faucet. But she didn't move. Her gaze was riveted on the empty sink. It rinsed clean. Why couldn't she?

Because she wasn't made out of porcelain. Stryke had gotten to her.

She backed up to the wall and sank to the floor.

He'd constantly put her first, not just with her body, but with her wants and needs. At times, it'd seemed like he'd known her better than she did. Her mind argued the reasons why—deception, underhandedness, trickery. But the part of herself she'd lost when Mitchell died, Stryke had fought for. And it wasn't from guilt. The only guilt she'd sensed from Stryke was how much his actions would hurt her.

She pressed her palms against her eyes. But Bishop was right. The demon's single-minded obsession with her wasn't healthy. She couldn't trust it. He'd given her the gift of discovering that her life didn't need to be an isolated endeavor filled only with duty and work, but she couldn't accept a male who didn't fight for a cause. Especially not one from the underworld. So many reasons to fight against oppression and evil, and he'd just coasted through until he'd seen her.

Blowing out a hard breath, she put her hands on the countertop and heaved herself up, feeling like she'd tripled in weight.

She scrubbed her face, straightened her hair, and brushed off her clothes. Adjusting her gear, she gave herself a steely-eyed look of determination. It was time to get back to work.

***

Quution hovered in the shadows and made room for Stryke to sneak a peek. The chamber Quution had brought him to was unnaturally dark. They lived in a dark world already, but one of the Circle had gone out of their way to conceal what was held here. Where torches lined the walls of the rest of the underworld, they were missing here. The energy of several wards traveled up and down his spine. In addition to being hidden away in the maze of the underworld and left with no chance of light, this chamber was guarded.

"Lest you think you're the only reason I want to destroy Hypna, Brother."

Quution managed to always sneer at that word, like he didn't want to get used to it. Stryke didn't care either way. He was back to the days where all the fucks he gave couldn't fill the palm of his hand.

Or was he? Part of him had to admit he wasn't just here out of curiosity.

"All I had to do was threaten a tiny part of Hypna's world and she turned to this." Quution extended his hand and wiggled his fingers. He'd donned another set of fake claws and they waggled as Q manipulated the wards around the cave to send a tiny energy ball shimmering into the middle of the open expanse.

Stryke jolted. The place was larger than he'd anticipated, but that wasn't what shocked him enough to rock him back on his feet. The place was littered with bones. Tiny little bones that had belonged to small humanoid beings.

"Babies," he breathed. Nothing Stryke had witnessed in his life sickened him as much as the sight before him. Piles and piles of baby skeletons were stacked as if they'd been discarded without thought, which was likely true. Various stages of rot were evident in the top layer of corpses. A rectangular, rust-covered platform rose from the floor in the middle of the cavern.

Bile crawled up his throat. Demons consumed without discretion. If these had been human babies, there'd be little left, but human babies were more trouble than they were worth, a horde of humans hunting for the baby snatchers when the little things were only a mouthful.

These remains were second-tier babies.

Quution stepped forward, his expression as grim as the situation. Stryke eyed him with clarity. This had been a test. How much would Stryke give a shit? He doubted Quution would've reneged on the deal they'd made, but Stryke's status would've been more of a gofer than a partner.

"I stumbled across this after I recovered from our sire's attack." Quution slowly swung his hand in an arc to highlight every morbid stack of remains. "The first thing that struck me was that not even the scarabs had cleaned up the leftovers because the chamber had been warded so well against bugs—why? Perhaps the wards were meant to keep everything out, or they were afraid of what was in here getting out. Unlikely, given the victims. I determined they were afraid of their secret leaking. After all, even demons would question their own young being murdered and not consumed."

"Yes, why not consume them and hide the evidence altogether?" Stryke wanted to gag just asking, but he had to make sense of what had gone on here and Quution seemed to have worked through all the answers.

A gleam darkened Quution's lilac eyes. "As gluttonous as our kind can be, not even they can eat this much without hurting their girly figures."

Stryke nodded. "What about the parents? With all the young in here—we'd have too many second-tiers missing."

"Unless they're in on it. More power for their Circle member, more benefits for the servant."

That was despicable. "There's only a handful of beings involved then."

"I've pinned Hypna, of course. After her brother's demise at Fyra's hand, she's been frantic to seize power. But it's not just her. This is one of the secrets all Circle members are initiated into. However," Quution stabbed his finger in the air, "I was not—my power already threatens them. I refused to be patient. I can't put a stop to this if I don't know enough about it."

Stryke glowered at the platform that must be the alter for sacrifice. Bits of information clicked into place. "*This* is why the Circle has made such progress infiltrating the human realm in the last few decades. They've been stealing second-tier babies to harvest power from them."

Quution's casual shrug wasn't what Stryke had expected. "Part of that is the vampires' own hunger for power. But it doesn't change that the thirteen need a prime vampire host who can handle their power. They still have to be summoned, and if they walk the realm in their own bodies, well, what dies in another realm stays dead. But," he flashed a sly grin, "I would guess their plans for all-world domination would be expedited if they didn't need the approval of their host, if they could, essentially, do what you do, only with more force and less finesse."

Those greedy bastards. When images of him being poisoned and secured in Hypna's dungeon bombarded his brain, he froze. "They aren't just stealing the babies. They're birthing them just to sacrifice them, like their own sacrificial factory."

"Ding, ding, ding. What better way to keep it on the down-low? We might assume they ate their own young but not sacrificed them to absorb their powers. Demons don't mind a little cannibalism, but don't you dare try to get ahead by stealing powers."

A moment of panic burned through Stryke's gut. "I'm still Hypna's servant until you officially transition control." Fuck, he hated feeling this damn powerless, would love to cut ties to the underworld altogether. Hellfire, he would abandon every other second-tier without a second thought, but not babies. Blame his rough start in life for making him a softie where vulnerable creatures were concerned.

This practice couldn't be allowed to go on. The mounds of bones mocked him. The complete disregard for life. All this had been going on under his nose. His own brand of energy demon was becoming rare. Was it because they were being killed for their power?

Quution grinned around his prosthetic fangs. "We know Hypna won't give up. Once she learns you're no longer bonded, she'll render the underworld to ash to get with your child. But that problem will solve itself when we kill her."

"We kill them all and create our own Circle?" That plan would be an instant death sentence if any of the other twelve caught wind. Hypna might be a one and done, but once the others started to fall, Q and Stryke's longevity would be instantly shortened.

Q's smile turned wicked. "It'll get easier as we implant our own members on the Circle. Sprinkle in a few second-tiers and I doubt they'll

242 · MARIE JOHNSTON

take kindly to their babies being power factories."

Stryke rolled a droll look toward his brother. "I'm not as confident in the altruism of my brethren." Once the oppressed population of the underworld sniffed a way to get ahead, they wouldn't give it up.

"You and I are horrified. You're friends with Fyra, a former second-tier. What would she think?"

Stryke chewed the inside of his cheek. Sweet brimstone, could they really pull this off?

Quution lightly patted him on the shoulder, keeping the sound down to not set off the wards. "We only need a few strong, morally solid-ish members to plant on the Circle. Then we can keep balance down here and," Q pointed to the ceiling, "up there."

"And we'd spend our life defending this realm and the creatures down here. We've never had a government with that goal before."

Quution removed his hand and sliced his palm and stuck it toward Stryke. "You would be dedicated to a worthy cause, my brother."

Stryke followed suit without hesitation, but a part of him died as he shook. Zoey's words registered in his mind. She'd been right, of course. He'd been nothing but blind devotion to her and that was unhealthy, had made him almost as worthless as he'd been before. Now he had purpose, a noble one, but he couldn't fool himself. He wasn't doing this to win her over, but because

it had to be done. He'd exhibited protective in-
stincts before. With Fyra. Lee. But never for
those he'd never met, who couldn't do a thing to
advance Stryke's plans. This act needed to be
stopped and prevented from occurring ever again
and it was like he'd been training his whole life
to do just that.

Maybe Zoey would be proud, but it didn't
matter. He'd just tied himself to the underworld
for the rest of his existence.

Chapter Sixteen

Zoey stood over Creed in his office, her gaze dancing between the monitors. Creed kicked his legs out and crossed them at the ankles, managing to remain seated on his exercise-ball office chair. He finished pointing out the new cameras. "So, now we have a complete view of the woods. Somewhat obscured be-cause...trees."

He squeezed a smiley-face stress ball in one hand. When she'd been in here last, she'd busted him watching the Blanchettes' place and Melody, but this time the monitors only contained images of the woods and the exterior of the compound.

"We could just get word out that you're no longer bound to Stryke." Creed tossed the stress ball up and caught it again. Zoey frowned at him but he wasn't being facetious. He was throwing an obvious option out and evaluating her response.

"Hypna would use me to drive him into the open. We can't take the chance she succeeds. You might not like him, but we're not the kind to set males up to get assaulted and put innocent babies at risk."

"Agreed." Toss, catch. Toss. Catch. He watched her. A lack of heat was present in his gaze. He cared for her but no longer had any sexual interest.

Toss, catch. Toss, catch.

With a disgusted snarl, she snatched the ball and pitched it toward the far wall. It ricocheted and hit the ceiling, then bounced off another wall. Creed stretched out, caught it before it took out a monitor, and held it firmly in his grip.

She sighed. "Don't you dare ask me about him. I'll be fine doing my job."

"I wasn't concerned about that. You always get the job done." He paused and she ripped her gaze away to stare aimlessly at his desk. "You're different."

She slid her gaze back to him.

He held up his hands like he was an innocent victim and not flirting with a left hook. "Serious, but like not in a bad way. I'd like to say you've loosened up, but I don't think that's you and that's okay. I just think you've suppressed a side of yourself for a long time and you actually let her out to play. Then after the Synod bullshit, you shoved her back in. But you're not as okay with it."

"You heard what he did to Mitchell."

Creed nodded, his face solemn. "I did, and this has nothing to do with either of those males. I just… Never mind." He turned back to his keyboard and tapped a few buttons. The images on the screens changed to a different view of the woods.

"You can't drift off like that and leave me hanging."

He turned back, wariness in his gaze. "You've always been a female with your own mission. You didn't let Mitchell sway you, and we all know how much he tried. You didn't let Stryke sway you. But the Synod makes a few grunts about not liking you hooking up with a demon they don't know shit about, and well, you bend immediately."

"You said it there. Demon. It doesn't matter what we don't know about him. He's a demon."

"And you know that's bullshit. Just like us fearing Fyra turning against us is a pointless concern. Remember, this isn't about Stryke or his obsession with you. It's about you doing what you believe in. You found someone you started to believe in, and the Synod shakes their head and you're done."

Her face went numb as blood drained away. No. No, that wasn't it at all. She'd believed in Stryke? She'd barely believed him, period.

Except…had she?

"Damn you, Creed. I had this all figured out. I had a good reason for—" Movement in the woods stole her words.

Creed spun around to see what'd stopped her. "Shit." He tapped the radio. "Boss, we have action. Standby."

He zoomed, but the image grew grainier.

Zoey leaned over his shoulder. "Humans or vampires?"

"Nightfall is an hour away. Could be both if the vampire is powerful enough. And Yancy would be."

A male took a long, bulky object from his back and kneeled.

They both strained to make out details when the male rested it on his shoulder and aimed one end toward the compound.

"Hellfire. Is that an RPG?"

"Not on my watch." Creed tapped a few buttons and muffled gunshots could be heard from the office.

Plops of dirt scattered around the male as he dove to the side. Creed lay on the trigger and from the comfort of the compound, he fired shot after shot toward the male. The figure jerked and rolled, eventually falling still. Creed eased off the button. A yawning, black chasm opened. Brittle branches cracked and whipped around it and snow flurries swirled in the air. Then all went still.

"Good. You hit him." She peered at the other monitors and stabbed at a suspicious blur. "There. Another one. Female this time."

Creed was punching in a few buttons to re-calibrate the mounted guns when Zoey gasped. The exterior door had flung open and two young boys tumbled out. Ari and Xavier were giggling and dodging each other, oblivious to the danger around them.

Zoey tore out of the office, Creed right behind her. They raced through the halls and up the stairs toward the exit.

A shrill female voice was calling out the boys' names. Melody.

Creed had been absolutely right. Having to protect her on top of containing the boys was a nightmare.

Laughter drifted in through the open door and Melody shrieked.

Zoey put on a boost of speed and Creed almost shoved past her. They both barreled out of the door. Ari and Xavier frolicked in the snow and were already near the tree line. Melody was jogging toward them, like she was pretending to join in on the fun, but was really going to corral them. Zoey instinctively broke for the boys, while Creed tackled Melody.

Gunfire rang out from the woods and the boys went quiet.

Zoey was just yards away when a female appeared between them. Yancy—possessed by Hypna, no doubt.

A wicked grin lit Yancy's face as she stared at the kids. "Oh my. You two are just adorable. So yummy and tender." She stooped to greedily sweep them into her arms, but they darted away. More gunshots echoed and Yancy straightened. "Quit shooting, idiots. You're scaring the bait away."

Ari sprinted for Melody with Xavier trying to keep up. Creed released Melody to rush and meet them. Ari dodged, thinking it was all a game.

Zoey yanked her gun out and aimed at Yancy's head, but the female disappeared.

"Fuck." She circled around.

Yancy appeared ten feet in front of Ari and lunged for him. Zoey slowed her breathing, Yancy in her sights.

Exhale. Fire.

Yancy's shoulder flung back and she snarled. Ari pivoted with a shriek and spun in another direction. Creed had reached Grace's brother and cradled him in his arms. He reached a hand out to snag Melody, but she'd taken off for Ari.

"Melody, dammit," Creed growled. "Get inside where it's safe."

Melody didn't slow. Zoey flashed in front of her and spun her around. "Go inside!" Melody stumbled, taking several steps to regain her balance.

Ari screamed. Zoey whipped around, her stomach plummeting. Yancy held the boy by the arms.

Zoey swallowed and flashed again. Landing behind Yancy, she slammed an elbow into the crook of the female's neck. Yancy shouted in pain and dropped to her knees, releasing Ari. She tucked and rolled before Zoey could grab her.

Ari ran away, crying loud and hard. Xavier was screaming in Creed's arms. Melody was closer and rushed for Ari.

Yancy jumped up and flashed. She was probably going for Ari again. Zoey concentrated to flash. She disappeared and reappeared in time to see Melody shove Ari behind her and yank a stake from her waistband. Without hesitation, Melody struck.

Her aim was stellar and her speed was fast for a human.

The dull *thunk* of the stake reached Zoey's ears before Yancy's shout. The vampire stumbled backward and tripped.

Dammit, Melody hadn't been strong enough to plunge the spear into Yancy's heart, just injure her. Zoey kicked into motion to finish the deed, but Melody beat her again.

"You don't touch my kids," the girl screeched. She dove onto Yancy's chest as the vampire fell. Melody clutched the stake with both hands. Using her body weight, she dropped anchor on the piece of wood and sent it straight to its target.

A gurgling howl cut off as Yancy's body *poofed* into ash.

Melody bounced to the ground as the body disappeared. She raised both arms in a whoop. A shot resounded from the trees and Melody flinched. Zoey gasped. A tiny hole blew open in Melody's sweater. The silly, courageous, infuriating girl looked as shocked and scared as Zoey felt. As red bloomed out from the hole, another horrifying thought occurred to Zoey.

Creed beat her with the warning. "Melody, move! Get the fuck out of there!"

Spurred into action, Zoey closed the distance to rescue Melody, but a little body beat her.

"Melwo-dee!" Lines of tears streaked down Ari's face. He sought comfort from his nanny and it was putting him in greater danger than before.

The chasm was opening right under Melody, but she didn't notice. Her stunned gaze was on her shoulder and she touched the bullet hole and winced.

"Melody, move!" Hellfire. Zoey snatched Ari up and he fought, not knowing Zoey well enough when Melody was within reach.

Zoey reached for the girl, intending to flash all of them away, when Melody slumped to the side. The vacuum of the groaning opening rustled dried leaves and hunks of snow. All inched in the direction of the portal. The force increased, toppling Melody inside.

Zoey met Creed's horrified gaze, his hold still tight on Xavier. His gaze beseeched her, asking if she could just find a way to save Melody from the awful fate that awaited her when she landed in the underworld next to Hypna. But Zoey had to save the child. She flashed with Ari to Creed and rushed them both through the exterior door and out of range of the gunfire.

***

Stryke stepped through the trees and eyed his brother. Ironically, they'd found a set of twin men, midforties, sporting impressive beer guts, to possess. The men had both divorced within months of each other and were new depressed bachelors living together. Easy finds with their broken energy patterns acting like a beacon to creatures like Stryke and his brother.

The dudes had been good choices, though—they were avid sportsmen of the shooting variety, shooting trophies and awards lining the walls of their barren apartment. Stryke and Quution were each packing handguns with plenty of ammo and their car had no less than three loaded shotguns.

The compound and the fight he'd heard raging around them came into view. Stryke stopped in his tracks, willing his eyes to be wrong about what he'd just seen. A young human girl had been sucked into the underworld with Hypna. Zoey and Creed had saved the children at least, but the human would suffer dearly.

Familiar woods surrounded Stryke, taunting him with the time he'd camped close to this very spot to keep watch over his female. He'd possessed a sense of duty, a small amount of optimism, and complete blindness. He could argue he'd been doing the right thing, but perhaps he'd been doing it for the wrong purpose. Again, he found himself with innocent beings who didn't know they counted on him for their safety, but unlike Zoey, current and future babies couldn't defend themselves. This cause was right, Stryke felt in every fiber of his being. Yet it didn't assuage the deep sadness weaved into his every fiber. Because one thing he hadn't deluded himself about were his feelings toward the vampire. They were real.

But they weren't returned. So be it. He had shit to do, a human girl to save, and a wicked demon to kill—and that was only a start.

"Demon balls. Did you just see that?" Quution breathed next to him. "That little blonde is fucked."

Stryke shifted to peer around the trees. Other human hosts were roaming the woods and he wanted to locate the one who'd shot the girl. "If we can save her, the vampires will be more likely to work with us."

"How convenient," Quution murmured with a smirk. "Saving her will involve killing Hypna. Win-win." His keen gaze scanned the trees like Stryke's had. "I sense five hosts. You break right."

Worked for Stryke. He took off to his right, wanting the shooter. He hadn't met the human, but he knew her story and anyone who could leave everything she knew and serve another species—willingly—ranked highly in his book. He obviously had a soft spot for people who cared for children.

When had kids become a thing with him?

He toed through the woods. His host wasn't in the best shape of his life, but he'd kept active enough that a late-night hike didn't wind him much, beer gut aside. Still, Stryke took it slowly. The host he was after was crashing through branches and leaving visible footprints in the snow. Stryke could only assume from his circular trajectory around the compound that he was attempting to open fire on it. But Zoey, Creed, and the kids were behind closed doors.

Stryke pulled his gray turtleneck higher and crouched down. The douche was coming back this way and hadn't sensed Stryke yet.

Either Quution had dispatched his targets extremely quietly, or he hadn't engaged yet. Either way, any noise Quution made shouldn't hurt his chances. If his target was put on alert, he had a long way to go before becoming stealthy. The guy was twitchy as fuck.

"I can smell you, demon."

Ah. So he did sense Stryke. He didn't bother concentrating his energy and dampening his smell. Then the second-tier he stalked would suspect it was him.

Stryke smiled to himself. But they would be ever so surprised to find Quution hunting them in the woods. His second-tier brother who made all quake, thinking he was a loose-cannon pureblood.

How quickly Stryke's opinion of Quution had changed. But then he'd been more open-minded as soon as Quution had quit trying to kill him. Stryke frowned. Actually, Quution had never tried killing him per se. His brother had been angry and filled with resentment, but his tactics had been more attention getting.

Enough pondering. The host was closing the gap between them and all Stryke had to do was wait.

In the distance, a muffled roar filtered through the trees. The sound of a portal opening. Stryke sent out energy feelers. His brother's similar power answered. Good. One down and—

The host spun around, just feet from Stryke, his eyes wide, growing impossibly wider when his gaze landed on Stryke.

"You," he hissed, revealing a mouthful of half-rotted teeth. He swung his gun up.

Stryke slapped the barrel skyward. A shot went off in the air. Stryke ignored it and pulled the attacker toward him. The guy lobbed a punch, but it was so slow and cumbersome Stryke batted it away and spun the man around.

He broke the human's neck easily enough, stripped him of his weapon, and shoved him away as hard as he could. The body collided with a tree trunk, branches cracking, before falling limply at the base.

Stryke strode away as soundlessly as possible in his hiking boots. He sent his feelers out again, the portal causing all kinds of energy alarms to go off.

The last three were easy to find, just as not stealthy as the one Stryke had just taken care of. They were deeper in the trees, heading toward the road, fleeing after hearing the portals opening and witnessing the demise of Hypna's host. Stryke knew exactly where they'd parked. He and Q had scoped them out before choosing their own spot—after deflating some tires first.

Swearing and yelling coaxed a smile out of Stryke. He spotted Quution off to his left. His brother caught his gaze and nodded. They both checked their weapons and changed course to their targets' cars, guns raised.

They began firing as soon as the hosts were visible in the trees. Two women and a man. From this distance, their greasy, ratty hair was obvious, along with their general lack of hygiene.

The women snarled and ran around the opposite side of the car for cover. They returned fire, but their blood stained the air. The man slid against the car, leaving a smear of blood across the teal paint. He had wrestled his weapon out and hit the trigger several times before making contact with the ground. Stryke stalled long enough to aim. The gunshot hit the man between the eyes.

But no time to mentally award himself a shooting trophy; the women's accuracy was improving. Bark flew off the trees around Stryke. At least he was far enough away to not worry about the portal sucking the man's demon home.

Quution grunted in pain and dropped to a knee but kept up constant suppressive fire.

Stryke took cover behind a narrow trunk that offered only enough cover for his ear and spine, but it was enough.

The air ripened with gunpowder and blood. None of his host's blood yet. One woman dove into the car while the second laid down cover fire. The engine fired up and just as Stryke was about to gloat that they wouldn't get anywhere with four flats, the second shooter dove into the back and the car lurched away. Rubber flapped against the ground. Soon, it'd be shaved away and the car would be chugging along with nothing but rims throwing up sparks. Stryke debated if it was worth the effort sending an energy jolt to the battery and stopping it dead.

He didn't have to decide, though. The driver slumped and the car careened off the road, bumping through the ditch right into a tree trunk. A crack wrenched through the tree and the telltale groan of a portal resonated from the holes in the window. Then another.

A twofer.

Quution limped toward him. "Their wounds caught up with them."

"Yes."

"Are drug dens always a popular place to recruit hosts?" Tension pinched around Quution's eyes. He was feeling his host's pain, and his human would follow the last five hosts if the bleeding continued.

Stryke tore at his undershirt until he freed a strip of fabric. He crossed to Quution before he walked any more blood out of himself and tied the cloth around his thigh, above his wound. Quution hissed when Stryke knotted it with extra force.

"I'm sure the hosts are coerced with promises of drugs, money, or food, but they're only paid in death. Come on." Stryke nudged his shoulder under Quution's. "I don't want to wait while you find another host."

Together, they hobbled to the road and turned to head toward their hosts' pickup.

He heard the rumble of the engine with his human ears almost as soon as the SUV was on them, but he couldn't whip around without upsetting Quution's balance.

"Stryke?"

Stryke's eyes drifted shut for a heartbeat. The sexiness of her voice shouldn't affect him so. He halted the thrill that surged through him that she sensed it was him even though they were no longer bonded. Stop that shit before it started.

"I guess we'll face the vampires sooner than later, Brother." Quution's wry chuckle only irritated Stryke further.

With halting steps, they swung around. Zoey was in the passenger seat, her face filled with dismay and dare he hope...anticipation?

The SUV screeched to a stop. Creed hopped out and slammed the door behind him. He marched toward the brothers as he drew his sidearm. "Which one of you fuckers do I need to kill to get to the underworld right now?"

Stryke's brows popped up. Of course, he'd known Zoey's team would attempt a rescue, but Creed was a little more...impatient...than he'd expected.

"We do not wish these hosts any more harm than we've brought to them," Stryke said.

Creed's expression said he didn't give a shit, he'd gut them and crawl inside before the portal opened.

Zoey exited the SUV, her advance more cautious. "Who's that?" She jutted her chin toward Quution.

Even without that damn bond, his blood still sang for her. Like it wanted to present itself on a silver fucking platter for her to sup on. But that train had left the station and he had to try to find a way to work with her without upsetting his balance. Without wanting to shuck everything to the curb the second she beckoned for him in any way.

Back to the question. The muscles between his shoulder blades cramped and not from bearing Q's weight. Because how was this explanation going to go over?

"Not out here," Quution said. His face was pale, but not gray and ashen. They had time.

"He's right. This explanation cannot take place in the open."

Creed was on him in a second, a cold barrel pressed to Stryke's temple. "How fucking convenient. Are you trying to get inside the compound because Yancy could only abscond with Melody?"

His voice cracked slightly on the girl's name.

Well, wasn't that enlightening. Suddenly, any hostility Stryke had toward the male drained away. The male no longer held a torch for Zoey, but he'd be a lot less screwed if he did. Stryke's own bad odds had proven insurmountable. A vampire and human combo had even less of a chance. Just like Melody in the underworld.

Pity must've shown through his host's eyes because Creed's aim wavered until he finally dropped his arm. He didn't holster his weapon but looked around. The crashed car and blood-stains hinted at the battle that had taken place.

Creed's words were bleak. "Did you get them all?"

"Yes."

Zoey had reached them and was watching Creed closely. She must've come to the same conclusion Stryke had about the male's feelings toward the doomed girl.

"Why?" she asked.

"Because I've found a cause I can get behind," Stryke said more snidely than he'd intended. He tightened his hold on Quution and prompted him to start limping to the SUV, which was closer.

They loaded Quution in the backseat. The tourniquet was working, but if they didn't get the host to a hospital, he'd lose his leg and maybe his life. The two vampires jumped in and Creed punched down the gas as he squealed a U-turn and sped toward the compound. Zoey had her phone out, texting furiously.

"Just park in the garage so we can talk securely," Stryke ordered. "This man needs medical attention soon."

Creed glanced at him in the rearview mirror. "You just killed five humans."

"Regrettable." And, he found, it actually was. Those hosts had likely been tricked into agreement. Their fate would've been the same, unfortunately. "However, I'm sure Zoey has explained how I can enter a host without their permission. These two hosts did not acquiesce."

Creed inclined his head, his eyes going back to the road.

Sure she had. Spilled everything. Probably even spilled about her blood disorder. No, he couldn't be resentful about that. They needed to know before she became a detriment in the field—for herself and others.

"These hosts don't need to perish," Quution gritted out, his leg straightened across Stryke's lap.

"What? Like you'd feel guilty." And Creed was back to directing his hostility toward him and his brother.

"Yes. Does that surprise you? That I give a shit about more than myself and..." Stryke's gaze flicked toward Zoey when he trailed off.

"Shit shouldn't catch me off guard any-more," Creed muttered. "Not after having Fyra under the same roof for over a month."

The compound loomed in front of them. The garage was already opening, shadows moving around inside. Zoey was nothing if not efficient.

Cap the damn bitterness.

They pulled in and Creed flung open a door so the others could hear. "Start talking."

Chapter Seventeen

Melody's ragged breathing filled her own ears as searing pain blazed through her shoulder.

Oh god. Was this how awful her father had felt when he'd died? No wonder he'd wanted to go.

She whimpered and rolled to her knees. Why was it so dark? She'd been proud of how well she'd developed her night vision since caring for two vampire boys, but only torchlight flickered where she was now.

Torchlight?

Ohmigod, ohmigod, ohmigod.

She wasn't where she thought she was…was she?

Ohmigod, ohmigo—ouch.

Looking left and right had irritated her shoulder, ratcheting up the pain to unbearable levels. She cradled her left elbow in her other hand and swayed to a stand. Only all those years hunting with her dad kept her on her feet. A girl didn't get weak after tromping through the woods and forests for days at a time in search of big game.

The temperature was pleasantly warm here, whereas she'd been chilled blasting out of the compound in a sweater and jeans.

All those long talks with Grace rushed back. Host death. Portals. Her stomach heaved and she wanted to throw up. She released a shaky breath.

"Oh hell. I'm in Hell."

No wait. Just the underworld.

Melody chuckled, then winced. "Just" the underworld. How tilted had her world become?

Her dear, sweet employers were going to blame themselves so hard for Melody's predicament when it was her own damn fault. She'd only left Xavier and Ari for two minutes to fix a snack while their parents took a breather and enjoyed some alone time. Creed had said he'd rigged the door so it was childproof. But Creed didn't have kids, probably hadn't been around many, and didn't realize that no device was childproof, just child-delaying.

Creed.

She drew in another tremulous breath. Her knees quaked. Was she going into shock? Thinking about Creed didn't normally cause this strong of a physical reaction.

That was a lie—it used to. But her raging crush had diminished after she'd overheard his conversation about her with Rourke. She was another forgettable human, according to him. Between her short life span and the epic amount of money he came from, nothing was going to happen.

Can't a girl have a healthy case of hero worship and not get vehemently insulted?

Wooziness hit her hard. She stumbled around, looking for a place to sit before she passed out and ate dirt.

She squeaked and flattened her hand over her racing heart. A giant female demon was watching her with a disgusting tilt to her lush mouth. The gender was obvious because—no clothes. Not a stitch. Heavy breasts drooped from her chest, and the junction of her thighs... well, she had all the standard pieces. The female had—oh dear lord, were those *horns*? Turgid, purple shanks jutted out from the demon's forehead. And—holy smokes!—they moved like tentacles. And—Melody gulped—wickedly curved claws tipped each finger.

"Oh my—"

"Shut your mouth." The demoness enunciated around a mouthful of pointed teeth and made it look effortless. "Don't speak such language."

Melody snapped her mouth shut with a squeak. She clutched her elbow, her shoulder was on fire, and her tremors were growing stronger. What was going to happen?

The demon's blazing emerald eyes drifted shut and she dragged in a deep breath. Melody recalled her name. Hypna. "Mmm. I love the smell of blood in my home."

Melody glanced around as if she'd find another source of blood. As if her sweater weren't saturated and tacky as new blood mixed with drying blood.

The demon cocked her head. "Such a little thing. And all that hair reminds me of obnoxious summer sunlight." Her horns speared toward Melody, jolting her back. From this close, the iridescent drops draining from the tips seized Melody with desperation. She feared she'd hurl and it'd ignite her injury further and piss off the she-demon.

For once, Melody was speechless.

Hypna advanced, the tips of her sharp horns tracking Melody as she backed up.

"You work for them, yes? The vampires?"

Melody's eyes grew as round as the clay discs she'd used trapshooting.

"Yes," Hypna purred. "You are valuable to them, otherwise they wouldn't employ you. Or!"

Melody jumped and her back hit the wall. Another wave of nausea rolled through her as it jarred her painful bullet wound. The point of Hypna's horn lifted a curl stuck on Melody's face.

"Or…you're their toy? Yes?"

Was it better or worse to let the demon think that? On the one hand, she'd didn't want to be seen as complete garbage to be cast aside or worse, if Hypna thought she was worthless. On the other hand, after what Creed had said about her, Melody was loath to pretend to be his, or anyone else's, toy.

Hypna tugged hard on her hair. "Answer me!"

"I w-work for them."

"Eh, good enough." Hypna clapped a hand on her good shoulder and dug her claws in.

Melody's knees gave out, but she didn't fall with the demon's hold on her.

"Now, let's wrap you up like good little bait." Her lips curled in a cruel smile and roots shot out of the wall on each side of Melody's head.

She let out a startled gasp as the spindly vines wrapped themselves around her. As more and more roots birthed from the dirt surface and fastened her to the wall, Melody's tremors had no way to express themselves in her tightly secured body.

Her wail started as a moan and turned to a full-throated scream, accompanied only by Hypna's evil laugh.

***

Zoey had stayed in the passenger seat of the SUV. The story spilled from Stryke. Quution panted, doing the demon equivalent of Lamaze through his painful leg cramps.

Demetrius, Bishop, and Rourke surrounded the vehicle. Her door hung open and Creed's window was open.

"What are they going to do with Melody?" Creed asked. "She's not a baby. She's a fucking human. Is she dead already? Would Hypna try to fuck her, too, before she kills her? Would she kill her trying to fuck her? Oh hell, she has that poison shit, right?"

Zoey laid her hand on Creed's arm. He was rattling rapid-fire—exactly like Melody would when she was nervous. His panic diverted her attention from Stryke and his brother. Their tale was probable and she'd love to believe that he was truly dedicated to saving babies. But she'd have to trust Quution for that and she'd been burned, literally, by him before.

Their theories would explain a lot. The recent spike in activity. What was a demon's gestation time anyway?

"Is the power cumulative or does the spell wear off?" she asked. Stryke sat right behind her so she shifted in her seat until she was sideways.

Foolishness twined around her heart. She'd been afraid to look at him, but he was in his host, talking with his host's voice. His presence filled the cab like he was in his true form… which he couldn't do because she'd forced him to break their bond.

Quution answered, his voice strained with pain. "The young are sacrificed and the power transfer is permanent, albeit smaller as they haven't grown into their abilities. It's why we don't sacrifice adults. The transfer could kill us. Sometimes it's tried temporarily, but unless one side submits, it usually fails." He drew in a ragged breath. "Demon balls, won't this leg ever go numb? I didn't think humans were so resilient."

"Take us back to our car," Stryke said. "We'll drive somewhere and call an ambulance, then jet back home and find your girl. But…" His gaze found Demetrius standing by the driver's door. "We need Fyra or the big guy to come with."

"Why?" Bishop and Demetrius asked at the same time.

Stryke held up his hands to indicate his body. "I can no longer travel back and forth between the realms. Melody will need someone to transport her, if—" He cut off with a grimace.

Creed jumped on the change. "If what? If she's alive?"

Stryke leveled him with a serious stare. "If she can even get back. She's human. I don't know that any have escaped the underworld."

Before they perished, Zoey finished mentally for him.

"Then we both go with," Bishop rumbled, his arms crossed over his massive chest. "Two of us will have better odds transporting her. Meet us in her old chamber."

Stryke and Quution both nodded.

"It's decided, then." Creed fired up the engine and opened the garage door.

Demetrius knocked on the hood. "Go to the intersection of the highway and head north five miles. I don't want the humans sniffing around here. We already have a mess to clean."

"Wait." Zoey swung her legs back in and shut the door before Creed could back it out of the garage and take off. "Bishop, can you and Fyra get me down there, too?"

Her hand was still on the door handle and she squeezed until her knuckles turned white. She couldn't be left behind. Yeah, there was work here to do, but she needed to save Melody, needed to be with Stryke—to check out his story.

She was not going to be pathetic about this. The situation was urgent and a friend was in trouble, but Zoey had been hoping for more than a cool reception from Stryke. He and his brother—geez that was weird—wanted to form an alliance. He hadn't come back to rekindle anything with Zoey. She'd thought they'd last parted with him saving her. Had she been in any real danger?

At the time—yes and no.

Stryke's gaze flicked to her. It was the host's eyes, black from possession, so unlike Stryke's real eyes, and packing none of the heat he used to reserve just for her. "They shouldn't waste their power. Like Demetrius said, you have plenty to do up here."

"Fuck that." Creed cranked the wheel around and stomped on the gas. They peeled away from the compound, bumping along the road to Quution's groans. "We're finding some damn second-tier to burn and get a one-way ticket."

Stryke gripped the front seat and leaned forward, careful of Quution's leg. "And if you do, how will you get back?"

"You two can do the bond thing again."

Zoey's chest froze and she stared. Stryke remained immobile behind her. Even Quution had silenced his agony.

"She's made her choice," Stryke said in a flat voice. "I've made mine."

"You can change your mind." The speedometer needle rose as Creed gave the gas pedal all he had. "There's a life at stake."

"Along with Zoey's. You recall she'd lose her station if she stayed with me. And I've sworn myself to another."

Zoey whipped her had back before she could stop herself. "So soon?" Derision dripped from those two words.

"Relax, Zohana," Stryke chided. "Remember, once severed, I cannot bond myself to another. But I've sworn myself to aiding the underworld's young."

"There's a life at stake," Creed repeated.

A metallic glint in the bare tree branches was rapidly approaching. It'd only taken Creed minutes to find the spot. He skidded to a stop.

Zoey clenched her jaw as she opened doors for Stryke to haul Quution out. He cradled the host all the way to the hidden truck where Zoey did a repeat of her doorman duties.

Stryke levered himself behind the wheel. "Tell Bishop ten minutes, we'll be there."

"I'll find a way down."

Creed honked the horn and she tossed him a scowl.

"No, you won't." His tone wasn't belittling, just accepting. "Because you have a job to do. Yes, young Melody is in danger, possible even dead already. But you're on the Synod to protect many more than just her. If you chased me to the underworld, you might not get back to do your job. You'd be in danger constantly. You're committed." He reached out to gently tug the door from her hands. "And so am I."

She stepped clear as he angled the car out of the trees and onto the blacktop. She watched him drive away and jumped when the SUV pulled up inches away from her.

"Are you walking back or finding a way down to the realm?"

Zoey was back in her seat before she could think. What if they were successful and they found a way to the underworld? The Synod wouldn't fault her for saving Melody.

Or would they? She was human and they would be risking a lot of their team going after a girl who might no longer be alive.

But then to get back, what would she do? She'd had her true mate. She'd had her demon bond. Stryke said it was one and done.

Hellfire, did she care if she made it back? She'd be on the run in the underworld…but Stryke was there. Yet he had formed an alliance with Quution and she was no longer his concern.

"Call it in." Creed's hard gaze was pinned to the windshield as he flew to town to look for a host. "But tell Demetrius I'm going. I don't care what he fucking says."

D picked up on the first ring. "Bishop and Fyra are gone. Where are you two?"

Zoey's hand tightened around her phone. "We're going to look for a way into the underworld."

"Figures. The Synod's not going to like you being this active in the field—trying to get into the underworld."

Her first thought was, *They can suck it*. But she said, "I'll deal with it later. Melody's a friend."

"And you're working closely with a demon male you were once bonded to. Who's admitted to killing one of our own."

"You heard the story," she said quietly and gripped the "oh shit" handle as Creed careened around turns without letting up on the gas.

"I did. I almost believe him, too. But you and Stryke have a helluva convoluted history and you're rushing after him instead of trusting Bishop and his mate to deal with it."

"It's the underworld, they're massively out-numbered," she said tersely.

"You don't have to convince me, Zoey. You're an adult. You've been my friend longer than most humans live. Your mate was my friend. Stryke is not my friend, but I trust your gut. You don't get stupid over males. The Synod may fear it, but I know you."

The back of her throat burned as emotion choked her. D had almost driven Bishop away because of Fyra. But here he was declaring Zoey of sound mind and body.

"But," Demetrius continued, "I don't trust Creed not to drop some IQ points over this Melody ordeal. So you stick with him and you both get your asses back in one piece and I'll back whatever you do."

Zoey grinned and then it faltered. Her friend had just put himself out there for her and Creed. His own standing with the Synod could be affected, and he'd almost lost it once already. But he'd throw caution to the wind over and over again for his people.

She hung up with him and called Ophelia.

"It's me," her friend answered. She almost never answered or replied to messages, but somehow, she seemed to know when she was needed.

"We need some possessed hosts worthy of being put in the ground. We need a ticket to the underworld."

Ophelia was quiet for a heartbeat before she rattled off a few prime names, including Yancy. "They're off and on as hosts for some of the thirteen. They might have some lackeys hanging around, but they also might be too attention grabbing."

"Cross Yancy off that list. Melody staked her."

"The chatterbox? Well, then… Rumor has it the primes' brokers have been hitting up crack houses and lingering around drug dealers for new recruits. I heard Nadair mention the halfway house in downtown Freemont. You'll find the name in the paper. It just got a huge donation," Ophelia's tone went taut, "from Nadair's family."

"Has he been a host yet?" No one knew what Ophelia was doing, other than gathering intel for them. But she'd stuck close to her on-again, off-again lover. Zoey was going to pry as much info as possible as long as she was talking. She trusted

Ophelia, though her tactics might raise eyebrows, but she'd been coming out from undercover less and less.

"He hasn't hosted…yet."

That she knew of. She'd have to sit Ophelia down and catch her up on all the latest.

Ophelia killed the line after Zoey passed on her thanks. They had reached Freemont and Creed was already weaving through traffic to get to the halfway house. Vampire hearing could be efficient sometimes.

Tall, glass buildings flashed by. Streetlamps lit up the roads, and traffic was sparse on this side of midnight.

"Saving Grace."

"What?" Zoey glanced at Creed. His profile hadn't changed.

"That's what the place is called. The halfway house. But I don't know the address. Look it up."

She did as he demanded. This side of Creed didn't often emerge, the bossy, intense warrior. He'd worked so hard to appear aloof and lost in his technology. But this felt more genuine. Like a little of the real Creed had snuck past a long-closed door.

She rattled off the address and within minutes, Creed parked in a spot about a block away. Square, official buildings lined the street on either side, but smaller, more pedestrian businesses were interspersed. Freemont's major hospital was only three blocks away, and the law enforcement center and jail were five blocks away in the opposite direction. A prime spot for a halfway house.

"It'd be faster if we split up to search around the property." Creed hopped out so fast Zoey had to scramble to keep up with him.

"No way."

He shot her a sharp look and she shook her head.

"The mindset you're in, Creed, I don't trust that'll you wait for me before you shank the first host you find." Or that he'd discern whether the host should remain living.

"I just feel guilty, that's all." His features clouded over, his blond brows so low they cast shadows over his blue eyes. Yes, she'd need to stick close to him before he did anything they all regretted.

They circled the house, but all was quiet for the night. The sunshine-yellow craftsman home, so different than any other architecture around it, seemed to fit in. Like it belonged and the other buildings didn't.

"This is fucking pointless," Creed said as they stomped another circle around the block. "Are you sure Ophelia knew what she was talking about?"

From the corner of her eye, Zoey detected two shadowy figures. She tapped Creed's elbow and he glared in her direction. It was his default expression the last two hours. She cocked her head down the street and they both changed direction.

Sure enough, a woman stumbled along behind a man. He had a firm grip on her arm and a clarity in his eyes the woman lacked.

"Think he's possessed?" Creed murmured.

Zoey inhaled deeply. A trace of brimstone was in the air, but she couldn't pinpoint which human carried it. "One of 'em is."

"Good enough for me." Creed started for them, but she put a hand on his arm.

"You know we can't just kill her."

"Your boyfriend didn't stop and check before he and his brother killed five hosts." Creed glowered at her, his muscles bunched like he was going to break free of her grip.

A flare of anger tightened her hold. "The demons inside were trying to kill us and them. And we don't know whether they were coerced or willing. But I never said I agreed with it. He's not my boyfriend and he's not under my control." Or the Synod's.

Why was that such a point in Stryke's favor?

He finally relaxed with a quiet sigh. "I promise I won't kill anyone who doesn't deserve it."

She relinquished his arm and was speared with a moment of alarm when he ambled off in the couple's direction.

Cold air numbed Zoey's nose and fingers. Good thing she had a stash of Gatorade in their ride. The scent of snow lingered in the night as temperatures noticeably plummeted before dawn. Scraps of paper and pop bottles littered the sidewalk, along with a thousand cigarette butts. As they neared the humans, they passed pockets ripe with human urine, a little cat piss, and a whole lotta bird shit.

The man was casting furtive glances their way and as they grew closer, the woman's struggle was more apparent.

"I need to go back," she whined and shook her head, stringy hair flying. "No. No, I can't do this."

Suddenly, the woman's head snapped up and she stared straight at Zoey. Her irises had been swallowed up by darkness. "Evening." She grinned and half her teeth were missing.

Had to be a meth addict. Zoey crushed her pity, it did no good in a fight. They'd try to save the woman and hope her foray with a demon didn't kick her back a few steps in her recovery.

Zoey smiled. "Morning. We're a little lost. Can you help us out with directions?"

"No," the man sneered and tried to walk around them. He kept his gaze downward. Afraid his black eyes would give him away?

"Where's the nearest broker?" Creed asked.

The man froze. "I don't know what you're talking about." He made huffing sounds, like he was trying to sniff out their scent but the human's olfactory senses weren't equipped with the ability.

"That's so weird, Creed," Zoey said with false wonder. "I've never run across a broker who's possessed himself."

The man released the woman and faced them. The lady followed suit, probably stood straighter than she had in years thanks to the second-tier inside her ignoring her aches and pains and debilitating cravings.

A knowing glint lit the man's eyes. "Vampires. I thought I smelled waste." He straightened his threadbare coat. "Yes, well, your kind tends to prefer being behind the scenes."

"What'd you promise the human?" Creed asked.

All right. That was direct, but Zoey waited for the answer.

The man grinned, displaying even, white teeth. His hair looked vibrant and healthy, and he stood with confidence. He was definitely the slick broker.

"I only needed to ask. Don't you just love it when hosts cooperate—"

Creed withdrew his knife and buried it in the human's throat mid word.

The addict snarled and leaped toward Creed, but he shoved her off. Relief washed through Zoey. She flashed behind the woman and wrapped her in a choke hold. She fought, but even with the demon's help, she couldn't compare to Zoey's strength. Once the familiar groaning signaled a portal opening, Zoey thumped her on the head and pushed her as far away as possible.

She flashed by Creed just in time for him to take her hand and jump into the blackness.

Chapter Eighteen

The trip to the underworld was seconds longer and highly more disconcerting than a flash. When Zoey flashed the great distance to the Synod, it only required milliseconds longer than a trip across town and an extra bottle of Gatorade.

Aw hell. The Gatorade. Well, she had Creed. And Stryke was down here somewhere. She knew without doubt he'd help her—because that's who he was.

He'd been listless in the underworld most of his life because he had serious hero tendencies and had been born in the wrong life to help.

Or had he?

If Quution was to be trusted with his intentions, then Stryke was the perfect demon for the job.

The feeling of weightlessness ceased and a dim cave formed around her. Or she formed in the cave.

"You okay?" Creed asked, rubbing his head.

She almost chuckled when she realized she was rubbing her own temples. She clocked in to her body—no weakness, the light-headedness was fleeting, and her salt cravings were idling. "I'm good."

"Fuck, where are we?"

Faint torchlight flickered from the hallway, or whatever was outside the opening, but it was enough for her acute eyesight to make out the empty cave they were in. A rectangular slab was attached to the far wall, and a fetid smell emanated from a hole in the ground in the corner. She wanted to gag, wouldn't be surprised if fumes wafted up from the opening.

"Is that the shitter?" Creed went over to check. "Uck, yeah. Is this, like, the underworld equivalent to an efficiency apartment?" He turned back to her. His eyes went wide, and his hand landed on the butt of his gun.

Zoey spun around, ducking at the same time. It was her first mistake. The second-tier they'd driven back down here had his head lowered to spear her with his horns. Unlike Stryke's warm-chocolate horns, this male's horns were blood-red with spikes up and down the sides like thorns.

She flung herself backward, but the spikes caught her across the forehead. Searing pain ignited from the wound. She palmed the knife in her tactical belt and buried it in the male's gut.

He roared in pain and dropped to his knees. She withdrew her knife and readied for another blow, but Creed was already next to her, burying his knife to the hilt in the male's eye. The male dropped.

Creed wiped his hands off on his pants and eyed the body. "Can they come back from that?"

"Dunno." The male was smaller than Stryke, with the typical humanoid form of a second-tier, but not as…pleasing as Stryke's. He was as naked and pink as the day he was spawned. "What about those bugs Bishop said eat carcasses?"

"I don't want to wait around to find out."

Zoey ran her forearm over her brow. Dammit, those wounds bled horribly. She squatted down and grabbed the male's feet and dragged him to the hole in the floor.

"Good idea. No being would want to come back from that. Leave my dagger in him, though, to make extra sure the bastard stays flushed."

Together, they wrestled the body into the latrine.

Zoey was breathing hard and regretting it by the time they were done. She swiped her forehead again. Her sleeve came away saturated with blood.

Creed frowned and touched his fingertips to the skin around the wound. "You're not healing yet. Do you think he had some sort of anti-coagulant?"

"That'd be my luck."

"Totally would." He used his backup knife to cut the seam by his shoulder, then he ripped his sleeve off and handed it to her.

She used it first to clear the drops of blood rolling past her brows before tying it across her forehead.

She glanced at Creed. "Do I look badass?"

"Like Rambo." His smile was gone as soon as it had appeared, and he went to inspect the mouth of the cave.

It was good to have her friend back. Would've sucked to have lost him, too.

Speaking of males she'd lost, time to find Stryke.

Creed signaled the all clear and they crept into the passageway. According to Bishop, and she could see it was obviously all accurate, the underworld had few identifying features. It was caverns and dirt and tiny roots sticking out of the walls. Torches dotted the underworld system, casting soft light and even more shadows throughout the passageways.

She let her senses flare. Could she sense Stryke? Melody? She'd been incredibly close to Stryke, had fed from him. Closing her eyes, she listened for an inner thrum, an intuitive suggestion, hell, just an itch on one side of her body.

Nothing. She blinked her lids open as sadness engulfed her. For months before Stryke had charged into her life and dragged her unconscious body away from a portal, she'd been plagued with a sense of anticipation. Afterward, when her feeling had come to fruition, she'd been confused, upset, and…secure, filled with a sense of rightness and finality that she…dammit, that she absolutely missed.

"Fuck. I don't know. This way." Creed chose to take a right and stalked off.

Scowling at his back, her frustration with herself swelled. Stuck in the underworld, unable to make a damn decision. This wasn't her. She'd always been confident and focused. Now, she dithered about whether to take a left or right and the significance of not being able to decide.

She squared her shoulders and palmed her dagger, afraid the noise of a gun would attract too much unwanted attention. Brimstone clogged her nostrils and she wanted to gag as they walked through intermittent pockets of rotting-garbage stench.

They approached a fork in the path. Skittering sounds echoed from one side. Creed ducked into an opening on their left and Zoey slipped in behind him.

No torches glowed in the cave they'd popped into and they were shrouded in darkness. The scratching grew closer and Zoey could make out garbled words from a rough female voice.

"She said you were propositioned when you were last in the realm."

"She knows not what she speaks," a male with a high-pitched nasal voice replied.

The female coughed, or maybe it was a laugh. "That's true, but she's been after you for a while."

The male's derisive chuckle was loud in Zoey's ears as the couple passed in front of their hiding spot. "Lover, she's after everyone."

"True. She is shameless. 'Tis what most males like about her."

The voices faded and Zoey was tempted to step out and stare after them. She'd caught a glimpse of bipeds as they'd crossed the opening but couldn't see much beyond that. Her best assumption was that they were two second-tiers in a committed relationship.

How odd.

She'd thought Fyra was an oddity. Then Stryke had come along. And Quution, whose sincerity was yet to be tested. Now, a couple who seemed more concerned about infidelity than cruelty.

Creed shot her a look with an arched brow like he'd been thinking the same thing. Zoey shrugged and peered out. Clear.

They resumed their search, pausing at the fork. Another right? Left?

The couple had left a trail of brimstone musk. Zoey wrinkled her nose. Had they just fucked?

It was stronger from the left passageway. She and Creed simultaneously readjusted their trajectory to the right. If the two demons hadn't been worked up about anything, hopefully nothing of interest lay in that direction.

More of the same greeted them. Frayed roots, torches, stench, and enough sulfur smog to burn her nose hairs.

How had Stryke maintained his pleasing wood-fire scent surrounded by this smell?

How would she manage to get a damn thing done thinking about Stryke all the time?

She was about to brush off her thoughts when a faint electrical sensation thrummed down her spine.

Wait. She knew that feeling—when Stryke trailed his fingers down her back.

She increased her pace until she had to shoulder past Creed. He let her, sensing she must be onto something.

The feeling stayed faint until she caught a whiff of a male's scent that curled around her center and woke up her desire.

"He's this way." Zoey was nearly running, only holding back enough to maintain her stealth and avoid running headlong into stupidity.

***

Stryke and Quution located the sacrificial chamber.

"No one's here," Quution growled. He stomped his hidden platform boots. Walking in those couldn't be comfortable, but he believably towered over Stryke.

"Hypna's chamber." Stryke spun and took off at a trot. Quution shuffled behind him.

Stryke had to hand it to his brother. He was committed to his ruse. Staying in that atrocious getup was more convincing than his willingness to help Melody.

"Do we wait for Bishop and Fyra?" Quution asked.

Stryke didn't slow. "Fyra knows where Hypna lives. She'll find us."

They wove through passages, avoiding other demons when possible. The few instances they crossed paths with a second-tier, Quution snarled at them as they bowed in reverence. Stryke didn't bother trying to cover for anything—or himself. He was in his typical underworld uniform of buck naked. And being with Quution would be understood once Hypna was dead and he "worked" for his brother.

He slowed as they neared Hypna's cavern so Quution could quiet the noise he made. Melody's tremulous voice drifted out of the entrance to the cave. His brother came up even with him, his breath not as labored as his journey had sounded.

Stryke sent his energy feelers out. Melody's terror was the first vibration he sensed. Hypna's conniving glee. Pain. Must be from Melody. The walls trembled and Stryke knew that feeling well. Hypna had used her powers to compel roots to the surface. He could guess Melody was wrapped as tightly as those Christmas presents humans coveted this time of year.

He glanced at Quution. His brother's eyes were narrowed and his horns angled forward. Was he testing for energy with those cumbersome things?

Stryke had never used his horns like that. Or for anything, really. They were just horns— barely worthwhile.

Thanks for the biology lesson, dear Mother. He brushed his sarcastic thought away and straightened his horns.

He jerked. Hellfire. They were like amplifiers.

In the multitude of sensations streaming in like they had a direct line to his brain, only one was significant enough for him to filter it out.

The electrical buzz he sifted out reminded him of a salty-sweet dessert. Zoey.

Quution's gaze flicked up to Stryke's horns, then he raised a brow in question and cocked his head toward the far end of the corridor.

Stryke nodded that yes, he detected Zoey.

He couldn't worry about her when facing off with Hypna. Concentrating on the cavern, he formed the massive amount of energy waves into a picture.

Melody was cocooned to a wall with the root system Hypna could manipulate. With her injury, it was probably for the best to have the compression. Hypna paced, her anger sending hard vibrations out from all around her like a homing beacon.

And Melody talked. And talked. And talked.

Stryke tucked his horns back in and he and Quution inched closer.

Melody's voice was surprisingly strong despite the amount of blood Stryke smelled. "That's a really cool trick. I don't know what I'd do with plant powers. I mean, I kill anything I come across. I think the aloe plant growers have a 'most wanted' sign with my picture. I killed an aloe plant in twelve hours. Can you believe it? I left it outside overnight last spring and it froze. To be fair, it took a few days to completely die, but I knew it was toast. It was my third plant. I had a transplant from my grandfather's aloe plant. I should've known that if I couldn't keep that one alive, I just shouldn't try. I mean, he was so damn proud of that plant. It took a few months, but it died. I just couldn't put it in a spot with enough sunlight." Melody chuckled weakly. "I guess growing aloe's a lost cause with vampires, huh? Why do I keep wanting to try? I guess because they're so useful. Have you ever burned yourself? What am I asking? Look at all the torches, of course you have."

"Wench, if you don't shut your mouth, I will stuff it so full of roots they'll crawl out your eyeballs." Hypna paused. "That might be fun. Tell me, human. Do you think you would die from that?"

The squeak from Melody was her confirmation. "I'm sorry. I talk a lot. It happens when I get nervous. My parents used to fight a lot and by that I mean, they'd say something insulting, then not talk for days. One time it was a week—"

"Wench!" Hypna's power ramped up. She was going to follow through on her threat.

Stryke nudged Q. His brother nodded and soundlessly drew a knife as long as a sword from a scabbard on his back. Stryke had nothing but his bare hands and that was all he needed to rip Hypna apart. If she pumped him with that toxin of hers, he'd shred his dick to kill her.

She sought to destroy his young. He wasn't going to subject any child of his to a mother like her, or a sire like his own. His apathy from earlier washed away and he embraced his rage.

Melody's words melted into a yell and Stryke made his move.

He pounced into the cave. Hypna's back was to him and he plowed forward. He didn't grab her around the neck or tackle her. He went straight for her horns. Wrapping his hands around their warm lengths, he jerked her head back and shoved a knee into her back.

She cried out and tried to twist but fell to her knees.

Roots sprouted from the floor, but she was too distracted to direct them. Quution appeared in front of her, his knife drawn back, ready to attack. Stryke wrestled with her and one horn slipped free. As fast as an eel, the ugly purple thing reared backward and grazed him along his neck.

The sting of her poison seeping in only spurred his strength. Clenching his jaw, he caught the horn again and wrenched it with a mighty twist. It cracked like a bone and Hypna unleashed a stomach-curdling scream.

He did the same with her other horn. They were still attached, but she sagged with a wail.

He loosened his hold. A mistake. With an enraged snarl, she twisted on him and punched him in the gut. Her strength and anger poured into her hit and dislodged Stryke. He stumbled back. Quution swung, but she ducked and tried to yank his feet out from under him. He danced back, but lost his balance and cartwheeled back into the wall next to Melody.

Twines gagged the girl and the vines along the floor started to flourish. Stryke sent his energy through his feet to zap them in mass quantities. They wriggled and recoiled but recovered quickly, like their master.

Hypna screeched to her feet and held her arms out to beckon her weeds. With her horns incapacitated, it was her only weapon left.

Quution lobbed a ball of energy toward her head. She lunged left and the ball went right and headed for Stryke.

Stryke threw his hands up like he was catching a kid's rubber ball, but before contact, he shoved it back toward Hypna's center mass. She wasn't paying attention while crouched to attack Quution. The mass of light knocked her in the back of the head and she dropped.

"Mistress!" One of Hypna's second-tiers rushed into the cave and pulled to a stop. A second lesser demon crashed into her back.

Hypna groaned and rolled to her hands and knees. "Don't just stand there, dolts. Kill them!"

The female dove for Stryke, her fangs bared. Stryke's first thought: he hated fangs. Hated getting bitten. With one exception. His next thought: ooh, she's female. Damn Hypna's poison. Stryke had zero interest in sex at the moment, but his body was helpless to the effects. He also had nil interest in any female in the chamber, and again, his body didn't care. He used his fingers like guns and shot energy at her heart. She dropped like a stone and he chuckled. He'd always disliked the rest of Hypna's second-tiers.

Quution did nearly the same with his attacker, but Hypna had recovered. She reared up, her claws elongated to talons, her fangs dripping poison. An ability he hadn't known she possessed.

Her sinister chuckle echoed in the sudden silence. "Are you happy to see me, Stryke? We used to have some good times together."

He centered his energy, ready to unleash hell on the demoness. "No, we didn't."

"I'll make you a deal. I don't care which of you impregnates me, but I'll let the girl go if one of you does."

"It's not just the girl," Quution said, his voice back to guttural grunts. "I'm putting a stop to the sacrifices."

Her lips curled in a sneer. "Who do you think you are?"

An evil smile darkened Quution's face. "The one who's gonna show you what it feels like."

Stryke paused, his orbs hovering above his hands. Could his brother steal her abilities without her acquiescence? One of them would end up dead.

Quution began a chant. A strangled gasp left Hypna. More shouts carried in from the corridor, jerking all their attention away.

Hypna slowly turned her head back to Quution, who'd stopped mid incantation. "Looks like you might have to wait on that."

Blood roared in Stryke's ears as a salty-sweet scent caressed him. His erection raged, painful and full. He wanted to vomit and rut at the same time. The orbs disappeared as he slammed his palms to his eyes and crashed to his knees.

Sweet brimstone. Zoey was outside the room and he wanted nothing more than to pin her against the wall and fuck hard, no matter who or how many people were around. The thought sickened him further and he dropped to his hands to retch. The power of Hypna's toxin, his raging libido for Zoey, the seedy voice telling him it didn't matter as long as there was vagina to thrust into, and the fact that they were fighting for Melody's life, Q's secret, Zoey's life—it all mixed into a putrid mixture in his stomach.

He couldn't be fucking useless. Not now. So many more beings counted on him than just his project of the moment. Stryke wanted to help and he'd been handed the opportunity. He blinked and craned his head up.

A flash of Zoey's ever-tight bun went across the opening. She fought a second-tier and had just gutted him. She crossed into to the room and ripped a bloody strip of fabric off her head. Her gaze landed on him and he calmed himself enough to read her expressions. Relief, a flash of heat, and blankness. Her gaze had fallen to his erection. Her gaze narrowed on Hypna and her knuckles whitened around the hilt of her bloodied knife.

Creed pushed around her. His clothes shone with patches of dried and fresh blood. He crossed to Melody in record time. Her eyes were as round as a full moon and she strained to holler for him around her gag. The chrysalis she was wrapped in undulated with her movement.

Stryke let out an anguished cry, his body shaking while he kept himself from jumping the female he'd wanted so badly to call his own. Zoey stepped toward him and stopped, the corners of her mouth pulled down like she was unsure if she'd make it better or worse. He wished he knew, too.

Quution's voice cut through his sensual haze. His brother had resumed chanting.

Hypna roared and rushed Q. He settled in a defensive position and maintained eye contact, an arrogant tilt to his mouth. She grabbed a dangling horn and drew back.

Stryke's lust-induced fog lifted. That bitch was *not* going to hurt his brother. He took off from his hands and knees like the gun had gone off for a race. Tackling the demoness, he ripped her away from his brother before her horn made contact. They tumbled to the floor.

Quution's voice cleared and rose in volume. Stryke wrestled the demoness until they ended up with him on his back and her back pinned against him. Hypna thrashed, throwing her elbows back. The jostling against his cock was absolutely unwanted, but again, his cock was morbidly satisfied it was getting touched at all. It was enough to fuel Stryke's fury. He wrapped his arms around Hypna's head to snap her neck, but she went rigid, her threats and barks cut-off.

Her body shook and flopped, but Stryke didn't let go. She vibrated with energy, her body warming until Stryke had to mentally prepare himself for holding her while she scorched him.

Oh fuck. Her power was gathering to transfer to Q. Stryke wasn't sure how he felt about his brother risking himself, but there was no time to analyze anything as Hypna's body lit up like a nest of fireflies had found realty under her skin.

Quution's brow popped. Had he not been sure it'd work? He swayed on his feet and his face drained of color.

An occasional elbow would dig into Stryke's side. His dick was bookended between them but it was better than being in her, so he wasn't going to complain.

Another nightmare-inducing sound ripped from her throat and she redoubled her efforts as she grew brighter and hotter.

Enough of this. He wasn't going to let his brother kill himself destroying Hypna. Stryke would break her neck and decapitate her, let the scarabs feast.

Dirt rained down from the ceiling and the torches flickered but didn't blow out.

"The energy's too much for the cave!" Stryke snapped her neck before half the underworld fell on their heads.

Strong hands gripped his shoulders and pulled. The dirt shower started filling with bigger and bigger chunks.

"I don't have Melody free yet!" Creed yelled.

Quution hit a crescendo as he finished the chant. Hypna's body twitched and stiffened.

Stryke managed to get to his feet with
Zoey's help and he shoved her behind him. Q
was riveted to his spot, his morbidly curious gaze
glued to Hypna. The spell was going to work
whether Hypna was conscious or not. And maybe
Q would survive without Hypna's resistance.

Beams of light shot out from all directions.
Creed glanced over his shoulder. He only had
Melody's bloody top partially freed, but he
grabbed her in a bear hug. The veins stood out in
his neck as he strained. Her mouth gaped open in
pain, but he didn't let up.

The energy hovered for a second, like
Stryke's orbs did when he was directing them,
only this energy formed a line pointing to his
brother. Her powers were going to transfer to Q.
The whole cave shook.

With a desperate roar, Creed extracted Melody, but his momentum with Melody's sudden
weight unbalanced him. He tripped backward and
overcorrected. Melody dropped from his arms,
but her legs couldn't hold her and she fell on top
of Hypna. The light sucked back in with the in-
terruption. Hypna's body glowed and vibrated
under Melody.

"No, no, no," Quution shouted. "She can't
interfere. Get her off—"

A sonic boom dropped a chunk of ceiling,
nearly clipping Melody's head.

Then it all went silent.

Melody lay limp over Hypna, smoke tendrils
rising from her body. Quution remained rooted in
his spot, his mouth open in disbelief, displaying

his garish prosthetics. Stryke's lust haze rammed back into him and he dropped back to his knees to keep from mounting a fully clothed Zoey. Zoey didn't help by resting a hand on his back and asking him what was wrong.

"Hypna…her powers." Quution's words crept into Stryke's ears past his internal struggle. "Her power was outside of her body, but when the human interrupted the spell, it tried to get back into Hypna but settled in the next closest life source."

For the second time, it all went silent. Not even Stryke's screaming dick could move him.

Melody had absorbed Hypna's power? Creed's face went ashen. Zoey hadn't moved and Quution was good as a stunned statue.

"Oh god," Zoey breathed. "Is she alive?"

They all watched while Creed gently lifted Melody and cradled her in his arms. She flopped, arms and legs lifeless. He touched her brow and bent his head to listen to her heart and check for breathing.

"She lives." Creed spoke so low he was barely audible.

With the relief, Stryke's libido came roaring back.

Quution sensed the change and crossed to him, glancing at Creed monitoring Melody's pulse. "He was poisoned. You need to leave or he'll attack you."

Instead of backing away, Zoey squatted down. "Will it pass?"

"No," Stryke croaked. "Not for hours."

Zoey craned her neck around. "Are we safe here, or will other members of the Circle find us?"

Quution lifted his faux-saggy shoulder. "They've sensed her death, no doubt. I can go and answer for it." His gaze touched on Melody and softened. "I will, of course, not go into detail about the circumstances."

"Where's a place I can take care of him?" Zoey asked.

Stryke's head popped up and he went temporarily deaf as his body screamed at him to take his female this instant. But she wasn't his female, and he wouldn't defile her in front of witnesses and not on a dirt floor.

"Are you certain?" Quution asked in a measured tone.

"No!" It was the only word Stryke could get out.

"Yes. And we need a safe spot to care for Melody and figure out a way to get her and Creed back home."

Quution's eyes swept over Melody's limp, sunshiny hair. "I'll take care of the girl." His lips flattened. "And the vampire. Come."

Zoey tucked her hands under his shoulders to lift him. Stryke tried to struggle, but his body would follow Zoey anywhere.

His feet threatened to tangle up on themselves, but he remained upright as Zoey tugged him along by the hand. Quution swept out of the cave with a quick word to Creed to stay put.

In his haze, he had no idea where his brother was leading them. All he registered was Zoey's sugar-tinged scent, and his gaze constantly tracked the curves of her body, the arch of her neck, the way her hips swayed.

Chapter Nineteen

Was she really doing this? In the under-world?

Zoey clamped onto Stryke's hand harder as he fought weakly to free himself. He was in severe pain, she could see how his shaft pulsed for release, and he was a danger to himself and others in his situation. She had no doubt he'd hole himself up somewhere and suffer alone where he'd be a target. Other females might find him.

Zoey growled. Stryke was hers.

Quution ducked into an opening and stepped back out. "I'll weave an energy ward for you until Stryke can raise one himself."

Zoey towed Stryke inside. "Why are you doing this?"

"I admit to a foreign fondness toward him because we're related. While I do hold some resentment toward him for leaving me in that hellhole, he didn't know I existed." Quution straightened his dirty clothing. "And you and rest of the vampires are necessary to carry out our plans. Simple as that." His lilac eyes flicked to where Stryke paced the cave as if waiting for an opening. "We've sworn allegiance to each other."

Was that a challenge or a warning? "I've heard. I don't plan on interfering." Her heart fell. She'd had her chance.

With a curt nod, Quution left. Zoey's skin tingled as the energy wards went up. Nice power to have.

She eyed the opening. Did the opening keep others away? Would they walk by and know what was going on in here but not get in?

She sighed and started unbuckling her weapons belt and harness. Setting them by the hard dirt bed, she continued to her clothing.

Stryke faced away from her, his back taut, his buttocks tense and rounded. Liquid heat pooled into her belly. Hellfire. She wanted this. Her shirt came off, then her pants.

"Get dressed." His guttural words sent more heat to her core. She'd missed him. Wanted more time with him to sit on the couch and chat while watching TV. Wanted fucking matching pajamas. Wanted to sup on his blood and split a Gatorade with him.

Could they still do that while she did her job and he did his? Could she walk away from the Synod without regrets, without feeling like she was letting her people down over a male?

She could. She wasn't leaving it for him, she was leaving for her.

"Come here, Stryke."

His head twitched to the side. "I'm not taking you like this."

"I want you to." She closed the distance between them and slid her hands over his hot shoulders. Stepping closer, she pressed a cheek to his back. He flinched.

"I can't do this again." The pain in his words drove straight into her heart.

"I don't just want to help you. I want to be with you. Always."

Tremors shuddered through him. "You can't mean that. You're stuck down here—you need me." The words were full of bitterness.

She drew back. After a beat of anger passed, she recognized the fear in his voice. "Have you ever known me to be the type of girl to sleep with a male out of pity or fear?" She waited for an answer and sensed his defenses dropping. "And you know me better than anyone," she said softly.

He finally turned around, his manhood wedged between them, but she didn't touch it yet, needed him to accept this act between them as more than a quick fuck to take the worst of the poison's edge off.

"So we have sex. Then what?" His violet eyes swirled with uncertainty.

She reached up and plucked the pins out of her hair and let it cascade down her back. Fire ignited in his gaze. "I was thinking… Why could I have both a mate and a bond to you? Has any demon tried bonding a second time?"

He paused. "They usually try avoiding the first time."

"What if we try again?"

Disbelief crossed his face, followed by suspicion. He didn't trust her intentions.

"I want us to make this work and it can't work down here. I'd be too big of a target. But I want you, Stryke." She wrapped a hand around his hot, pulsing shaft.

The muscles in his arms bulged as he resisted reaching for her. "And if it works, what about the Synod? They won't allow you to remain bonded to me."

"Fuck 'em." When his gaze narrowed incredulously, she continued, "I was doing exactly what I'd been determined not to do my entire life. I was letting another dictate what I was and wasn't allowed to do, and it didn't just affect my job, but my life…and yours."

A low rumble started, but his eyes remained narrowed. The sound grew until he growled and banded his hands around her biceps. Twirling her around, he pressed her up against the wall and hooked her legs around his waist. His gaze swept up to her forehead.

"Were you injured?"

"A little."

He shoved inside in the next second.

She wasn't as prepared for him as usual. Pleasure/pain filled her and he stilled.

"Dammit, did I hurt you?"

"Keep going," she gasped and smashed her mouth against his. His wood-fire taste filled her senses and he thrust once before he came for the first time.

He continued to piston in and out. She didn't try to match his rhythm but let him take her with complete trust. Their tongues tangled, but he pulled away and kissed a hot, wet path down her neck.

His fangs nicked her and she shivered. He lapped at the drops of blood and slammed into her and stopped. "Promise yourself to me."

Her eyelids fluttered open and she had to re-orient herself from the ecstasy coursing through her body. It was no problem to acquiesce. "I'm yours."

He struck, piercing her vein. Zoey bowed as much as she could between the wall and Stryke as her orgasm slammed into her.

Stryke released in a second orgasm but kept pumping.

"I don't feel anything different," she gasped, barely able to think around the ecstasy.

"Because it didn't work," he growled.

No. It had to work. It had to. She wanted to be linked to this male, wanted it more than anything. She didn't care about her safety, didn't care if she returned to Earth. Sure, they could be a couple, but she wanted the damn link!

"Use your energy."

He stilled and looked her in the eye, his gaze the clearest she'd seen since she reunited with him. His forehead crinkled in concentration and his eyelids fell shut.

Her lips parted as faint tendrils of energy warmed her insides. "I can feel you."

With a groan, his hips undulated. "Zoey, I can't hold back. If this works, it's for real. *I'm not letting you go again.*"

Hellfire, she hoped not. She cupped his face. "Do it. I'm yours. For all time."

As he filled her body with his energy, a special, singular bond linked them and she relished the feeling of completeness it created. She had him back. She didn't want to be without him.

He closed off the wound and bared his neck for her. She caressed his face instead. "I love you, Stryke."

He met her gaze and stilled. The change was instantaneous. He wrapped his arms around her back and turned them away from the wall. With her wrapped around him, still connected in the most intimate way, he settled onto the rectangular platform, not letting Zoey take the brunt of the hardness.

Zoey stretched over him and he cradled her head into his neck so she could feed. She rode him in a steady pace, located his vein, and reveled in the changes that had taken place between them. They made love and bonded in the underworld.

**

His body was his own again, thanks to his female.

His female. Zoey was his once again, willingly this time. He couldn't believe it had worked. This bond was different, like a current ran between the two of them.

But would she stay? She no longer had the bracelet to demand he release her, but he would if she asked. He'd catch and release her until he exhausted his bond-forming abilities.

She was dressing and he shouldn't watch, because he was hard again. He had no clothes to don, so he waited. She twisted her hair into a bun, but this time it didn't seem like a defense against the world, but a way to keep from having it used against her in a fight.

Finishing with her hair, she started on her weapons. "Between you and me, can we get Creed and Melody back?"

"Dunno. Don't think it's ever been tried before." He wasn't supposed to be able to bond again, either.

"What if we can't?"

"Q and I will hide them until we figure it out."

She dropped her hands to her side, her expression solemn. "You two are really doing this."

He bobbed his head. They were. And it felt right. He and Zoey felt right. But were the two mutually exclusive? "Ready?"

When she nodded, he wove his fingers through the air and dismantled Q's wards. The energy waves were so like his own, he marveled over it every time.

They maneuvered back to Creed and Melody. Fyra and Bishop had arrived and were hovering over the couple on the floor. The girl was still ashen and limp in Creed's arms. Quution brooded in the corner. No one was speaking to each other. As they entered, the energy vibrated with hostility, desperation, and curiosity. Only desperation emanated from Creed. From the way Stryke's brother watched Melody, that answered the curiosity question. From the way Quution's gaze clouded when he looked at Creed, there was the hostility.

Was his brother crushing on a human?

"How do we do this?"

Quution pushed off the wall. "We link hands like some kumbaya human bullshit." His brother had flicked his concerned gaze toward Melody at the word "human."

Stryke glanced at Zoey, who'd subtly raised a brow toward him.

They crowded around Creed. If the male cared that they were there, he didn't show it, and they had to wrestle their hands around his because he wasn't letting go of the blonde.

The sight of Zoey's hand in Creed's no longer bothered Stryke. It was obvious there was nothing but friendship between them. Any ill feelings toward Creed would no longer originate in Stryke at least. He couldn't speak for his brother.

"What do I do?" Zoey asked.

Stryke gave her hand a squeeze. "It's probably like flashing. Envision the place you'll arrive. We'll go to the compound, right by the door where the fight for the kids took place. You and I will try to transport with them and Quution will push us with his energy."

Fyra's brilliant gaze assessed all of them. "Let's do this."

Zoey closed her eyes.

Stryke kept his open, along with Quution. Creed watched them with both hope and suspicion. Then he glanced at Fyra and Bishop as if for reassurance. Stryke latched onto his bond with Zoey, his first priority to get her home.

A familiar draft of displacement wafted over him. He and Zoey disappeared, a wave of Quution's energy riding behind them.

Her eyelids flew up and Stryke clenched his jaw. Fresh, cold air with the crisp smell of winter surrounded them. Fyra and Bishop stood next to them.

Until Quution's hologram appeared. "Well, that didn't work."

"They didn't budge." Stryke hadn't felt any willing energy from the couple they'd left behind.

Quution sighed. "I will hide them, then. The girl needs time to recover."

Zoey drew her phone out and started messaging. "We'll work on finding a way to help Melody, to remove her power."

Bishop guided Fyra to the compound's door. "We'll update D." They disappeared inside.

"I can try the transfer spell again." A muscle jumped in Quution's jaw and his prosthetic teeth ground together. "But I doubt she'd survive the attempt." He drew himself up straighter. "Brother, to ward the place, your assistance is required."

And Quution threw down the first test. Would Stryke say fuck them all and stay with Zoey?

She'd paused on her phone, and her gaze met his.

"I will be back when I can."

Zoey blinked. "Oh, of course. Um…yeah. Demetrius will want to talk with Quution. We need to come to an agreement."

"And I'm your main line to your missing friends," Quution tacked on. "Got it."

He vanished and Stryke felt like he should say more, explain when he was going to be… home? Back? When he'd return?

Did he lean in and give her a good-bye kiss?

Zoey seemed to sense his indecision and she gave him a little smile. "I'll be here when you get back."

Okay. So that was it.

***

Two days later, Stryke threaded through the hallway of the compound to Zoey's apartment in the early morning hours. Fatigue weighed on him, and he hadn't even stopped to steal a pair of sweats. He would've broken into the compound, but Fyra had met him at the door and let him in, muttering about not having access for him yet because without Creed's help, she'd fried the computer. He gave her the quick rundown of how they'd stashed Creed and that there'd been no change in Melody's condition. She was comatose but breathing fine on her own with a steady heartbeat. He rattled off a time and place for his brother to hologram with Demetrius. Fyra had said she'd pass it on in case he was, wink, wink, busy.

Would he be? He approached Zoey's door.

Would he be welcome here? Was their bond truly more than a work arrangement? Her only experience with him was when he'd have done anything for her, but within an hour of recommitting herself to him, he'd disappeared. Her mate had given up everything for her. Now Stryke sacrificed his time and safety for others. Would she truly be okay with that?

He tested the doorknob with his senses and was surprised to find it unlocked. He opened it and went in.

Zoey was cross-legged on the couch with a big bowl of popcorn in her lap. Her hair was down in soft waves around her face. The TV was playing a cartoon movie with colorful clown fish. Her doe eyes lit up and she smiled.

A pang of guilt nailed him when he looked back down at the bowl. She'd been resorting to dietary salt because he hadn't been available for blood. That would be the way it was for them. He'd be away for work. She'd be away for work.

"Hey, you're home—here." She chewed her lip. "I mean, this can be your home, but you don't have to…"

He frowned and scanned her place. It was the same, but different. His gaze landed on the eggplant lampshade, the rainbow lap blanket, and the throw pillows with cats all over them.

She was back to worrying her lip. "I, uh, since… I had some extra time since I no longer have to attend the Synod meetings, so I went shopping. It was too plain in here."

She stood up and the shorts with cartoon cats became visible. His heart warmed but not much as blood rushed to his cock.

He held his desire at bay. "The Synod removed you."

"I removed myself. They don't get to dictate my life. I have my work with the team. Now that we've identified another population the brokers are targeting, I have plenty to do."

The tentative wall he'd built wavered. "How has your salt supply been?"

Genuine confusion crossed her face before understanding set in. "Same as always." A slow smile curved her lips. "I've lived like this my whole life. You're kind of like dessert. Don't worry when you're gone. The guys have me covered if shit goes to hell."

He didn't like the idea of not being there to help, but for Zoey, it was life, it was how she preferred it. His wall crumbled and his arousal bloomed.

Heat simmered in her eyes when she noticed his manhood growing. "I have the matching sweats for you, but it looks like we might not need them for a few hours."

And she was cutting her playful side loose. "You're really serious about us?" he asked, his voice thick.

She shed her top and stepped out of her shorts as she reached him. "I am. I know your

time will be split between here and the underworld, but we'll make it work. I think it'll be
good for us." She hesitated, as if testing what she
was going to say next. "I'm proud of you."

He shoved the door closed behind him and
sent an electric bolt to lock it. The next shock he
sent out tickled across Zoey's ass.

She yelped, her eyes widening in surprise before she threw her head back and laughed.

Stryke's gaze followed the smooth column
of her throat to her smiling, beautiful face. He
wrapped his arms around her and caught her
mouth in a kiss. He was finally holding his mate,
his true mate.

ABOUT THE AUTHOR

Marie Johnston lives in the upper-Midwest with her husband, four kids, and an old cat. Deciding to trade in her lab coat for a laptop, she's writing down all the tales she's been making up in her head for years. An avid reader of paranormal romance, these are the stories hanging out and waiting to be told between the demands of work, home, and the endless chauffeuring that comes with children.

www.mariejohnstonwriter.com/

Facebook: Marie Johnston Writer

Twitter: @mjohnstonwriter

The Sigma Menace:
Fever Claim (Book 1)
Primal Claim (Book 2)
True Claim (Book 3)
Reclaim (Book 3.5)
Lawful Claim (Book 4)
Pure Claim (Book 5)

New Vampire Disorder:
Demetrius (Book1)
Rourke (Book 2)
Bishop (Book 3)

Pale Moonlight:
Birthright (Book 1)

Ancient Ties (Book 2)

78998888R00188

Made in the USA
Columbia, SC
23 October 2017